PROTECTING JOSIE

SEAL OF PROTECTION: ALLIANCE
BOOK 3

SUSAN STOKER

Edited by Kelli Collins

Cover Design by AURA Design Group

Manufactured in the United States

CHAPTER ONE

Nate "Blink" Davis swore as he lay on the floor right where his captors had dumped him, kicked the crap out of him, then, thankfully, left him alone.

It was safe to say his second mission to Iran had been just as much of a shitshow as the first one, when his teammates had been killed and injured.

No, that wasn't true. This time, the team had completed their objective of finding and taking out the terrorists they'd been sent to eliminate. And strangely, Blink wasn't pissed that he'd been taken captive. Probably because he'd done what he'd failed to do the last time he was here.

Save his SEAL teammates.

At least he hoped. They'd been surrounded with no way out. It was déjà vu. But he'd determined this time wasn't going to be like the last. Even knowing exactly what would happen —he'd either be caught or killed—Blink took off running.

He only prayed the SEALs had honored his sacrifice and done what they needed to do to get away.

So no, Blink wasn't freaking out that he was now a "guest" of the Iranian Armed Forces. He'd come to terms with his decision because it hopefully meant good men would live. But his actions hadn't been a suicide mission. He wanted to live too. Thanks to a lot of introspection after his last mission to Iran, and with help from his therapist, he'd realized that just because his friends had died, that didn't mean *his* life was over as well.

Saving Remi also had a hand in that realization. If he hadn't been in the right place at the right time, she'd be dead. And seeing his team leader, Kevlar, so happy with Remi, the love of his life, renewed Blink's determination to use his experience and abilities to help others.

Now, like then, some sixth sense deep inside him screamed that what he'd done was meant to happen. It seemed corny as hell...but Blink couldn't dismiss the feeling that he was right where he needed to be at the moment.

Which was ridiculous. Who in their right mind thought that being locked in a cell, with torture definitely on the schedule by those who'd dragged him in here, was fate or some such stupid shit?

A noise had Blink turning his head, but it was dark in the cell and he saw nothing. It hurt to turn his neck, he noted. His ribs also ached, but he didn't think they were broken... yet. Blood was dripping down his arm and his temple, places where he'd been struck, and he was thirsty. So damn thirsty. But he was alive. That was all that mattered.

A SEAL never left a SEAL behind, and he had no doubt

someone would be coming for him. He just had to endure whatever these assholes dished out in the meantime. Which he had no doubt he could do. He'd trained for this. To be a POW. Sort of fucked up, but that was just how the world, *his* world of special forces, worked.

At first, Blink wasn't thrilled to learn he'd be expected to wear a damn tracker, like he was a fucking dog or something, when he'd joined his new SEAL team. But now? His lips tilted upward in a satisfied grin. A man named Tex was out there watching, probably planning his rescue already. Blink hated that someone else would have to put their lives on the line to save his damn hide, but he couldn't help but feel grateful.

He heard something again, and Blink realized he'd gotten lost in his head for a moment. It was something he did a lot now. It was the only thing that kept him sane when he'd been processing what happened to his previous friends and teammates.

Forcing himself to stay in the moment, he squinted, trying again to see through the darkness. There was a small bit of light coming in through the bottom of the door that entered into this makeshift prison. He hadn't noted much when he'd been dragged inside...a couple of cells, no windows, the smell of mold, mildew, and maybe not surprising, body odor. There was one door to the room, and when his captors left, it slammed shut with a finality that would strike fear into most prisoners.

The rustling sound happened again, and Blink called out, "Is someone there?"

He got no response.

But he hadn't imagined the sound. Groaning, he did his

best to sit up. His wrists were shackled to a chain around his ankles. Thankful that he hadn't been hogtied with his hands behind his back, Blink swayed as he tried to identify what he'd heard in the cell next to his.

Using his shoulder to wipe away some of the blood trickling down his temple, he waited for his eyes to adjust more fully to the darkness. A couple minutes passed before something finally started to come into focus.

Blink wasn't sure what he was looking at. An animal? A child? Whatever was in the cell next to his wasn't speaking. Wasn't moving at all. It was huddled in the far back corner, wearing something...maybe brown or black.

"Hello? Do you understand English?"

Still no response. Blink asked the same question in Spanish, French, German, and then in Arabic. He didn't speak any of those languages, but had studied enough to be able to ask the simple question.

Whatever it was, it didn't utter a word. Or even move.

Blink sighed and lay back down on the concrete floor. His head throbbed with pain. He'd probably imagined whatever he thought he saw. Lord knew he'd been up for forty-eight hours with no sleep, and with the beating he'd received, along with the lack of water—or food, for that matter—he was nearing the end of his rope.

Besides, it didn't really matter what, or who, was in that other cell. They were as fucked as he was.

Closing his eyes, Blink let himself relax for the first time in a week. Maybe he should stay awake, explore his cell, see what weaknesses he could find, try to figure out a plan of escape. But being shackled as he was, and with his reserves as low as they were, he wasn't going anywhere. Not right now.

Getting some sleep so he could be as prepared as possible when rescue came was the best thing he could do at the moment. And if the torture he knew was imminent began before his rescue, he'd need to be ready. And that meant letting his body recharge as much as it could by sleeping.

* * *

Josie England stared at the man in the cell next to hers. It had been so long—how long *exactly*, she had no idea—since she'd heard anyone speak English. Or even heard someone talk to her who wasn't yelling or ordering her around.

The first thing out of his mouth was the F-word, after their captors had left him alone in the cell. Which amused her as much as it surprised her. Then, when he'd asked if anyone was there, she *wanted* to answer him. But she couldn't. She'd even opened her mouth to speak, but nothing came out. It was as if her vocal cords were frozen.

When she'd first been taken captive, she'd screamed. Then begged and pleaded. But nothing she'd said or done had made a lick of difference to the men who'd taken her.

Memories flooded back as she watched the man in the next cell lay back down and close his eyes.

Ayden, her boyfriend, was in the military. Had been on R&R in Kuwait, and he'd begged her to fly over to see him. Things between them hadn't been great for a long while, but Josie didn't want to send him a "Dear John" letter while he was deployed. Didn't want to break up with him when he needed to concentrate on what he was doing.

She'd told him no; it was crazy for her to fly halfway across the world to see him during a short break, but he'd been extremely insistent. He'd even talked his sister and mother into trying to convince her. Genevieve—or Gen, as she liked to be called—and Millie had succeeded where Ayden hadn't. Gen, his sister, had told her all about her own trip to visit her brother a few months prior. She'd made it sound wonderful... and perfectly safe. And Josie agreed that seeing a part of the world she'd probably never have a reason to visit ever again sounded kind of fun.

So, she'd agreed.

Even though her gut screamed not to, she'd taken time off work and gotten on a plane.

Even knowing Ayden was sleeping with a woman in his platoon, she'd still gone.

At first, things between them were good. She'd even briefly reconsidered breaking up with him. But after a few days, he'd turned back into the guy she'd come to know throughout their relationship. Selfish, derogatory, vain.

When he suggested they go on a boat ride so he could show her the area, Josie was already over the "vacation." Even if that hadn't been the case, she didn't think a boat ride was a good idea. She knew enough about the area to know the waters around Kuwait weren't exactly safe. Of course, Ayden just scoffed and talked down to her. Told her she didn't know what she was talking about. Said she was a homebody who hadn't ever been anywhere, who didn't know anything about the world.

In the end, she'd let him pressure her into it. She'd gotten on the boat he'd rented for the day in her bikini and cover-up, pretending that everything was fine. Except it wasn't. Ayden had driven recklessly, showing off, and wanting to see how close he could get to Iran.

Stupid. So damn *stupid*.

The boat motor died, he hadn't been able to restart it... and the next thing they knew, a boat was coming at them, fast. Josie had been frozen in fear. The men in the boat didn't give them a chance to say or do much of anything.

Ayden held his hands up to show them he was unarmed—and was shot on the spot.

Two men boarded the boat, threw Ayden's body overboard, and hauled her onto *their* boat before heading back the way they came.

Josie had been terrified she was about to be assaulted, was reeling from what happened to Ayden. She'd begged them to take her back. Told them she knew nothing, was nobody, but all the men did was laugh. When they arrived at a ramshackle dock, they'd hauled her onshore, not caring that they were hurting her as they half carried, half dragged her through the city streets. She'd lost her flip-flops along the way and the stones under her feet left bruises and cuts that had taken weeks to heal.

They'd brought her to the cell where she still resided, and threw her in, seemingly amused by the terror on her face. A few men entered and beat her, yelling all the while. Josie had screamed and begged, to no avail.

The only positive throughout her entire ordeal was that she hadn't been raped. She didn't know why. Supposed it didn't matter. The men left her on the concrete floor, much as they had the man now in the cell next to hers, bleeding and hurting.

Someone came back the next day, threw a little metal cup at her, along with a piece of bread. He returned off and on for the next few weeks or so, but then the visits to her cell stopped entirely. Josie didn't know why. It was a relief...but no visits also meant no food.

At four foot nine, Josie had never been a big person. Now with no food for who knew how long, and only water dripping ever so slowly down the wall into her cup to sustain her, she was nothing but skin and bones.

The bikini, which had fit so perfectly back in Vegas when she'd bought it, hung off her gaunt frame. The cute little pink cover-up that made her feel so pretty was tattered and torn. It was also a muddy brown color now, the spaghetti straps constantly slipping off her bony shoulders.

And her hair...Josie didn't even want to think about what it looked like. The blonde strands were caked with dirt and who knew what else from the floor of her prison. She'd done her best to comb through it with her fingers to try to keep it from clumping together, but the longer she was here, the less she cared. Her finger and toenails were cracked and had black gunk caked underneath.

She was a shell of the woman she used to be.

More animal than human.

She was going to die here. One day, her captors would come in and be surprised to find a dead body lying in the cell. Or maybe they wouldn't be. Maybe that was their goal all along. It wasn't as if they could get any money for her. Or use her to exchange for someone the United States was holding captive. She was simply a stupid tourist who'd made the colossal mistake of getting on a damn boat with a cocky soldier.

She'd wondered more than once what Millie and Gen were going through. They had to have been notified by now that Ayden had disappeared. Had his friends told their superior officers that he and Josie had gone out for a boat ride? Did they even know? Had the boat floated back into Kuwaiti waters? Had Ayden's mom told anyone that Josie was visiting her son?

She had no idea. Millie had never liked Josie much, though she had no idea why. Josie worked hard, minded her business, and was polite to everyone she met. And yet, Millie just hadn't taken to her. Maybe she thought no one was good enough for her son. It made sense, she supposed, considering the fact that Ayden had always been a mama's boy.

The sound of the man in the next cell snoring slightly brought Josie back to the present. She had a tendency to get lost in memories and her thoughts...because what else did she have to do? Time crawled here. She had no idea if it was night or day. She could hear life going on as usual outside the walls of her prison. In the early days of her incarceration, she'd yelled and screamed, trying to get someone's attention, but all that did was make one of her captors come in and scream at her...and one time, enter her cell and beat the hell out of her. That had ended any desire she'd had to bring attention to herself.

Her eyes had adjusted to the low light long ago, and Josie

could see the man fairly clearly. She figured she was part mole now, living in the darkness and filth as she did.

The man had a beard that wasn't bushy enough to have been growing more than a few weeks, a mustache, and fairly full lips. His fingers were long, and he had large biceps. He was wearing a T-shirt and a pair of camouflage pants, and that was it.

Her attention was drawn to his toes. It was silly, but his skin seemed to glow. He wasn't covered in dirt, as she was. He looked...clean. And looking at his clean feet made Josie's heart clench. It wouldn't be long before he was just as dirty as her.

He looked like he was someone important. And he was in handcuffs. So the men who'd brought him here had to be a little scared of him. Of what he could do.

As she watched, he licked his lips in his sleep and moaned a little as he shifted on the concrete floor.

The *drip drip drip* of the water into her little cup made Josie glance at it. It was almost full. It took two days to get a full cup. She usually tried to wait until then, so she could drink it all at once and trick her belly into thinking she'd given it food.

This man had no leak on his side. No cup to collect water.

But surely he'd be given food and water. If he was as important as she figured he might be, their captors would have to take care of him if they wanted to exchange him for a political prisoner or hold him for ransom.

Still...unease sat in her gut like a lead ball. What if they didn't? What if they left him there like they did her? With his hands cuffed to his ankles, he wouldn't be able to move very well. And a man as big as he was would need a lot more suste-nance to stay alive than she did.

It wasn't fair.

That she was here. That she'd been left to rot. That this man had been captured. Nothing about what happened to either of them was fair. And Josie felt anger rising up within her. She'd suppressed that emotion over the weeks. Suppressed *all* emotions. Because being mad, or scared, or feeling *any* heightened emotions wouldn't help her situation. Being desperate and angry and terrified had only earned her beatings. So she'd learned to feel nothing. Think about noth-ing. She counted how many drips of water fell into her cup for entertainment.

But now this man's arrival made her emotions well up once more. It was uncomfortable and scary. Josie didn't like it. She wanted this man to *go*. Leave. Be taken away and never returned. She knew what to expect in this hellhole when it was just her. But with his arrival, she had a gut feeling every-thing would change.

She just didn't know if it would be for better or worse.

Time passed, and Josie kept her gaze locked on the man. She memorized the shape of his face, how one ear stuck out just a tiny bit more than the other; the fact his beard was full, not patchy like some men's; the pattern of the blood rolling down his temple into his hair. The way his big toe canted in slightly on his left foot, but was straight on his right.

She had no idea how long she stared at the man, but it was long enough that she'd know him anywhere. She could meet him on the street years from now, and she'd immediately recognize him. Her mind catalogued every detail, tucking them all away. Why? She had no idea. But it felt...important.

Suddenly, the door to their prison slammed against the wall, making the man's eyes pop open.

And for some reason, they locked right onto her.

Blue. His eyes were light blue. His hair was reddish-brown. And with light pouring in, she saw that he had freckles. Lots of them. Over every inch of skin that wasn't covered by his beard. The captors heading for his cell were talking, saying words Josie couldn't understand. Still, the man didn't look at them. His gaze remained on her. Studying Josie as carefully as she'd examined him while he was sleeping.

Neither spoke out loud, and yet, it felt as if he could see down to her soul. Her black, withered, completely damaged soul.

The door to his cell opened and then their captors were there. Hauling the man to his feet, manhandling him, shoving him as they dragged him toward the door.

Josie lost eye contact with the man briefly, but as they dragged him past her cell, his head turned and he looked right at her once more. She was still huddled in the corner, doing her best to stay out of sight, to not draw the attention of men she had no doubt could end her struggle to live with ease.

"Showtime," he said—and winked.

The man actually *winked*. As if he was having fun! But the blood on his face was real. The pain his captors had inflicted was easy to see in his eyes, at least for her, because she'd experienced the same thing.

Then he was gone. The door was shut and she was in the dark once more. Josie opened her mouth to yell, to tell the man to be strong, to say *something*...she wasn't sure what. But once again, nothing came out. Only a faint growl.

Feeling as if she'd failed the man somehow, Josie curled into herself once more. She had no idea if he'd be back or not. She realized his being there had likely been her only chance to talk to another English-speaking human being before her death. To tell someone who she was, to be a *person* one last time. And she'd blown it.

Sorrow swamped her, and Josie tried to tamp it down but it was no use. Emotions sucked. Being numb made this hell easier to handle. Lifting her head, she stared at the place where the man had lain in his cell. Could see a dark spot on the floor where his blood had dripped.

Be strong, she thought. *Don't let them win.*

Then she closed her eyes and did her best to count water drops once more. Doing so was better than thinking about what the man might be going through.

CHAPTER TWO

Torture sucked.

That was Blink's main thought as his captors used their fists to beat on him. Then they switched to sticks, hitting the bottom of his feet, making them bleed as they jeered and taunted.

His second-most prominent thought—that was a *woman* in the cell next to his. Not an animal. Not a fellow military prisoner. But a woman. At first, he'd thought it was a child. But as he stared at her, he'd realized she was an adult. She was malnourished, filthy, and as skinny as anyone he'd ever seen who was still alive.

Yet, her eyes told him she was alert. Hadn't yet succumbed to whatever torture their captors had inflicted upon her. And that knowledge gave Blink the strength to withstand what they were dishing out at the moment.

He knew they were just getting started. He understood how being a POW worked. He'd been trained for this moment. It sucked, and no Navy SEAL ever wanted to be in his position, but he wouldn't crack.

It took longer than he'd hoped, but eventually his captors got bored, or tired, or needed to do something else. He didn't know which, and he didn't care. All he cared about was getting a reprieve. Blink had no doubt they'd start up again soon, but it wouldn't matter. He wouldn't tell these assholes anything about the planned extraction point of his team or if there were any other HVTs the SEALs were hunting.

They'd managed to break a finger or two, split his lip open, and the cigarette burns on his ankles and feet hurt like a bitch, but nothing they'd done would keep him from being able to walk when the time came. Even the wounds on the bottom of his feet wouldn't prevent him from getting the hell out of there. Trust in the fact that he'd be rescued helped Blink compartmentalize what was happening to him physically.

Thinking about the woman in the cell next to his also kept his mind occupied while he was beaten. Why was she in that cell? How long had she been there? Where was she from?

He had too many questions and no answers. He was impatient to be taken back to his cell. Not to lick his wounds or to sleep, but to talk to the woman.

Blink made sure to groan extra loud when he was dropped once more onto the floor of his cell, but his eyes immediately sought out the woman he'd gotten a glimpse of earlier.

She was in the same place. Didn't look like she'd moved even one inch. Huddled in a little ball, her knees up, arms around them, pressed into the corner. And like earlier, she was staring at him as if she could see right through to all his innermost thoughts. Her blue eyes bore into his own as he was once more locked into his cell.

None of his captors even looked in her direction as they left the room, shutting the door behind them, which Blink thought was odd. It made him want to know what her deal was even more.

A pained moan escaped as he shifted on the hard floor. He closed his eyes for a moment as he took stock of his injuries. He ached all over, but he'd live. Live to be tortured another day, which he was sure was the goal. But every day that passed was one closer to rescue. Blink knew that down to his toes. Help was coming, he just had to hang on until it arrived.

"I'm Blink," he told the woman, his voice seeming to echo in the room around him. "My name is actually Nate, but people call me Blink."

He waited but got no response.

"What's your name?"

Still nothing.

He sighed. "Can you understand me?"

Blink waited...and then he got it. A nod so slight, some people might've mistaken it as nothing more than the woman adjusting slightly. But he took it for what it was, an acknowledgement of his words.

He was elated, even as he felt sorry for her. And while he hated that she was in this situation—and obviously had been for a long while, if her appearance was any indication—he was even more curious, now that he knew she understood English. Who *was* she? How did she get here?

But he didn't expect to get any answers. Not right now, at least. She was obviously traumatized, which wasn't a surprise.

This was no place for anyone, much less a woman as slight as her. She looked like a stiff breeze could knock her over. He hadn't missed the way her collarbones protruded from her skin. The way her cheeks were hollowed. How her arms clasped her knees so tightly they seemed to be the only things holding her together.

Blink made a decision—he wasn't leaving her. Rescuers wouldn't be expecting to liberate a second person, but in no way was he the type of man who would leave any living being in this shit hole.

The longer he lay there on the cold, hard floor, the more his body throbbed. He would kill for some water right about now. Or even one of the crappy MREs that he'd been eating for the last week. But his captors obviously weren't concerned about feeding him.

He shifted on the floor and grimaced. Looking back over at the woman, he could barely make her out in the darkness, but he saw she hadn't moved. Not even an inch. She was still looking in his direction as if waiting for something.

The possibility that their cells were being monitored occurred to him, but as he looked around, he didn't see any blinking lights indicating cameras. And judging by the condition of the place, he wasn't sure the men who'd nabbed him had a terribly sophisticated security system, which would work in his favor when help came.

Still, he wouldn't discount the idea that they were being watched. He wanted to talk to the woman. Wanted to put her at ease. But he couldn't tell her that help was coming. That the tracker Tex had insisted he wear was still safe and secure inside the waistband of his underwear.

"As I said before...I'm Nate. I don't know about you, but I'd kill for a huge cup of coffee. No, a caramel macchiato. I know, that's not usually a drink you'd think a guy would like, but I'm addicted to the things. Besides, it's caramel...who doesn't like that? My friend, Safe, he makes the *best* coffee. He has one of those fancy machines you see in coffee shops right in his house. The first time I went to his place and he fired that thing up, I almost knocked my other friends out of the way to get to the first cup of coffee. Oh, and you know what else I miss?"

Blink was talking more to himself than the woman; it was comforting to hear something other than the oppressive silence or his captors yelling at him in a language he didn't understand.

"Cheetos. Not the puffy kind, those are gross, but the real thing. The small, hard, crunchy bits. Flash makes fun of me for liking that crap, but I could live on them. Okay, probably not, because they're full of stuff that isn't good for me, but there's nothing like sitting on the couch watching football and getting my fingers all orange from eating those things."

It was ironic that Blink was in a situation where he had to do all the talking. He wasn't a talker. Never had been. But as he spoke, he swore he could see the woman across from him relaxing a fraction. As if his voice was comforting. Hell, she probably hadn't heard a friendly voice since she'd been thrown in this hellhole.

So he continued talking. About nothing. Stupid shit. But he couldn't seem to stop. It was as if a dam had broken.

"I have a twin brother. His name is Tate. Yes—Nate and Tate. Ridiculous, but what can you do? My mom left when we were young. Around four. Said she couldn't handle being a wife and mother anymore. When my dad got home from work, she met him at the door with her suitcase in hand and told him she was leaving. And that was it. She was gone.

"My dad though, he's amazing. I know it wasn't easy being left with two rambunctious four-year-old boys. We were hellions. I mean, I don't remember much from that time, but Tate and I competed with each other all the time, about *everything*. Who could eat the fastest, who could do their homework the fastest, who could fall asleep first, who would lose their first tooth...it went on and on. He liked the Dallas Cowboys, so I decided I liked the Pittsburgh Steelers. I joined the swim team, and he decided to become a runner. We were total opposites, and would do whatever we could to one-up each other. But he's also my best friend."

Blink stared up at the ceiling of his cell, watching the darker shadows move and shift above him. Thinking about his brother. He wondered where he was right that second. Whether he knew Blink had been captured. Probably not officially, but as many twins did, they had a connection. Many people would dismiss it as wishful thinking, but when Tate broke his arm when he was eight, Blink had known about it the second it happened. When Blink was in a car accident when he was seventeen, Tate had beaten him to the hospital.

"Asshole joined the Army when I decided to go into the Navy. I know he did it just to piss me off," Blink said with a small huff of laughter. Thinking about Tate was actually painful. He hadn't seen his twin in way too long, and right then and there, he vowed to fix that the second he got back to California. He had no idea if Tate was deployed at the moment, but he'd do whatever it took to spend a few days with his brother.

"Anyway, my dad...he was awesome. Didn't even pause when our mother left. He figured shit out. Got babysitters, found a job where he could be at home when we got out of school. Our old man didn't miss one swim meet or track competition. We could always hear him cheering from the stands. But he also didn't put up with our shit, either. The one time we snuck out to go to a party in high school, he was waiting up for us when we returned at three in the morning. Knowing we'd disappointed him, that the trust he had in us was broken, was enough for us to never want to do it again."

Hearing a slight sound, Blink turned his head and saw the woman had lowered herself to the floor. Her legs were still curled into herself, but her head was resting on one of her arms now as she lay on her side, still staring at him.

"He's still alive, in case you were wondering," Blink told her. "My dad. Lives in Florida like a king. All the ladies giggle and titter around him as if he literally *is* the King of England or something. But he never got serious with a woman after my mom left. He loved her. And she broke his damn heart. And honestly, I used to never want to get close enough to a woman for her to hurt me like that. But then I met Remi. She and Kevlar...they're..."

His words faded. Blink wasn't sure how to explain the relationship his team leader had with his girlfriend.

"Maybe I need to back up," he said. Then he proceeded to tell the mysterious woman all about Remi and Kevlar. How they'd met when they were stranded in the ocean together. About one of Kevlar's ex-teammates scheming to murder

Remi. He downplayed his role in the fiasco; he still had a lot of guilt that he hadn't figured out a way to stop the asshole before he'd actually put Remi into that hole in the ground.

"My point," Blink said with a small chuckle, "is that I want that now. What they have. I used to think what they found was a one-time thing. A fluke. But then Safe had to go and meet Wren."

He spent the next ten minutes explaining how another teammate of his had found *his* soul mate.

"She's out there," Blink said in a barely there whisper. "I don't know her name, her story, or where she is, but I just hope and pray that one day when we cross paths, I'll recognize her...and somehow manage to make her see through the stoic, boring shell I show the rest of the world to the man who will cherish her for the rest of our lives."

It was cheesy as hell. Melodramatic for sure. But Blink wanted what his father had been robbed of. Raising young boys wasn't easy, and he and Tate hadn't realized how much of a deterrent they'd been when it came to any woman wanting a relationship with their dad.

A low sound had Blink turning his head and looking at the woman once more. She'd lifted her head and was staring in his direction. As he waited, she made the sound again. It was a cross between a groan and a growl. For some reason, it made the hair on the back of his neck stand up.

He had no idea what she was trying to communicate. But the fact that she *had* made some sort of sound felt like a monumentally big deal.

"Right, I'm going on and on about nothing," he told her. "Believe it or not, I'm the quiet guy. The one who doesn't say *anything* unless something needs to be said. And here I am, blabbering my fool head off. You're probably over there wondering why the hell you got stuck with a cellmate who won't shut the hell up."

She made another sound deep in her throat. And this time Blink saw her actually shake her head.

"No?" he asked, feeling giddy. She was interacting with him! Not simply staring with those huge, wounded blue eyes. He wanted to sit up, throw his fists in the air, and exclaim *yes!* But he decided that would probably scare the hell out of her. And even if he wasn't shackled, he didn't think he could move his arm over his head. It hurt like hell.

"So you like hearing me go on and on about nothing?" he asked.

Blink waited patiently and was rewarded with her chin dipping down a fraction.

He smiled. Huge. Making his split lip throb. "Right. So, what else do you want me to talk about? My fascinating morning routine? How I only use cold water to wash my clothes because my dad once warned me about washing in hot water and how it would shrink my shirts, and I've been terrified of all my clothes coming out the size of toddler shit ever since?"

Blink could've sworn he saw the woman's lips twitch, but it was dark enough that he couldn't be sure. He smiled again himself though, and turned his head so he was staring up at the ceiling once more. "One year, my dad decided he wanted to take Tate and me on vacation. He didn't have a destination in mind, simply packed some clothes and some snacks and threw us in the car and off we went. Those two weeks are some of the best memories of my life."

Blink talked until his voice went hoarse. His throat hurt, he would do just about anything for some water, but he didn't stop. Talking about his family, stuff that was as far removed from this stinking cell as possible, helped him continue to compartmentalize, turn off his aches and pains.

When he'd finished sharing a memory about the first girl he'd ever kissed, when he was in the fourth grade, Blink turned to look at the woman. Her eyes were closed and she seemed to be asleep.

Some men would be annoyed that the woman they were trying to entertain had gone to sleep on them. But hearing her deep breaths in the otherwise quiet cells felt like a victory to Blink. Intellectually, he knew she had to sleep sometime. No human could stay awake forever. And knowing his voice was the last thing she'd heard before nodding off, and not the oppressive silence of their cells or the angry shouts of their captors, made him feel good.

It was a lame word to describe his sense of satisfaction, but his head hurt, as did most of his body, and he couldn't think of a better one at the moment.

Closing his own eyes, Blink heard the distinct drip of water coming from somewhere, the low murmur of men's voices on the other side of the door down the short hall leading to their cells, and the long, slow, deep breaths of the woman incarcerated next to him.

CHAPTER THREE

"Good morning!" a man's harsh voice called out.

Josie woke with a start but didn't move from her position on the floor. She opened her eyes to see the man, Nate, in the cell next to hers being hauled to his feet by three other men. This was the third day he'd been there, and every day he'd been dragged away and returned hours later, bloody and beaten to hell.

But this time was different. There was a man who spoke English. And instead of dragging Nate away to torture him, someone brought in a chair and plunked it down in the middle of his cell. They forced Nate to sit, and then began beating him right there.

Josie wanted to close her eyes. She didn't want to watch, but somehow she couldn't seem to tear her gaze away from what was happening. The man began to question Nate in English, wanting to know exactly what the US government knew about his organization. What other groups the US was targeting.

But Nate didn't speak, simply took whatever this man and his lackeys dished out.

The man speaking English—clearly a leader of some kind —got more and more frustrated. Eventually he lifted a foot and kicked Nate in the side, and he toppled over onto the floor like a sack of potatoes. He was facing Josie, and seeing the blood oozing out of his nose and from numerous cuts on his body made a growl escape from deep within her gut.

She wanted to cry out. To beg the men to stop, to leave Nate alone.

But all she could muster was that deep, hateful growl.

The terrorist leader didn't even turn her way. He hovered over Nate and stared down at him with a look so terrifying, so full of anticipation, it made Josie's skin crawl. This wasn't a man to cross, and Nate had done just that simply by remaining silent.

"That all you got?" he mumbled from his vulnerable position on the floor.

"You think you're tough?" the leader asked. "Big tough US soldier? We'll see how you feel tomorrow when we increase our techniques to make you talk."

"Waterboarding? Oh good. I *am* a bit thirsty," Nate taunted. "Your people seem to have forgotten to bring me any sustenance. I've come to enjoy Damavand water. It's produced right here in Iran, right? Delicious."

Josie could see the leader's lips turn down in a furious scowl. She wanted to tell Nate not to antagonize the man. For someone who claimed he didn't talk much, he certainly couldn't seem to keep his mouth shut at the moment.

"You want to be waterboarded? We can accommodate you," he said, before his leg swung back and he aimed his boot at Nate's head.

This time, Josie hissed. She couldn't stop herself. But thankfully, Nate jerked his head back at the last second, and the man's boot only grazed his temple.

The leader said something in his language to the other men, and they filed out of the cell, taking the chair with them and leaving Nate lying in the middle of the floor. His hands were still shackled and attached to his ankles, and he looked...broken.

For the first time in weeks, since the first days of her captivity, tears dripped down Josie's cheeks.

At the last moment, before he left the room, the leader turned and looked directly at her. Josie froze. Having someone notice her was something she both yearned for and dreaded.

He asked one of the other men something as he gestured toward her with his thumb. The other man responded with a shrug. The leader barked out what sounded like an order, then she was once again alone with Nate.

Shivering—Josie didn't like the look in the leader's eye as he left—she used her fingers to wipe her cheeks of the lingering tears. She was probably smearing dirt from her hands to her face, but what did it matter? She was so dirty, she didn't even think about what she looked like anymore.

Glancing over at Nate, she saw he hadn't moved. Was still

lying on his side, each breath he managed looking labored and painful.

She opened her mouth to say his name, to ask if he was all right, but nothing came out. It was stupid anyway; of *course* he wasn't all right. Josie had no idea what to do. But the truth was, she couldn't do anything to help him. They were both in big trouble, she knew that down to the marrow of her bones.

But then it occurred to her—something she *could* do to help Nate.

Turning, she looked at the cup of water at the corner of her cell. Nate had to be terribly dehydrated. Thirsty. He'd said as much to the leader guy. No one had brought him any water or food since he'd arrived. And he'd been beaten every day.

Her mouth felt as dry as cotton, her lips were cracked and bleeding from lack of moisture. But Nate was worse off.

Moving carefully, Josie picked up her precious cup and slowly scooted across her cell floor. This was the first time since Nate had arrived that she'd moved away from the wall she considered her safe base. But he was hurting. He needed this more than she did.

Nate must have heard her moving, because his eyes opened and he watched her scoot toward him.

"I'm okay," he slurred. "Piece of cake. Those assholes hit like girls. Wait, that was rude, I know some women who hit pretty damn hard. I'm not gonna break, if you were worried."

Josie kept her gaze on his as she approached. He was lying about three feet away from the bars that separated their cells. She carefully placed the nearly full cup of water on the floor and pushed it toward him.

Nate frowned. "What's that, Spirit?"

He'd started calling her that the day before, because even though she'd obviously been through hell, he could see her spirit shining through her eyes, refusing to give up. At least, that's what he claimed. He'd said he needed to call her *something*, and since he didn't know her name, that would work until she felt safe enough to share her real name with him.

But it wasn't a matter of feeling safe or not. It was that she literally couldn't speak. For whatever reason, every time she opened her mouth, no sound came out. A psychologist would probably have a field day analyzing her and coming up with all the reasons why she couldn't talk, but at the moment, it didn't matter. Nothing mattered but making sure this man lived. And he needed water to do that. And that was something she could give him.

She nodded at the cup, but Nate didn't even look at it, his gaze locked on hers.

He spoke again, but this time his words were barely a whisper. "They're coming, Spirit. It won't be long now, we just have to hold on until they get here."

Josie gaped at him, equally surprised by his words...and the swift anger they caused inside her. How dare he try to raise her hopes! Insist that some mysterious rescue team would just swoop in and take them out of here.

Brows furrowing, she impatiently pointed at the cup of water. But Nate's gaze didn't leave hers.

"I'm a SEAL," he told her. "I can take whatever they dish out. It's only a matter of time."

She didn't want to listen to what he was saying anymore. She leaned forward, stuck a hand through the bars and pushed the cup closer. When he *still* didn't look away from her, she growled, then lay on the floor to push the cup as close to him as she could manage.

It wasn't until it was practically under his nose that Nate finally glanced down. One of his brows lifted. "Water?" he asked, as if not believing what he was seeing.

Josie nodded, but his gaze was fixed on the cup. He licked his lips, probably unconsciously. Then he finally tore his gaze from the water and looked back at her.

"Where did you get that?" he whispered, almost in awe. She pointed at the corner of the room. He probably couldn't see the water dripping there, but he nodded anyway. Then he said, "I can't take this. You need it."

Josie huffed out an exasperated breath.

"I can hear your exasperation with me even in that small sound. I still can't take your water," he told her.

But she was done with his martyr act. She wanted to tell him that she'd had her usual cupful a couple days ago. That she could go another day or two without. But *he* couldn't. He needed the liquid so he could stay strong.

Instead, all that came out was a small hiss.

Annoyingly, Nate smiled at her. "You're like a small kitten, hissing in irritation."

Josie wrinkled her nose.

"Sorry, probably not the best way to describe you if I want to stay on your good side. Are you absolutely sure?" he asked, still not reaching for the cup.

Josie gave him a small nod.

"Thank you," he said simply, as he did his best to sit up, then reached for the cup with both hands. He couldn't move far, not shackled the way he was, but he managed to bring the cup to his lips. Josie watched as he closed his eyes when the first drops of water hit his lips. He didn't guzzle the liquid as she expected him to, as *she'd* done the first time she'd gotten enough to drink. Instead, he savored it, every swallow treated as if it was pure gold he was ingesting.

When the cup was empty, he placed it back on the ground and slid it toward her. His intense blue gaze met her own. "I will never forget this," he said solemnly. "It hasn't escaped my notice that you haven't been given anything to eat or drink since I've been here either. For you to give me the water that you so desperately need..." His voice trailed off and he took a deep breath, then winced. "Ouch," he joked. "Need to remember not to do that again.

"Sharing your water with me," he went on in that low, serious tone. "I've never had anyone do anything so selfless for me before."

Josie wanted to tell him it wasn't that big of a deal, but deep down, she knew it was. She would suffer for her good deed. But this man was suffering more than she was. At least she wasn't the recipient of their captors' ire.

Reaching forward and snatching the cup back through the bars, she quickly scooted over to her spot against the wall. She carefully placed the cup back under the drip, and the first tinny sound of water hitting the bottom soothed her. For her, it was the sound of life. Literally.

Groaning, Nate eased to the floor and onto his back. "Fuck," he muttered.

Josie couldn't help but smile. That was the first word she'd ever heard him say, and she felt a little nostalgic about it already. Which was stupid, but then again, this wasn't a normal situation.

Nate began to talk again, and Josie wanted to tell him to hush, to save his strength, but she couldn't deny that his voice soothed her. Made her feel not so alone. Gave her more of that dreaded hope. Even if hope was dangerous for a woman in her situation. A nobody. Forgotten, thrown away to rot.

Having Nate there, sharing her miserable existence if only for a few days, was a boon she never expected nor thought she deserved.

If there was anything she could do to help him, she would. Without reservation. Her body was giving out. She was well aware that she couldn't go indefinitely without food. Having water was keeping her alive, but eventually her organs would fail. One day, the captors would come in and find her rotting corpse. It was a morbid thought, but nothing much fazed her anymore.

But before she died, if she had the opportunity, she'd do what she could to help Nate.

* * *

Blink's mind spun. What he'd just experienced...it was humbling. Spirit was slowly starving to death. It wasn't hard to see. And yet, she'd still given up the only thing she had to sustain her life. To *him*.

He'd tried to tell her that help would be here soon, but he could see his words simply upset her. He still believed down to his soul that help *was* coming. Enough time had gone by to put together a plan for a rescue mission. He'd participated in more than his share during his time as a SEAL to know how they worked.

He was still thirsty, but that cup of water had given him new life. He could literally feel his cells soaking up the liquid. He would've been okay for another couple of days, but the fact that she'd given up something she so desperately needed hit him in a way nothing ever had.

As he lay there, contemplating how big her sacrifice really was, Blink heard a sound that was completely out of place for his situation.

Forcing himself to sit up, he stared at the wall where the sound was coming from.

He gasped at what he saw. To many people, it would look like an alien tentacle or something equally as foreign, but he knew exactly what it was.

He grinned and waved at the thing like a total dork.

It disappeared in an instant, but Blink wasn't alarmed.

Within seconds, a small black earplug was shoved through the hole, falling onto the floor. Suppressing a groan, Blink scooted on his ass, moving closer to the wall. He leaned against it as he placed the earpiece into his ear.

"Hey, Blink! How the hell are ya?"

"Flash? Is that you?" he asked in a voice so low, it was almost a whisper. But he had no doubt his teammate would hear him. The technology in the radio receiver was that good.

"It's me," Flash reassured him. "You done with your little vacation yet? Want a ride home?"

"Fuck yes," he said, relief swamping through his body.

"Right. Saw the jewelry you're wearing, and we'll have to get that off first thing. But we're gonna make a hole into your cell, pull your ass out, then head off into the night. The natives are restless, so we're gonna try to do this quietly. Got you a nice disguise to put on and with any luck, we'll get to the taxi stand without attention."

Blink frowned, and his gaze immediately went to the woman in the cell next to him. "Got a friend," he told Flash.

There was silence for a moment. "Shit. All right. Where?"

"Ten feet to my right."

He wasn't surprised when the fiberoptic camera at the end of the fiberscope returned through the tiny hole and was pointed toward the other cell.

"Intel?" Flash demanded.

"Not much. Small, under five feet. No shoes or appropriate clothing. I'm not leaving her."

"Roger. This changes plans. Can you hold on a few more hours?"

Blink would hold on as long as it took for Spirit to be rescued alongside him. "Yes." He wouldn't think about the torture his captors had in store for him. He'd take whatever they wanted to dish out if it meant getting out of this hellhole.

"All right, we'll be back. Be ready."

"I was born ready," Blink told his teammate.

There was a pause, then Flash snorted. "Are you sure you're Blink? You're awfully talkative."

"Just get us the hell out of here," he told his friend. "We'll be ready."

"Roger."

Then the camera disappeared through the hole once

more, and Blink knew his friend was gone. He looked over at the woman.

And just as he thought, her eyes were open and she was staring at him from her spot along the far wall. Moving painfully, Blink scooted toward the bars separating their cells. He spoke in a low, even tone. "That was my team. They'll be back tomorrow to get us out. Don't know the plan yet, but all we have to do is go with the flow. Do you think you can walk?"

Her serious eyes bore into his own, but she didn't respond. Didn't move. He didn't think she was even breathing.

"It's okay if you can't. You're tiny. I can carry you easily enough."

She finally moved, lifting her foot and pointing to it.

Blink was thrilled she was communicating with him. It was surprisingly easy to have a "conversation" with her, even without her saying a word. "My team will take care of shoes and clothes for us both."

Her gaze went from him, to the door of their prison, then back to him.

"They're devising a new plan, but whatever it is, it'll work. I trust them with our lives, Spirit."

She frowned and looked toward the door once more, then back at him. She curled her fingers into a fist and swung it in the air.

"Oh, them? It's fine. They aren't going to kill me. I'm too valuable."

The woman growled deep in her throat once more. As if arguing with him.

"Did you hear me? Talking to my teammate?" he asked.

Her chin dipped.

"I could've left tonight. They were ready to implement their plan. But I'm not leaving without you. I can take whatever that asshole wants to do to me, but what I *can't* take is knowing you're still here while I'm free. Not happening, Spirit. So tomorrow, I'll deal with whatever they have in store for me, then we'll get the fuck out of here. Okay?"

Her eyes were big in her face as she simply stared at him.

"Right. I need you to take this," Blink said as he reached into his ear and took out the tiny receiver. "I can't have it in my ear when they come to beat on me some more. They'll find it, and then we'll *really* be in a world of hurt. Put it in, and if you hear my team talking, let me know. I realize you can't talk back to them, but if you tap on it, they'll hear and know we've got ears, even if we can't respond."

The woman didn't move. Her gaze went from his to the receiver in his hand, but she made no attempt to come toward him.

Internally sighing, he wished he could touch this woman just once. Reassure her that they really *were* going to be rescued from this prison. But he had no idea what she'd been through. It was possible being touched was the last thing she wanted from anyone.

Thoughts of this tiny woman being at the mercy of the assholes who'd been beating on him for the last few days made a red haze descend over Blink's vision. But he forced himself to stay calm. She needed him in control, not out of his mind with anger.

He reached between the bars and placed the small receiver that looked like a little earplug on the floor. She couldn't know how hard it was for him to give up the connection to his team. For a SEAL, communication was everything. And being in the dark about the plan made his skin crawl, but it couldn't be helped. If his captors discovered the device, he was as good as dead. And it would suck to be killed right before a rescue.

Blink moved away from the bars and lay down on his back once more. The position took some of the pressure off his aching ribs. He didn't know how much longer he had before the assholes came back to torture him some more. But he'd be ready. He had no choice.

CHAPTER FOUR

Josie stared at the small black device for what seemed like hours. Nate hadn't moved since lying down, and finally she moved across the cell and snatched it up before returning to her place at the wall.

Glancing at what looked like an AirPod but smaller, memories rushed over her, almost painful in their intensity. How she'd used something like this on the plane ride to Kuwait. The music she'd listened to. How naïve and carefree she'd been, with no idea of the hell that awaited her.

Closing the door firmly on her memories, Josie put the device in her ear. She heard nothing. No static. No one talking. Nothing.

Looking over at Nate, she bit her lip and thought about what he'd done. His people were there to rescue him. He could've left hours ago. But he hadn't. He'd stayed. Because of *her*. Thinking about what he'd done made her chest hurt. Even knowing he was probably going to be freaking waterboarded, he'd actually told his friend, teammate, whatever, to come back later, when they had a plan to get her out too.

It was overwhelming. Unbelievable.

She wanted to trust that rescue really *was* on the way. But given how her life had gone lately, she was still having a hard time wrapping her head around how much things had changed from the day-to-day boredom and terror she'd experienced for who the hell knew how long.

For the first time in weeks, she allowed herself to think that maybe, just maybe, she'd get out of here. It was likely she'd probably die in the escape attempt, but if she was going to die here anyway, she'd rather die doing anything she could to escape the people who'd locked her away than simply give up and fade into obscurity, with no one ever knowing where she went.

Not that she had too many people back home who'd bother filing a missing person's report. Maybe the guy she worked for would wonder why she'd never reported back in after her vacation. But he probably just assumed she'd decided to quit. And she hadn't told anyone where she was going, because she didn't have anyone close enough to really care.

If someone investigated, they'd see that she'd used her passport and entered Kuwait, but what could a police officer from the US do? Nothing. Someone would have to talk to the Kuwaiti police, and they probably weren't too concerned about a missing American woman.

But the Army *should've* missed Ayden. They'd have done an investigation, and maybe, just maybe, they would've found out about her. But then again, she and Ayden hadn't hung out with any of his military buddies after her arrival. That was yet another red flag she'd ignored.

Trying to stop beating herself up for the decisions she'd made in the past, which she couldn't change now, Josie concentrated on the present. There wasn't much water in the cup after giving what she'd had to Nate, but she picked it up and swallowed the mouthful that had accumulated. She needed all the help she could get if she'd be expected to run when she got out of her cell.

How the hell were they getting out though? Josie had no idea how that was going to go down. Would his friends dress like their captors and literally come through the door? Would they shoot their way inside? How would they unlock the cells?

She had so many questions and no answers, so she did what she'd done over the last few weeks to try to stay sane. She closed her eyes and retreated deep within herself. It was easier to be numb and think about nothing than about all the horrible things that had already happened, and might still happen in the future.

Jerking awake, Josie had no idea how much time had passed, but once again there were men in Nate's cell. This time they had no chair, but one man held Nate's feet against the floor, another held one arm and a third held the other.

The man who spoke English was there as well. "You wanted some water?" he asked with an evil smile. "We'll give it to you."

A fourth man knelt at Nate's head and covered his face with a filthy towel, pulling it tight—and the leader proceeded to pour a bucket of water over the cloth.

Josie had never seen anyone waterboarded before. Didn't

even know how one went about torturing someone with the technique, but she was getting a firsthand education now.

It went on for what seemed like forever. She could hear Nate gasping for air under the wet towel as water was poured over the top again and again. It pooled on the concrete floor under him, creeping over into her cell as well.

Inside, Josie was screaming in horror. Nate was drowning right in front of her, and there wasn't a damn thing she could do about it! She could draw attention to herself somehow, but what good would that do? Instinctively, she knew it wouldn't do anything. These men were enjoying themselves too much to let anything stop them.

And they weren't even asking Nate any questions. They were simply torturing him to torture him, because they could. And the fact that he'd voluntarily put himself in this situation was what hurt Josie the most. He could've been long gone from here. And yet, he'd stayed, knowing this torture was coming.

It was more than she could bear. Closing her eyes, feeling cowardly, she did her best to block out the sight and sound of Nate's suffering.

Finally, *finally*, the men seemed to get tired of messing with their captive. The guy who spoke English whipped the towel off Nate's face and sneered down at him. "Had enough?" he asked.

"Enough," Nate croaked.

His response seemed to please the leader tremendously.

"Maybe in a few hours you will answer our questions," he said. "If not?" He shrugged. "We can have some more fun. How long will you last, I wonder?"

Nate stayed silent, which was a relief for Josie. She had a feeling he wanted to cuss the guy out. Tell him to bring it on. But he didn't say a word, simply glared at his torturer.

The man who seemed to be in charge laughed, then gestured for his men to follow him out of the cell.

At the last minute, before the door to the cell closed, Nate said, "Thanks for the water. I needed that."

The leader looked furious when he spun around. He strode toward Nate and began to kick him. Over and over his foot made contact with Nate's body. He'd curled himself into a ball to try to protect his head, but he wasn't able to keep the blows from landing everywhere else.

Blood mixed with the water on the floor, turning it a sick color of pink.

"Fuckin' Americans!" the man said, then spat on Nate before turning and slamming his cell door shut. Before he left the room, he told Nate, "I think next time, we'll start with *her*. See how long you can hold out when she screams."

Josie shivered as the man's words sank in and the door to their prison slammed shut.

"Don't listen to him," Nate slurred. "He's not going to touch you. Give you my word."

She wasn't so sure. If the leader came back, there wasn't anything he could do from his side of the cell. But his words still made her feel a little better.

"Anything from my team?" Nate asked, pointing to his ear.

Josie was confused for a moment, then realized he wanted to know if she'd heard anything through the receiver in her ear. She shook her head.

"Okay. Give me a little bit to get my bearings, and I'll take that receiver back. It won't be long now, hear me, Spirit? We'll be out of here drinking a pink drink with an umbrella in it before you know it."

Josie didn't smile. She couldn't. Nate might've made light of what just happened, but she'd heard his gasps for breath. Had seen the panic in his eyes when the towel was removed from his face. He'd been through hell...for *her*.

Moving before she knew what she was doing, Josie scooted to the bars that separated their cells. She held her hand out toward him, not even sure what she was doing or asking of him.

Amazingly, Nate maneuvered himself slowly across the floor, through the pooled water, toward her. To her shock, when he got close enough, he put his cheek on her outstretched hand. His beard was surprisingly soft against her palm.

He sighed. A long sound that seemed to reach out and grab hold of Josie's heart and squeeze it tight.

He was hurting, that was obvious. And somehow, her touch seemed to relieve some of that pain. They stayed like that for several moments. His cheek resting against her hand, connecting as human beings in a situation that had tried to suck out every ounce of their humanity.

Then Nate lifted his head and pierced her with a fierce look. "We're getting out of here, Spirit. I'd never let them put one finger on you. I'd do whatever it takes to make sure that doesn't happen, but I won't have to do anything, because Flash, Smiley, Kevlar, and the others are coming. Soon. I'm going to lie here and try to regain some strength, but I'll be ready when they arrive. Come hell or high water, we're getting out of here. Together."

He couldn't know the affect his words had on her. His reassurance. His protectiveness. His absolutely certainty that they were going to escape. His vulnerability in admitting his current weakness.

This man had turned her life upside down, and that was saying something, since it was already pretty well fucked.

Okay.

Her mouth had moved with the word, but no sound escaped her throat.

"Okay," he replied, as if she'd spoken out loud.

Then he stretched out his bound hands toward her. Resting them on the concrete floor, inches from the bars. He closed his eyes, attempting to recover from the torture he'd just endured enough so he'd be ready for whatever his friends were going to do to get them out.

Josie stared at his fingers. A couple looked like they were bent at a funny angle, and his fingernails were just as dirty as hers now. It was that, more than anything, that gave her the courage to reach between the bars once more. She placed her hand over one of his. His skin was warm, while hers felt cold. His fingers twitched but he didn't grab at her. Didn't move much at all. Except for his lips. They turned up in a small smile as he lay on the floor of his prison cell.

Now that she'd worked up the courage to touch him, Josie didn't want to let go. She lowered herself to the floor and kept her hand where it was. Covering his, trying to let him know without words how much his being there meant to her.

CHAPTER FIVE

Blink hurt. Everywhere. But it was the feeling of drowning that had him unable to sleep. Waterboarding sucked. There was no getting around it. Intellectually he knew he wasn't drowning, but the soaking-wet towel on his face was enough to give him the feeling of not being able to breathe, of being underwater. He'd had extensive training in the torture technique, but that didn't mean it still didn't suck.

Now, he was lying in an extremely uncomfortable position, but it was the small, cold fingers wrapped around his hand that kept him as still as possible on the floor. He wouldn't move unless he had to. Touching him was a *huge* step for this woman, and they both knew it.

And it was all the proof he needed that he'd made the right decision yesterday.

Flash and the rest of the team probably could've come up with a new plan on the fly, but the odds of succeeding would've been drastically reduced. It was better that they

44

regrouped and came back ready for two POWs instead of one. He'd go through ten more waterboarding sessions if it meant they both escaped.

The thought of her experiencing two seconds of what he'd been trained to withstand made Blink want to fucking kill the asshole who'd threatened her with his bare hands. He'd do whatever was necessary to keep her safe.

Suddenly, she jerked her hand off his, hitting it on the bars hard enough that Blink winced. She stared at him with wide eyes, reaching up to her ear.

"Ah, they're here?" he asked.

She nodded, a much more aggressive nod than he'd gotten from her ever before. Instead of opening his hand for the receiver, Blink moved closer to the bars and tilted his head in her direction. "Can you put it in my ear? That asshole fucked my arm up with one of his kicks."

It wasn't exactly a lie. Something *was* wrong with his arm, but Blink wanted to feel her touch again, strengthen that small bit of trust she'd shown him.

She hesitated, then she reached toward him.

Her fingers brushed against his earlobe, and goose bumps broke out on the back of Blink's neck. She didn't hesitate, didn't dally, just gently placed the earbud inside his ear then backed up.

"...in ten. You copy, Blink?"

"Sorry, no. Repeat," he told Preacher.

"Plan is to quietly and carefully take out a few of the cinder blocks in your current abode. We'll take you out that way, put them back, so it'll look like you disappeared into thin air. Gonna get to you in ten."

"And my friend?" he asked.

"We'll get to her the same way, at the same time," Preacher said.

"You'll only need to remove half the bricks to get to her," Blink said.

"Know that. We all saw her. We've got burkas for the two of you. It's not ideal, I realize, but neither of you can walk around in what you've got on without drawing the wrong kind of attention. Things are still extremely hot out here. No one's happy about what went down."

Blink thought that was an understatement. He and the SEAL team he'd been with had taken out two very high-ranking men in the area. Men who were longtime terrorist leaders. But he couldn't think about that right now. "Shoes?"

"Sandals. Had to guess at her size."

Blink nodded. He felt the woman's gaze on him and looked up. "We'll be ready," he told Preacher.

"Roger. Out."

Blink took a breath, then quickly said, "It's time. My team is going to take out some cinder blocks in our cells. We'll go out that way. They have burkas for us to put on. Then we'll simply walk away."

He saw her swallow, then nod. This woman had more courage in her little finger than many men he'd worked with in his SEAL career.

"We can do this," he told her.

Again, she nodded.

Not for the first time, Blink wished she would or could talk to him. Ask all the questions he saw swirling in her gaze. But for now, it was enough that she wasn't panicking.

The sound of scraping seemed loud in the otherwise quiet room, and Blink winced, praying the men on the other side of the door wouldn't hear.

The woman in the cell slowly stood. She walked over to where the cup was sitting on the floor under the water drip that had literally kept her alive. She picked it up, looked into it, then back up at Blink.

She held it up, as if asking if he wanted the water that had accumulated.

His chest hurt, and not because he'd been beaten time and time again. Blink shook his head. "You drink it, Spirit. Things are about to get pretty intense. Just stay calm, do what my team and I tell you to do as soon as we ask you to do it. All right?"

She didn't nod, just tipped the cup up to her lips. Then she lowered it to her side and held it with what looked like a death grip. He could see her fingers go white as she gripped the thing. It would be smarter to leave it, but since it had literally kept her alive, he understood her need to take it with her.

About two minutes passed as his team worked to remove enough cinder blocks so they could crawl out of their cells. Spirit's was completed before his, which wasn't surprising, since the hole didn't need to be as large.

"Tell her to come on out," Kevlar said in Blink's ear.

"Go on," Blink encouraged the woman.

But she didn't move. She stayed where she was, staring not at the hole in her cell, the path to freedom, and not at him... but at the progress his team was making to the hole on his side. It was hard to believe she wasn't bolting the first chance she got.

Instead, she was waiting for him.

Determination swelled within Blink once more.

No one was going to hurt this woman again. No fucking way.

"I think it's big enough. Get your hairy ass out here," Safe said through the radio receiver.

"Ready?" Blink asked the woman. "Together."

She nodded, then moved toward the hole on her side. Out of the corner of his eye, he saw her lie down, and then his team pulled her out with no fuss. It wasn't quite as easy for him. Blink lay on his back, since his hands were still cuffed in front of him. He wiggled his head out of the hole and then had to turn this way and that, as Kevlar and MacGyver struggled to get his shoulders out.

Blink wanted to scream in pain as the rough bricks scraped over the many wounds he already had on his body, but he didn't even grimace as he was finally pulled out of that hellhole and hauled to his feet.

"You look like shit."

"Wow, someone had a little too much fun rearranging your face."

"Good thing you have that beard to hide your ugly mug."

But Blink wasn't listening to the banter his team was known for, especially in stressful situations. He only had eyes for the woman who'd been his rock. She'd kept him calm, gave him a purpose while waiting for rescue.

She was standing in the alley next to the building where they'd been held. Filthy as hell, wearing a fucking *bikini* under a brown cover-up that was at one time probably some pretty pastel color, holding on to that damn cup as if her life depended on it. Her toes looked dainty and fragile in the dirt and trash that was all around them.

"Here, get this on. You can be the mom, she's the kid, and Kevlar's the dad. Keep your head down and be ready for anything," Safe said as he shoved a pile of material at Blink, even while Smiley worked to remove his shackles from around his wrists and ankles.

He figured out how to get the burka on and saw MacGyver helping the woman cover herself. The mesh screen across his face made it difficult to see clearly, but his team would be his eyes for him.

"Eyes open, everyone," Kevlar said through the radio. "We aren't out of here yet. Taxi's waiting, let's get the hell out of dodge."

Without thought, Blink took a step toward the woman. He couldn't see her eyes anymore, which bothered him for some reason.

"Stay one step behind me, Blink," Kevlar told him. "And keep hold of the woman. She looks like she'll blow away with one gust of wind."

Kevlar wasn't wrong. Blink reached out a hand and, to his surprise, she latched onto it with startling strength.

"If you have any trouble walking, let me know. I'll carry you. We've got this, Spirit."

To his amazement, Blink felt her fingers tighten around his, as if in confirmation of his words. Again, the thought of how brave she was hit him hard. She wasn't crying. Wasn't bitching about the sandals on her feet that he saw were obviously too big. She was doing what she had to do in order to survive.

But he had no time to think, as they were moving fast. And to his chagrin, *Blink* was the one having trouble walking. He felt himself swaying back and forth as if he were drunk. The beatings he'd received were catching up with him.

He felt the woman sidle up next to him. She held his hand even tighter, as if she could hold him up by sheer force of will. It worked. Having her walking so close helped Blink steady his stride.

They'd gone only a few blocks when they heard loud shouting from the next block over.

"Shit! Let's get the hell out of here!" Safe exclaimed through the comms.

And just like that, adrenaline flooded Blink. He no longer felt his injuries. No longer felt weak.

"We'll go north five blocks then west toward the water. There are three boats waiting," Kevlar told him, bringing his weapon up, ready to use at the slightest provocation.

Blink didn't need to explain to Spirit that something was wrong. Her body was tense and she could hear the shouting as well as he could.

"Easy," he murmured softly.

Knowing if they ran they'd look even more out of place, Blink walked them behind Kevlar as they went as fast as they dared toward the extraction point. Getting out of the city was going to be dangerous as hell.

As soon as he had the thought, he heard rapid gunfire echo through the streets around them.

"*Fuck*. Can you run?" Kevlar asked, addressing the question to both Blink and the woman at his side.

Spirit nodded, and that was all Blink needed to see.

He wasn't dying here, and neither was she. Every step hurt like hell. The shoes his team had brought him weren't great for running, and Spirit's were even worse. But if they didn't get on one of those boats, the condition of their feet would be the least of their worries. And just getting to the boats wasn't a guarantee they'd make it out of the country. Until they were out of Iranian waters, the possibility of being captured again was high.

Shouts sounded behind them—dangerously close.

They weren't going to make it to the boats.

Frustration and anger swam through Blink. He'd promised Spirit he'd get her out of there, and he wasn't going to be able to keep that promise.

Suddenly, Spirit tugged on his hand. Hard.

Almost falling, he glanced at her through the mesh of the burka and saw her pointing toward a house. A woman was standing in the doorway, motioning frantically for them to come closer.

"Kevlar. House!" Blink hissed, letting his team leader know what Spirit had spotted.

Every instinct told Blink to keep moving. To get to the boats. But the sounds of men searching the streets were louder now. Any second, they'd come around a corner and see them.

Kevlar nodded at him and they ran toward the house.

The door had just shut behind them when they heard the pounding of boots pass by. The woman who'd invited them in held a finger to her lips. Blink had no idea if she knew he was a man, that Spirit wasn't a little girl, but he wasn't about to blow their cover.

He could feel Spirit shaking next to him and without thought, he pulled her close. Her head barely came to his shoulder, and despite the dangerous situation, Blink felt something click into place deep inside as the woman leaned against him. It was a feeling he'd never had before.

A sense of rightness. Of coming home.

They were in the middle of a completely fucked-up rescue mission, as vulnerable as he'd ever been, and yet somehow, everything felt right in his world.

"Blink?"

Jerking at the sound of Kevlar's voice, he turned.

His team leader looked completely at ease. As if he wasn't running for his life with two very weak people who, at this point, were liabilities to his survival. He motioned to the earpiece they were using to stay in touch with the others— the one he'd completely ignored because he was too busy feeling blown away by his connection to Spirit.

"The team took two of the boats. We need to get to the third. Our contact is still there. Just in case we get separated, it's a brown speedboat. Looks like shit but she's got enough power to outrun anyone who might follow. He'll wait until dark if need be. The plan is to get to the boat and the second we get out of Iranian waters, we'll be picked up by a bird."

Blink nodded, not liking their odds at actually making it to the boat at this point. And he wasn't even going to ask Kevlar what he planned on doing if they *did* get separated, and he and Spirit took the boat that was waiting.

As if he'd been working with Blink for years, rather than the short time they'd actually been on the same team, Kevlar said, "We're getting out of here, Blink. We still need to have words about you sneaking off in the middle of the night without us."

He nodded. He realized he was breathing hard and adrenaline was still coursing through his bloodstream. They were so close to getting out of there, but the most dangerous part still remained. They had to get to the water and hope the pilot and the boat were as good as Kevlar claimed.

The woman who'd invited them into her house said something in rapid-fire Persian, then pulled on Spirit's burka and pointed toward the back of the house.

None of them had any idea what she'd said, but it was obvious she wanted them to follow her. They walked through the small house to a back door. She opened it a crack and peered out. Then she said something else to them and nodded, holding open the door.

Blink would have preferred to wait a little longer to make sure their pursuers thought they were gone, but it looked like they were leaving now. He nodded at the woman who'd helped them and stepped outside with Spirit and Kevlar once more.

"Doing good, Spirit," he told her quietly, as soon as they were back on the city street. "Just a little farther."

His feet hurt. His legs hurt. His fingers and back hurt. But nothing would keep Blink from getting to the water. He thought about the rest of his team, who'd been willing to come after him. About his former teammates, who'd died and been injured fighting against evil. And he thought about the woman who'd just risked her own safety to hide them. She didn't know they were Americans; all she probably saw was two parents and a child, scared and about to be caught in the middle of something dangerous. Blink had no idea if the woman thought they were the ones being chased, or if they were simply in the wrong place at the wrong time. But her kindness had allowed them another chance to get home. He would forever be grateful.

That was the thing about war. About the missions he did. Even though they might be in a hostile country, there were always innocents. Civilians who were merely living their lives. They weren't hardened terrorists, didn't want to kill or be killed. They were simply trying to survive in whatever situation life had handed them. Women, children, and men who loved and wanted to be loved. Who had goals and aspirations. Who didn't agree with others who were willing to kill for power. The woman who'd let them use her home as a momentary refuge was one such civilian.

Blink didn't know exactly where they were going, but he trusted Kevlar, and he could smell the water as his team leader steered them toward it. It didn't take long to reach, and there was a lot of action around the docks. Men yelling and pointing toward the gulf.

Scanning the boats, Blink spotted what had to be their ride. A man sat in a brown boat, and Kevlar was right, it looked like it would sink if it tried to go anywhere. Instead of looking concerned about the commotion around him, the guy appeared calm. He wasn't fiddling with fishing gear. Wasn't doing anything but sitting at the back of the boat with one hand on the control stick of the outboard motor.

But if this *wasn't* their contact and their way out of there, and Blink, Spirit, and Kevlar hopped into his boat, they were fucked.

Kevlar stopped with his back against the wall of a building not far from the dock, and Blink did the same, noticing he didn't even need to instruct Spirit to sandwich herself between them. She followed his lead without questions, without hesitation.

"See that boat?" Kevlar asked them, pointing out the exact one Blink had already spotted.

Spirit nodded, at the same time Blink said tersely, "Yes."

"That's our ride."

Spirit immediately looked up at Blink and shook her head.

He wished he could see her eyes better, but with both of them wearing burkas, he couldn't. "It's okay," he told her.

Instead of nodding, she shook her head again.

He wasn't sure why she was hesitating. He needed her to be onboard with this. He could carry her, but it would bring attention to them, attention they definitely didn't want or need. He squeezed her hand reassuringly, realizing yet again just how small and fragile she really was.

He didn't wait for Kevlar to explain why their only option at this point was getting into that boat. Spirit was looking to *him* for reassurance. "The helicopters can't cross into Iranian airspace without triggering a major international incident. Out in the desert, sure, they can manage to sneak in, drop off special forces, then sneak out, but coming into the city just isn't possible. We have to get out of the country so they can pick us up. Kevlar assures me that the boat can get us where we need to go in order for a chopper to pick us up. I trust him with my life. But more importantly, I trust him with *yours*. We can do this, Spirit. Hell, this is easy compared to what we've already been through."

He had no idea if what he said was getting through. She stared up at him, and it didn't feel like she was even breathing.

Then she shocked the hell out of Blink by sagging toward him, her forehead smacking against his chest. Her arms wrapped around him and held on so tightly, he winced from the pressure she was putting on his bruised ribs.

But he didn't hesitate to put his arms around her in return. She was shaking, obviously scared out of her mind. He wasn't sure why...but he was beginning to think it was because of the boat.

"Is that what happened to you? How you ended up here? A boat?" he asked quietly.

She nodded against him, and Blink's heart bled for her.

As much as he loved having her lean on him—he was a protector, after all—he knew they couldn't stand there forever. Someone would notice them.

He pulled back but didn't let go of her. "You aren't going back there. I give you my word as a Navy SEAL, and as a man. We're all getting the hell out of here. And when we get to the carrier where the rest of my teammates are waiting, I'll make sure you have the biggest, juiciest hamburger I can find. With all the trimmings. Oh, but if you're a vegetarian—which is fine, I mean, there's nothing wrong with that—I'll fix you the biggest salad instead, with every vegetable known to man."

She made a sound, and if Blink wasn't mistaken, it was a laugh of sorts.

Then...finally she nodded. It was a tiny movement of her head, but he saw it. She continued to impress the hell out of him.

"Right. So, let's go catch our ride. It's going to be bumpy. And fast. But all we have to do is keep our heads down and it'll be okay." Blink was talking out his ass. He had a feeling this was going to suck, *hard*. He had no idea if their pursuers —he had no doubt they'd be chased—would stop once they crossed out of Iranian waters, but their bird would be there. *That* he knew without question.

He felt something hard against his side, and realized she was still holding the little metal cup. "I have some pockets in my pants. If you trust me with it, I can put your cup in there. It'll free up your hands...just in case."

Blink had no idea how badly he'd wanted her to trust him with the precious cup until she held it out to him. It was smaller than it had seemed back in their cells. But the thing had saved her life, and probably his as well. Moving quickly, he shoved it into one of the many pockets of his pants. They were usually full of all sorts of things, but his captors had taken everything from him before they'd beaten the crap out of him the first time and thrown him into his cell.

"All right. Let's do this," Kevlar said.

Blink held out his hand and, once again, the world seemed to shift when Spirit placed her small hand in his larger one. Their fingers were filthy, his were bloody and bent from the torture he'd received, but somehow seeing their hands clasped felt like a good omen.

They were in this together.

CHAPTER SIX

Josie felt sick. She was terrified. She'd dreamed about being out of that cell for weeks, but now that she was, she wanted to go back. Back to where she knew what to expect, where she didn't have to worry about being shot or hunted like an animal.

But...she wasn't alone anymore. And that was better than what she'd endured while in captivity. Nate was larger than life, both physically and metaphorically. He kept himself between her and danger. Had constantly checked on her, reassured her. He didn't treat her as if she was a liability, which Josie knew she was.

She'd lost the sandals his friends had given her the minute they picked up their pace, and hurrying through the streets was extremely painful. It felt as if she'd found every pebble and sharp stone as they'd fled. But if Nate could endure without any sign of the pain he had to be in, so could she. There was no way she would slow him down.

But finding out they'd be escaping by boat? That nearly broke her. Memories assailed Josie...seeing Ayden shot, his body carelessly thrown overboard. The panic and terror when those men had grabbed her and dragged her onto their boat.

Out on the water, she, Nate, and Kevlar would be sitting ducks. She knew that better than anyone. There'd been nowhere to hide when the men had overtaken her and Ayden. No running away. She could swim, but in the middle of the gulf, where could she go?

And now she had to get back on another boat. A *smaller* one. And they'd surely be chased. It was her worst nightmare all over again.

But she had no choice. None. Nate was right; it wasn't as if a helicopter could come in and get them on the docks.

Her breaths were coming too fast as terror swam in her veins. But when Nate took her hand, and he and his fellow Navy SEAL stepped away from the shelter of the buildings, she had no choice but to follow. Her ears were ringing, and it felt as if she was seeing the world through a long dark tunnel. It didn't help that the mesh over her face blocked her peripheral vision. Someone could be sneaking up on them and they wouldn't even know.

"One step at a time," Nate said softly from beside her.

She squeezed his hand in acknowledgement, and feeling his fingers tighten around hers in return made her feel not quite so alone. Not quite so scared.

They stepped onto the dock leading to the boat—and that's when the shit hit the fan.

Someone yelled something from behind them, and without Nate or Kevlar having to tell her, Josie ran. They bolted toward the brown boat, and the man sitting next to the engine stood and gestured wildly for them to hurry.

Thankful that it was the correct boat, and they weren't about to jump into the vessel of some stranger who didn't know what was happening, Josie felt almost numb with relief as she ran faster. Nate was practically dragging her, since his legs were longer than hers, but he never let go of her hand. Never told her she was being too slow.

When they got to the boat, the man had already started the engine. Josie didn't hesitate. She lifted her leg to jump in, but promptly tripped over the vast material of the burka. Thankfully, she fell right where she wanted to go anyway—into the boat. She felt the craft lurch as Nate and Kevlar followed behind her.

Before she could sit up, she was pinned to the bottom of the boat as their driver gunned the engine.

"Hang on!" Nate yelled over the sound of the powerful motor.

Josie couldn't see, she couldn't breathe, all she could do was hold on, as Nate had instructed. She bounced slightly every time the boat went over a wave. She heard nothing but the piercing sound of the engine as she lay on her stomach and tried not to throw up.

After a few minutes, Nate lifted himself up and off her. Josie stayed where she was. Her heart was hammering and it felt as if she was having a heart attack. The boat didn't slow. In fact, it felt as if it was speeding up.

To her surprise, Nate turned her and began trying to get the burka up and over her head. The second it was removed, even though they were in no way safe, Josie immediately felt as if she could breathe again.

"We're doing it," he said, his words almost whipped away by the wind. "We're outrunning them!"

Looking behind them, Josie saw three boats in pursuit but, to her relief, it didn't seem as if they were gaining.

"You did good, Spirit," Nate told her.

Josie wasn't sure at first that she'd liked the nickname Nate had given her, but it was growing on her. Of course, she wished she could tell him her real name, but since her voice still didn't seem to work, it wasn't exactly possible at the moment.

Kevlar reached up to his ear and seemed to fiddle with the receiver, then half-yelled to be heard over the rushing wind, "We're on our way with tangos hot on our heels. Roger, we'll be ready. It'll be good to see you too. Out." He looked at her, then Blink. "Hold on, you two, we're almost there."

Josie swallowed hard and glanced ahead of them. All she saw was open water, but she knew somewhere out there was the "safe" zone. They just had to get to it before the men giving chase caught up to them.

She saw it before she heard it. A helicopter. It seemed tiny in the distance, but as they got closer and closer, it grew in size.

"That's it. Our way out of here!" Nate shouted.

Something occurred to Josie then. How the hell were they going to get *into* the helicopter? She wasn't sure, with no one out here patrolling the waters, that the people chasing would care about a borderline. She watched with trepidation as they raced closer and closer to the chopper.

Soon it was above them. The huge machine banked to the right and circled around so it paced them, heading in the same direction as the boat they were in kept driving at the same breakneck speed it had been, never slowing.

A door opened on the side of the helicopter—and a rope dropped from the opening.

Oh hell no!

Josie was not climbing up a freaking rope while driving a million miles an hour! She wasn't a circus performer. She couldn't do it!

But she should've known Nate would never ask something like that of her.

"All we have to do is hold on," he told her, his mouth close to her ear. "They'll pull us up with a mechanical wench. Just hold onto me and I'll keep you safe, Spirit. I give you my word."

For some reason, she believed him. He hadn't broken any of the promises he'd made to her so far. She was terrified, scared shitless, but then again, *everything* that had happened to her recently was scary and horrible. Why would this be any different?

And yet, it was. She wasn't alone this time. Ayden hadn't been able to protect her; honestly, he hadn't even tried. He panicked when he realized what he'd done, that he'd accidentally taken them into Iranian waters. He even tried to blame *Josie* when the men had boarded. Of course, it hadn't done any good. He'd been shot seconds after unsuccessfully trying to throw her under the bus.

But this man? He didn't panic when things went wrong

minutes after they'd been freed from their cells. He was calm, cool, and had done everything to protect her as they fled.

Nate stared down at her, as if waiting for her agreement on what was about to happen. That was another thing she respected about this man. He didn't force anything on her. Made it seem as if she had a say in what was happening. She didn't, but she appreciated the effort anyway.

She finally nodded.

"Good. Hamburger or salad. They'll soon be ours," he quipped, then looked up at the dangling rope. He stood, and Josie did her best to brace his legs. Which was ridiculous. It wasn't as if she had the strength to keep him from falling due to the erratic motions of the boat. Still, it made her feel as if she wasn't quite as helpless as she felt to be helping in some little way. Thankfully, Kevlar was on his other side, further stabilizing Nate as he reached for the rope.

To her amazement, Nate quickly manipulated a portion of the long rope into a loop and secured it around his hips. Then he motioned for her to stand. Apparently, they would be going up first. Joy.

Josie stood up—and immediately fell back on her ass as the boat went over a fairly large wave.

He frowned and held out his hand. Josie gripped it and, with his help, managed to get herself up against him. He and Kevlar looped the rope around her waist, and then under her butt. "Hop up!" he yelled against the wind.

Josie didn't understand. She frowned at him.

He didn't explain further. Instead, he simply put his hands on her butt and lifted. Automatically, Josie wrapped her legs around him, locking her ankles together at the small of his back.

"Hold on!" he yelled.

It was then that she realized all three of them would be going up at the same time. While Nate had been helping get her situated, Kevlar had quickly attached himself to the remaining length of rope that she'd thought was just "extra." He'd be dangling under the two of them.

Josie had a moment to pray that the rope was strong enough to lift three bodies at once. That it wouldn't break and send them all plunging into the water. That whatever mechanical contraption would be hauling them upward would be able to function with their combined weight.

Then her terror was suddenly focused elsewhere. Over Nate's shoulder, Josie saw several men in the boats that were pursuing them, aiming what looked like rifles on steroids straight at their boat.

A squeak left her throat. She wanted to yell for Nate to watch out. To point out the fact that they were about to get shot, but her voice wasn't cooperating.

She hissed as she felt pressure on her ass, and suddenly they began to ascend at a rapid rate. To her horror, they were about a dozen feet up when she saw the man who'd driven them to freedom fall over in the bottom of the boat.

He'd been shot!

Sorrow filled her. She hadn't said a word to the man, and he hadn't talked to any of them, but he'd risked his life to help them escape. Now he'd been *shot* because of them.

Closing her eyes, she buried her face in Nate's neck. She

tightened her legs and arms around him and prayed he wouldn't drop her.

They spun in circles as the chopper lifted high into the sky and away from the boats, bullets flying around them. Josie felt dizzy, and she opened her eyes to try to get her equilibrium back. She instantly regretted it, as their position above the waves was way higher than she'd anticipated.

"Almost there!" Nate yelled.

Josie looked up and saw the skids of the helicopter getting closer and closer at an alarming rate. Once again, she closed her eyes, not wanting to see the collision that was about to happen. Except it didn't.

She felt the rope swing outward, which made her open her eyes. A man inside the helicopter was manipulating the rope so they avoided smacking into the skids. He made it look so easy to maneuver them...but she supposed he probably had lots of practice helping people into a helicopter flying a million miles an hour over a churning ocean while being shot at.

The thought made her internally roll her eyes at herself. It was weird the things the brain came up with to cope with stressful situations.

Then hands were touching her, and she felt something hard at her back. They were yanked inside, and she watched as Kevlar hauled himself inside the chopper with little ceremony and an efficiency built by experience.

"Go, go, go!" someone yelled.

Before she had a chance to feel relieved that they were inside the helicopter, it banked left, hard. Sending her and Nate careening toward the other side. His back smacked against the metal wall of the chopper, and then they were sliding forward.

"Fuck!" Nate cursed, but his arms tightened around Josie, not letting go, not trying to remove the harness he'd wrapped around them both.

The noise inside the chopper was so loud, Josie couldn't hear anything but Nate.

"Easy, bro!"

The cover-up Josie had worn for weeks slid up as, once again, the helicopter banked hard to one side. She felt burning on the back of her thigh, but before she could even register the pain, a loud *boom* echoed through the chopper, making it lurch, and for a second, Josie thought the engine had stopped.

"Fuck!" Nate yelled. Then he looked down at her. "We're hit."

The words didn't register at first. And when they *did* finally sink in, the terror Josie felt earlier—all of it...running from their prison, seeing the boat they had to get in, being chased on the open seas, dangling by what seemed like a thread from a helicopter—increased tenfold.

"We've got one of the best pilots in the Army flying this thing. We'll be fine."

Josie had no idea how the hell they were going to be *fine* when they'd just been hit by some sort of missile. She could smell the smoke now, the caustic scent of gas.

Nate managed to sit upright. While keeping his arms around Josie, he scooted toward a lone seat right behind one of the pilots. Even with the chopper moving from side to side, obviously trying to evade more weapons fire from the men in boats, he pulled himself into the seat with Josie still clinging to him. Kevlar had strapped himself to the side of the chopper and he was on his knees, pointing his weapon out the still-open door of the chopper.

To her surprise, Nate pulled a harness, a seat belt of sorts, around the both of them, snapping it into place. He had his arms around her back, and her face was pressed against the side of his neck. She was straddling his lap, her crotch pressed tight against his, her cover-up and bikini no barrier whatsoever. The position should've been awkward, but all Josie could think of was sticking as close to Nate as possible.

She was about to die in a fiery helicopter crash. And if that didn't kill her, water filling the interior as they sank to the bottom of the ocean certainly would.

She didn't want to be alone when she died, and as long as she clung to Nate, at least they would die together.

The helicopter trip was the longest of Josie's life. It could've been ten minutes or an hour. She had no clue. By some miracle, they didn't crash. Not into the ocean, at least. She vaguely heard Nate speaking but due to her fear, his words made no sense.

Then his arms tightened around her so hard it was difficult to breathe. She figured out why when the sound of the engine suddenly disappeared.

"This is it. Hang on!" one of the pilots called out.

Squeezing her eyes shut, Josie did as ordered.

The last thing she heard was a popping sound, and Nate saying *"fuck!"* before the world turned upside down and something hit her head—hard.

* * *

Blink woke to the smell of something burning. Everything returned to him in a flash. The crazy boat ride, being hoisted to the chopper, seeing his brother, Tate, behind the controls, then the helicopter being hit with an RPG. Tate swearing as he and his copilot fought to stay in the air. He heard him say something about going down in Iraq before the engine died and they crashed.

Feeling pressure on his chest, Blink looked down and saw Spirit lying bonelessly against him. He'd managed to get them both into one of the seats and strapped in. Thank God. If he hadn't, they'd probably both be dead right now. As it was, he saw blood dripping from the side of Spirit's head.

"Tate? Kevlar?" he called out, worried about his brother and the other pilot and his team leader.

"I'm good!" Kevlar said.

"Alive!" Tate replied. "You and the girl?"

"Same," Blink said. He felt little puffs of air on his neck, so he knew Spirit was breathing.

"Shit, man, that was intense," the copilot said.

Blink focused and saw they were all still sitting in the cockpit of the MH-60 Black Hawk helicopter. Behind him was nothing but open air. To his right, the door of the chopper was completely missing and above him, he saw sky.

"Good to see you, bro," Tate said, turning around with a small smirk. "But I mean, maybe we could've met over a beer at a bar or something instead?"

Blink couldn't stop the smile that spread over his lips.

"Can't help but be in the middle of a clusterfuck, can you?" he asked his twin.

"Heard you needed a ride, who was I to turn that down?" Tate said.

"If you're done with your brotherly reunion, Casper, I'm thinking we need to get the hell out of here. We left a trail that tangos on *both* sides of the border will be able to follow," the copilot said. "We need to be out of here when they arrive."

"Bro, this is Pyro, my copilot," Tate said.

Blink nodded at the other man. "This is Kevlar, my team leader," he said, introducing Kevlar to the pilots. "Where are we?"

"Mountains between Iraq and Iran. I tried to get us to the desert, but steering was fucked by that RPG. This was as good as I could get," his brother explained.

"Any landing you walk away from is a perfect landing," Kevlar told him.

"Tell that to Laryn. She's gonna be pissed I crashed her baby."

Blink eyed him. "Laryn?"

"She's a mechanic on the naval carrier working as a special contractor to the Army for the Night Stalkers who was in the area when we got word you needed a lift out of Iran," Pyro answered. "You're lucky we were around. The Navy asked for us to join them onboard...for a mission I can't talk about, of course. Laryn always warns Casper that if he brings this beauty back with even a scratch, he'll answer to her," Pyro said.

Blink nodded, then returned his attention to Spirit with a

frown. She hadn't stirred against him. He unclipped the harness then quickly released the ropes he'd used to secure her to him for their ride into the chopper. He scooted forward in his seat. The cockpit was sitting at an angle, and he marveled anew at the fact that they were all still alive. He always knew his brother was a damn good pilot, had to be in order to be a Night Stalker, one of the best of the best as far as helicopter pilots went in the Army, but this certainly proved it.

Kevlar helped him move so he didn't have to let go of Spirit, and every muscle in his body screamed as he scooted to the edge of the chopper and stepped outside with Spirit still limp in his arms. He walked a few steps away from the smoldering chopper and went to his knees.

"Spirit?" he asked, as he lay her down on her back on the rocky ground.

"Who is she?" Tate asked, crouching beside him.

"No clue," Blink said. "She was in the cell next to mine." He glanced briefly at his twin. "Look at her. She's been starved. The only reason she was still alive was because there was a fucking leak in the corner of her cell, where she was able to collect water. And she gave it to me. She had this little tin cup, and it filled up every couple of days. And after a torture session, she gave that precious water to *me*. She hasn't spoken a single word. I have no idea what her name is, where she's from, or anything about her...but she's *mine*."

Blink's words were fierce and guttural. What he was saying made no sense, but he didn't care. He was in awe of this woman. She'd done everything he'd asked of her and more. She had no reason to trust him, and yet she had anyway.

She'd been thrown away, forgotten, and somehow she'd survived. Her spirit still shone as bright as the fucking sun.

"Easy, Blink," Kevlar said, putting a hand on his shoulder.

Blink took a deep breath. Getting emotional and worked up wouldn't do Spirit any good. He needed to stay calm. Do what needed to be done.

Tate nodded. "Take your woman over there while Pyro and I do what we need to do. We'll get the emergency packs and then we'll be on our way."

"I'll help," Kevlar said without hesitation.

Blink should've known his brother wouldn't tell him he was being ridiculous. They were twins; Tate knew him better than anyone in the entire world.

"Tate," he said when his brother started to walk away.

"Yeah?"

"Thanks." Blink didn't know what he was thanking his brother for. Coming to get him. Landing the disabled chopper. Not telling him that he was ridiculous for claiming a woman he didn't even know by name.

His brother didn't need clarification. He simply nodded, then turned back to the helicopter.

Blink stood and carefully picked up Spirit, carrying her about a hundred feet away from the downed chopper. His brother, Pyro, and Kevlar had jobs to do. They needed to make sure no one was able to get any government secrets by dismantling the helicopter. They'd destroy what they could, then torch the rest.

Right now, he was more concerned with the fact that Spirit was still unconscious. He put her back on the ground and inspected the wound on her head. It was bleeding sluggishly, but when he brushed her hair away from the wound, he was relieved to see it didn't need stitches.

He was carefully inspecting her arms and legs when his skin prickled, and Blink looked at her face—startled to realize she was awake and looking right at him.

"Hey," he said in a calm tone.

As expected, she didn't respond, simply continued to stare.

"Can you sit up?" he asked.

He waited, but when she didn't nod or shake her head, decided to encourage her to move anyway. He got her to a sitting position, and she finally took her gaze from him and looked around. Her eyes widened when she saw the helicopter.

"Yeah, it was a hard landing," Blink said, with no intonation in his voice.

She made a strangled sound in her throat that he thought might be a chuckle, and he felt ten feet tall that he'd been able to do that. Make her laugh. "My brother is apparently a fucking wizard," he told her. Then sighed. "Right, so...bad news is that we crashed. But the good news is that we're not in the ocean, and we aren't in Iran anymore."

Her gaze swung back to him, and she lifted a brow. Now it was Blink's turn to chuckle. "Right, so we're in Iraq. But we aren't actively at war with them anymore. So all we have to do is take a little walk through the mountains and I'm sure Tex will have us picked up in no time."

Spirit tilted her head as if to ask who the hell he was talking about.

"Tex is a former Navy SEAL who has made it his mission

in life to watch over those of us crazy enough to do this job. I've got a tracker. In my underwear. It's how my team knew exactly where to find me, and how the chopper found us in the middle of the ocean. It might take a couple of days, but they *will* come and get us," Blink told her.

"We're almost ready to go," Tate called out.

Blink looked at Spirit. "That's my brother, the fancy-ass helicopter pilot. We're twins."

Spirit looked over at Tate, then back to him, then back at his twin. She wrinkled her nose, then shook her head at him.

"What? We are."

She shook her head again.

Blink couldn't help but grin. "You don't think we look alike? Literally no one can tell us apart," he informed her.

To his surprise, Spirit pointed at herself.

"You can?" Blink asked.

She nodded.

For some reason, he liked that. No, he freaking *loved* it. And as much as he wanted to sit here and chat with this woman in their entirely unique way, they needed to get moving.

"Right. Good. Well...that's my brother. His name is Tate, but he goes by his call sign of Casper. That's his copilot, Pyro. They have to destroy the chopper before we go, so there will be a loud boom, and we need to be moving when it happens so anyone who might come to investigate doesn't find us here."

He wasn't surprised when Spirit merely nodded once more, then tried to stand.

"Easy!" Blink exclaimed when she swayed on her feet. He

didn't feel much more steady himself, but it wasn't as if either of them had a choice to lay around and eat bonbons.

When she was standing firm, it hit Blink that she was practically naked. Yes, she still had on her bikini, but the cover-up was torn in several places. And when she turned away from him, he saw a nasty red mark on the back of her thigh.

She was hurt. And seeing that mark made him feel nauseous. It was a silly thing to worry about; they were *all* totally banged up from the crash. He should just be thankful they were alive. But still, seeing that mark on her leg made him realize how fragile she was, despite her iron will. She'd been tough as hell up until now, and would have to continue to be...and he hated it.

"Tate!" he called out.

His brother turned.

"Need some clothes here."

Without a word, Tate jogged over to where they were standing and dropped a large pack at his feet. "Not sure what's in there," he told him.

"I'll make it work. Thanks. How much time?"

"Five minutes."

"Roger."

Then his twin headed back to the helicopter to help Pyro and Kevlar pull out wires and set explosives.

Blink unzipped the pack and began to rifle through it. He pulled out a brown undershirt that the Army soldiers wore beneath their uniforms. It would be way too big on Spirit, but he didn't think she'd care.

"We need to get you dressed in something more appropriate. Can you take off that cover-up?" It was a huge ask, and Blink knew it. He stood between her and the other men. They weren't watching them, and it wasn't as if they didn't know exactly what she looked like. The cover-up was as good as useless, but he knew it was probably psychological protection at this point, more than anything else.

She met his gaze, then slowly peeled the torn, dirty piece of material over her shoulders and let it fall to the ground.

"Here, lean over," he told her softly. "I'll help you get the shirt on."

She bent forward, and he eased the material over her head. It fell halfway down her thighs. Blink hadn't missed the way her ribs stood out, how her belly was concave, how her hip bones protruded obscenely from her body. She looked like the pictures he'd seen of prisoners of war from Vietnam and World War II. It made him sick to think of what she'd suffered...and how many days she might've had left if they hadn't escaped. But the fact that she was still upright, still pressing on, impressed the hell out of him.

He turned back to his brother's pack before he did something stupid...like fall to his knees and vow to never let her go hungry again. The fact was, she *wasn't* his. For all he knew, she had a family waiting for her back in the States. A husband. Maybe kids. He was helping her escape and that was it.

But it didn't *feel* like that was all this was. He felt a connection with this woman that he'd never experienced before. They'd bonded back in those cells and when she'd given him her precious water, the only thing keeping her alive, it felt like she'd given a small part of herself to him.

Blink wasn't the kind of man to force a woman to do

anything, let alone stay with him. It was very likely she was grateful he'd helped her escape. Might even want to keep in touch because of the situation they'd been through together. But he wasn't sure she'd like the man he was in the real world. A homebody. An introvert. More likely to stand back and watch life pass him by than take part.

He pulled a pair of camo pants from the duffle and frowned. They were going to be huge on Spirit. There was no way he'd be able to modify them enough for her to wear. Especially not before they had to get out of the area.

"Fuck," he muttered, before stuffing them back into the pack and pulling out a pair of socks. Now these she could use. Blink turned back to Spirit.

She was staring down at him.

"These will be big too, but we don't have shoes for you to wear. I think if we double them up, they should cushion your feet enough that you can walk. But if anything starts hurting, let me know and I'll carry you."

She frowned at that.

"I know, I know, you don't want to be a burden. And you aren't—hear me?" he said almost fiercely. "You've been anything *but* a burden. We're partners. Teammates. And teammates help each other."

He saw her swallow hard, then nod.

"Good. Oh, and while the *last* thing I want is to see you in my brother's underwear, I'm thinking that's preferable to going without anything. They'll be like shorts," Blink said, pulling out a pair of olive-green boxers.

Spirit's eyes widened, and she eagerly reached for the

underwear. Even those were too big for her, almost falling off her hips.

"Here, let me help," Blink said, finding a piece of paracord in the pack and quickly tying it around her too-skinny waist as a belt. He folded the extra material from the boxers over the rope so it wouldn't scratch her skin. "There. Does that work? Can you walk all right?"

Spirit took a few steps in a small circle, then nodded at him. She looked both pathetic and kind of adorable in her new outfit. The oversized shirt, the boxers peeking out from under the hem, the socks pulled over her calves. It wasn't enough—not nearly enough—but the fact that he'd covered her a little made Blink feel better about their situation.

The boots in Tate's pack felt like dead weight after he pulled them on. He felt guilty that he had sturdy footwear and Spirit was in fucking socks. But there was literally nothing he could do about that right now. He hoped like hell Tex had already done his thing, and help was coming to them sooner rather than later.

"Okay, we're ready. Cover your ears," Pyro called out.

Instead of covering his own, Blink stepped close to Spirit and put his hands over her ears.

Then she surprised the hell out of him...by reaching up and covering his own with her tiny hands.

The loud explosion from whatever the others had rigged up was much bigger and louder than Blink expected.

"Time to go!" Tate exclaimed, as he jogged toward them with Pyro and Kevlar at his heels. "That's gonna be a bullseye for every member of the Taliban and other bad guys for miles.

They'll be pissing themselves to get here to see what they can find. She good?"

"She's good," Blink said. "And she can hear you just fine. Don't talk about her as if she's not standing in front of you."

"Sorry," Tate apologized immediately. "You got a name?" he asked Spirit.

She stared back at him without saying a word.

"She doesn't talk," Blink reminded his brother. "Not with words."

To his credit, Tate merely nodded. "Got it. The way I figure it, we need to move southwest. Make sure we don't accidentally cross into Iran. I'm guessing you've both had enough of their hospitality."

Blink snorted in response.

"Yeah, that's what I thought. It won't be easy, but there should be plenty of places to hole up if we need to. This part of Iraq is inhabited, but we can avoid any outposts. If you need a break," Tate said, looking at Spirit, "let us know. This isn't a matter of racing to any particular point. We just need to keep moving and watch our six for tangos. We'll be picked up as fast as the hands of diplomacy can manage."

Blink nodded. He understood what his brother was saying. No one would be happy with the events that had transpired. A US soldier being taken captive, then being shot down while not in Iranian airspace, then a Night Stalker helicopter crashing in Iraq. And now with both Army and Navy personnel in danger, all the stops would be pulled out to get them home safely. It was only a matter of time before someone came for them.

They just had to stay alive until then.

Pyro led them as they walked away from the crash. Looking back, Blink shook his head in amazement. If he was a cat, he'd definitely used up a few of his nine lives, but he felt as if he had the spirits of his former teammates looking after him. And he knew without a doubt that his *current* team was probably already seeking permission to come after him once more.

As long as they didn't run into any pockets of Taliban fighters—who would gladly kill a few Americans dumb enough to encroach on their territory—they'd be fine.

CHAPTER SEVEN

Josie felt like she was dying. She felt much better wearing the T-shirt, boxers, and socks that Nate had given her, but she still felt entirely too naked. And even though Nate had given her a whole canteen of water to drink all by herself—and she'd drank until the water sloshed around in her empty stomach—she still felt as though every muscle in her body was on the verge of failure.

She'd also nibbled on some beef jerky. It was extremely salty and now sat like an uncomfortable lump in her belly, but she was glad to have it all the same. Just that tiny bit was more food than she'd had in her stomach in weeks.

But it was taking all her concentration to put one foot in front of the other. The terrain they were walking through was rocky, hilly, and on top of it all, *hot*. Extremely hot. It felt as if every drop of water she drank was coming out her pores in the form of sweat.

Josie wanted to sit down and refuse to move another inch.

She wanted a real pair of hiking boots, that hamburger Nate had promised, and an hour-long shower. But since none of those things were going to materialize anytime soon, she just kept walking. Nate was behind her, and she kept her gaze on his brother's boots in front of her. She stepped where he stepped and did her best to keep her misery from the men, to avoid being a burden.

When Nate told her that Tate was his twin, she was surprised for a moment. In her eyes, they didn't look alike at all. Oh, she could see the resemblance. The obvious similarities in their facial features. She figured they probably had fun playing tricks on people when they were younger, pretending to be each other. Maybe it was because she'd spent so much time memorizing Nate's features, but she had no problem telling them apart.

Nate's eyes had a little more gold to them than Tate's. His ears were a touch more pointed, his hair a little longer, his beard definitely bushier. Josie guessed if they both shaved, it might be harder to tell them apart.

But it was more than just looks. With Nate, she felt as if she were...home. It was a ridiculous thought. She and this man were like ships passing in the night. They were sharing this intense experience, and when they were safe and back in the United States, they'd each go back to their own lives.

The problem with that was, Josie didn't *want* to go back to her life. After weeks of captivity, she wasn't the person she used to be. Just days ago, she would've said she was more frightened. Unsure of herself. Weaker. But around Nate, she felt *stronger*. As if she wasn't a shell of the woman she'd been before making the impulsive decision to fly to Kuwait.

Honestly, she wasn't sure *who* she was anymore.

And that *really* scared the crap out of her.

But watching Nate walk away? That thought terrified her. He'd been her rock. Her salvation. She supposed she had some sort of psychological connection to her savior that a therapist would tell her will fade with time. But Josie didn't think so. She was drawn to him in a way she'd never felt before. And not just because he was keeping her safe.

When Nate seemed surprised that she didn't think he and his brother looked alike, Josie wished so badly that she could tell him why. Explain that something about him called to something deep inside *her*. That she'd know him in a room full of red-haired, freckle-faced men even if she was blindfolded.

"I'm going to need to stop soon," Nate said from behind her.

Looking over her shoulder, Josie glanced at the man she couldn't stop thinking about. He looked...not good. Looked like she felt. He was pale, the freckles on his face standing out even more than they had before, and he was limping.

"Roger. Pyro, find us a place to stop for the night," Tate said.

Josie turned and stepped to Nate's side, putting her arm around his waist. She wasn't going to be much help if he suddenly keeled over, but she wanted him to know she was there for him, just as he'd been for her.

"Blink?" Kevlar asked, coming up to his other side. He'd been bringing up the rear, guarding them from behind.

"I'm okay," he said softly. "Just hurting."

Josie pressed her lips together in frustration. She wanted

to tell Kevlar and the others that Nate had been tortured, had water poured over his face, and was repeatedly kicked and beaten. But her stupid words still wouldn't come.

"What'd they do to you?" Kevlar asked, as he and Josie helped Nate navigate over the rocky terrain, churning up dust with every step.

"What *didn't* they do?" he returned.

"Talk to me," Kevlar ordered gruffly.

Josie felt Nate sigh more than she heard it. "Cigarettes, beatings, waterboarding...the usual."

Tate had obviously been listening, and he stopped walking and turned to face his brother. "Are you fucking kidding me?" he asked.

Nate shook his head.

"And you didn't say anything?"

"Would it do any good?" Nate countered.

They all knew the answer to that.

"Right. Give me a rundown of what hurts and where," Kevlar demanded, sounding like the team leader he was.

Nate chuckled. Josie felt it down to her bones. "What doesn't? Burns on my calves, ankles, and the tops of my feet. Ribs likely cracked. Bruises everywhere. A few broken fingers, and I think there's some water in my lungs. But I'm alive and upright, so I'm good."

"Fuck. And her? Sorry. You, miss? Are you okay?" Tate asked.

His concern surprised Josie. Especially after what he'd just learned about his brother. She nodded, trying to indicate she was fine, that she hadn't been tortured.

"She's not good," Nate countered. "But she's alive and

upright too. We just need to rest for a while. Eat something other than jerky. Reset."

"Found a place!" Pyro called out from somewhere ahead of them.

They all started walking again without another word, Tate ahead of them, looking back at them every few seconds as if to make sure his brother was still on his feet, and Kevlar and Josie still helping Nate along. Soon they arrived at a small cave, where Pyro waited.

"No footprints around it and nothing inside. Doesn't look like anyone has used it for shelter. So that's good."

"Agreed. Okay. Pyro, see if you can find some sticks for a small fire. I'll get my brother and his friend settled. Then we've got plenty of food for us all," Tate said.

"I'll help you, Pyro," Kevlar volunteered, and after dropping their packs, the two of them headed away from the cave without a word.

Josie looked after them in concern.

"They'll be back. Pyro won't get lost. He's got a great sense of direction. It's why he's such a good pilot," Tate told her. "Now come on, let's get the two of you off your feet."

Within minutes, Josie was sitting on a crinkly metallic blanket Tate had pulled out of a pack, with Nate at her side.

"Show me," Tate ordered his brother.

"I'm fine," Nate insisted. "I'd rather eat something."

"Not until you show me your fucking wounds," Tate growled.

For a second, Josie thought the two men were going to get into a physical fight, but eventually Nate backed down and leaned forward to take off his boots, pull up his pants legs, then he removed his shirt as well. Tate growled low in his throat as he began to clean the worst of his brother's wounds. He had dark bruises all over his body, which looked extremely painful. Josie was horrified all over again.

"Now can we eat, Mom?" Nate bitched after he'd put his boots and shirt back on.

Tate didn't comment, simply reached into his pack and pulled out a bag and threw it toward Nate.

He caught it without a word and smiled as he read the package. He held it up for Josie to see. "MRE. This one's meatballs in marinara sauce. It's pretty close to a hamburger."

Josie hadn't been feeling all that hungry. She'd gone so long without food that she'd simply forgotten what it felt like to feel anything other than empty. But when she heard the word meatball, her mouth started watering. Suddenly, she felt almost sick with the need to eat.

"Easy, Spirit, I've got you."

She watched Nate open the plastic bag, feeling like a feral dog might when presented with the possibility of real food. She wanted to snatch it out of his hands and stuff everything in her mouth as fast as possible. Her hands shook with a need for the calories she'd been denied for so long.

"Start with this," Nate said, holding something out to her.

Josie blinked. It was yellow and rather sickly looking, but she'd recognize it anywhere. Bread. She reached for it, not caring that her hands were filthy. That she was shaking.

"Fuck—wait."

She didn't want to wait! But Josie took a deep breath and did as he asked. She wasn't an animal, even if she'd kind of acted like one back in that cell.

"Give me your hand," Nate ordered.

She held it out and watched as he used a wet wipe to slowly and methodically clean as much of the dirt off her fingers as he could.

Frowning, he said, "It's not good enough, but we can't spare the water to wash right now. I'm sorry."

He was *sorry*? Josie's eyes filled with tears. No one had taken such good care of her in her entire life. He had to be hungry too, and he was hurting; she'd seen the results of the torture he'd endured. And here he was, tending to her hands as if she was made of glass. It was too much.

Emotions she'd pushed back to the recesses of her mind rushed forward. Swaying, Josie closed her eyes, trying to keep her tears at bay.

"Come here," Nate said, seeming to understand how close she was to the edge. Of *course* he did. It was as if he could read her mind. Knew what she was thinking and feeling.

She cried then. For the first time in a very long time. She'd cried the first week she'd been taken, but after that her tears seemed to dry up. Now they returned with a vengeance. Even as she cried though, no sound escaped her. Her chest heaved with sobs, and yet not one squeak left her lips.

When she was done, Josie felt as if she weighed a thousand pounds. She was so tired, she could barely lift her head.

To her surprise, Nate smiled down at her. "Feel better?" he asked.

Josie shrugged. She wasn't sure how she felt.

"Right. So...should we try this again? Start with the bread-stick as I get the meatballs ready."

He held out the bread, and Josie took it in her much

cleaner but still grubby fingers and stared at it for a moment, before opening her mouth and taking a small bite.

"Go slow," Nate warned. "It's been a while since you've had carbs, and you don't want to throw it up."

No, she didn't want to do that.

At any other time, the bread would probably be gross. It was a little hard, and whatever preservatives had been used to make it edible made it taste slightly off...but it was also the best thing Josie had ever eaten in her life.

She closed her eyes as she forced herself to chew slowly and not swallow the bite whole. It was as if she could actually feel the bread making its way down her throat to her stomach. She opened her eyes and looked at Nate. He was staring at her with an expression she couldn't interpret.

Josie wanted to stuff the rest of the bread in her mouth before anyone could take it away, but instead, she held it out to Nate.

"I'm okay. You can have it," he told her.

She shook her head and held it closer to his mouth. To her surprise, he didn't grab it. Just leaned close enough to take a bite.

"Oh my God, that is so good," he said with his mouth full and a small smile.

"If you guys think that shit is good, you *have* to be half starved," Tate said from across the cave.

Josie had forgotten he was there. She'd forgotten about everything but the food and Nate.

"You have no idea," Nate told his brother.

"I'm thinking you might even be able to choke down the beef sticks," he said with a chuckle.

Nate huffed out a breath. "No one is *that* hungry," he said, then looked at Josie. "The beef sticks taste like dog food. And before you ask me how I know what dog food tastes like, Tate and I dared each other to try it when we were around twelve. So trust us, we know."

Amazingly, Josie found herself smiling.

Nate stared at her for a beat with something close to awe on his face, before clearing his throat and looking down at the plastic pouch in front of him. "Meatballs are almost done."

The smell coming from the bag was absolutely amazing. It was so good, Josie actually felt kind of nauseous, which made no sense to her.

Nate opened the pouch and steam rose between them. He picked up a fork and stuck it inside. When he removed the fork, there was a decent-size meatball on the end. Josie restrained herself from grabbing his hand and stuffing the whole thing in her mouth.

He brought the fork to his own mouth and bit off half the meatball. It seemed incongruent from all the other things he'd done for her, making sure she had water first, not wanting to take the breadstick from her.

Then he opened his mouth and breathed in and out rapidly, saying, "Hot, hot, hot!" in a muffled tone. He swallowed and brought the meatball back to his mouth, but instead of eating the rest, he blew on it, trying to cool it off. Then he held it out to her. "That whole thing was too big for you to eat, but I had a feeling you'd try anyway. I also wanted to make sure it wouldn't burn your mouth."

Josie wanted to cry again. He wasn't being selfish by

taking the first bite, he did it to save her from herself—because once again, he could read her mind.

She lifted her hand, curling her fingers around his on the fork. Without breaking eye contact, she leaned forward and wrapped her lips around the meatball.

The spices immediately hit her taste buds, making her eyes snap shut as she moaned deep in her throat. Oh my God, it was so good! Josie had never tasted anything so delicious in her entire life. She could die right now a happy woman.

Opening her eyes, she found Nate watching her like a hawk. "Okay?" he asked.

She nodded immediately.

"Good."

They took turns, him eating half of each meatball to make the rest easy for her to eat in one bite. Josie was shocked to find that after only four bites, she was completely stuffed. She put a hand to her stomach—then gasped and quickly raised her shirt, even more shocked to realize her belly was distended, sticking out as if she were a few months pregnant.

Frowning in alarm, she looked at Nate.

"It's normal," he soothed. "You'll be hungry again in an hour or so. It'll take a while to work back up to regular-size meals. Instead, you'll need to eat small snacks several times a day."

She had no idea how he knew that, but she trusted him.

Pyro and Kevlar had returned by then, and Josie watched them and Tate open their own MREs and eat without fanfare. By now it was almost dark, and her eyelids felt as if they were made of lead.

"Lie down, Spirit. Sleep. We'll make sure you're safe. Nothing will happen when we're here. Promise."

Nate's words settled into Josie's soul. She hadn't even known she needed to hear them, but she had.

But before she went to sleep, there was something she needed to do.

She reached for the accessory packet that came with the MRE and pulled out the little plastic knife. Leaning over, she used it to write something in the dirt on the floor of the cave.

Nate looked at it, then up at her. "Josie?" he whispered.

She nodded.

"That's your name? Josie?"

She nodded again.

A small smile spread across Nate's face. "It's beautiful."

Josie wasn't sure about that. It was just a name. She'd never given it much thought. But not having a name made her feel like...less. Like a non-person.

"Tate, Pyro, Kevlar...meet Josie."

The other men nodded at her from across the way. She could barely see them, but she gave them a little wave anyway.

"Holy crap, she's just like you. How many times have you given me that dorky little wave when we part ways or meet up?" Tate said with a laugh. "Oh, sorry. I didn't mean that in a bad way, Josie."

"Whatever," Nate said with another smile as looked at her. "Josie," he said quietly. "It's so nice to meet you."

She returned his smile, feeling shy all of a sudden.

"Although, I still think Spirit fits you. Go on, lie down. Use me as a pillow if you'd like."

Josie frowned and shook her head, pointing to a few of his injuries. He was hurt. She wasn't going to lie on him. No way.

But Nate chuckled. "You weigh like two pounds. Having your head on me isn't going to hurt. Not in the least."

She still had no plans on using him as a pillow...but the next thing she knew, they were *both* lying down and Josie was on her side, up against Nate, with her head on his shoulder and an arm around his belly.

"Perfect," Nate said on a big sigh.

Josie could literally feel his muscles relaxing. They were lying in the dirt, in a cave in the mountains in freaking Iraq, and yet, she felt safe for the first time in weeks. She had no recollection of falling asleep, only of feeling a sense of rightness...then nothing.

CHAPTER EIGHT

"Try this."

His brother's voice woke Blink the next morning. He felt stiff and sore, but amazingly, better than he had the day before. Tate's fussing over his wounds had obviously done some good, as had the antibiotic he'd taken with dinner. He'd slept hard. Probably because with his brother and team leader there, he felt safe to completely let down his guard for the first time since he'd been captured.

Turning his head, he saw Josie and Tate sitting at his feet. His brother was encouraging her to try what looked like the cherry blueberry cobbler that was inside the MRE he and Josie had shared the night before.

Seeing Josie with his twin felt...good. She was skittish, with very good reason, but clearly not afraid of the other men.

Josie. Just knowing her name felt as if they were taking a step forward. It was a strong name, yet cute. Just like her. She still wore the brown T-shirt and the socks, was still caked with dirt and frightfully skinny, but her eyes were bright. And that she kept her food down last night, and was able to eat this morning, even if it wasn't very much, was a good sign that she'd be okay.

"That's the best part of the MRE," Blink said as he sat up.

Josie's gaze immediately found his, and she smiled. Blink would do literally anything to see that smile on her face every morning for the rest of his life.

She held the sweet treat out to him.

He shook his head. "No. You have it."

Josie shook her head stubbornly and wiggled the fork at him.

Chuckling, Blink shuffled his feet around and sidled up next to her. He took hold of her wrist, much as she had last night when she'd held the fork with the meatball, and brought the treat to his lips.

They held eye contact as he took a bite and chewed. The flavors exploded on his tongue. A little sweet for this early in the morning, but he didn't care. "Good," he said with a nod.

Josie smiled again and returned his nod.

"Sit rep?" he asked Tate, tearing his gaze from Josie's. As much as he wanted to revel in her infrequent smiles, he needed to get her to safety.

"Pyro and Kevlar are scoping out the area. Everything's been quiet."

Blink relaxed a fraction.

Until Pyro came back into the cave with Kevlar at his heels and announced, "We need to go. Now!"

Tate was moving even before Pyro had finished talking.

He stuffed the trash from the MRE into his pack, and Pyro balled up the emergency blanket Blink and Josie had used, putting it into his own backpack.

"What'd you see?" Tate asked, as Kevlar moved quickly and efficiently to erase any signs they'd been in the cave.

"About a dozen men moving this way. Doesn't look like they're actively searching for anyone or anything, but I don't want to take the chance that they found some indication of where we are."

"Agreed," Tate said as he shrugged on his backpack.

Blink had stood as the other men were talking. He turned to Josie and saw she was standing with her back against the wall of the cave, looking freaked way the hell out.

"Breathe, Josie," he told her gently. "If they knew we were here, they'd be making a beeline for us. We're okay. We just need to move out fast and silently."

Her eyes were huge in her face and it looked as if she was on the verge of bolting.

Blink stepped toward her with his hand out. "Give me your hand," he ordered.

She looked surprised at his request but immediately held her hand out.

He took it, marveling at how small and thin it felt in his own. "No one is going to take you captive again. I swear."

She didn't nod. Didn't do anything other than look at him with intense emotions swirling in her eyes.

"We need to move hard and fast. I'd like to carry you."

Josie shook her head aggressively.

"*Please*. Listen..." Blink said. They didn't have time for this, but the last thing he wanted was to have to throw her over his shoulder and carry her off without her permission. He felt as if he was just breaking through her thick shields. He didn't want to do anything that would ruin his progress. "You don't have any shoes. And your body isn't up for another hard day's walk. Not that I don't think you'd walk until your feet fell off and you couldn't take another step. You'd probably crawl if that's what it took. Let me help you, Spirit. Hell, the packs my brother, Kevlar, and Pyro are carrying probably weigh more than you. You can get on my back and help keep a lookout for tangos rather than having to watch where you put your feet. I'm not saying this to hurt your feelings, but we can move faster with me carrying you."

Josie frowned and pointed at his torso. Then his legs. Then his face.

"My injuries?" he asked.

She nodded.

"They're okay."

That earned him a furious glare.

"They are," he insisted. "I'm sore as hell, can't deny that those burns on my legs fucking throb and my ribs don't feel one hundred percent. But the day I let a few little torture sessions get the better of me is the day I give up my Budweiser pin."

Josie didn't react. Simply stood there staring at him.

"Please, Spirit. Let me help you. You aren't alone anymore. We're a team, the five of us."

"Casper," Pyro said warningly from the mouth of the cave.

But Blink didn't move. He heard the concern in the pilot's tone, but he'd stand in this cave forever if he had to and let Josie decide for herself what her next move would be. She'd had enough choices taken from her in however many weeks she'd been a prisoner. He'd be damned if he took her free will away the second she was free.

If she wanted to walk, they'd make it work. It would be riskier, there was no doubt, as she would slow them down considerably. But he wouldn't force her to do a damn thing.

After an agonizing second or two, she gave him a small nod.

Blink didn't sigh in relief or tell her that she'd made the right decision. He simply turned his back to her and crouched down. "Hop on. Let's get the hell out of here."

He felt her hands on his shoulders, and he helped her get up on his back. Just as he'd thought, she was lighter than most of the packs he'd carried on missions. Blink hooked his arms under her legs to help give her leverage and her arms went around his neck.

He nodded at the others, and the five of them set off, leaving the cave behind. Blink felt Kevlar at his back, ready to step in and take over carrying Josie if needed. Protecting their six. It felt good. Really good.

The mountains were beautiful at that hour of the morning, but Blink barely took notice. All his attention was on the woman on his back. The warmth from her body seeped into his and the farther they walked, the more comfortable she seemed to get.

Her body weight evened out, and she rested her upper body on his back as they walked. They were making good time, were moving probably twice the speed they had yesterday. They had no destination in mind as far as Blink knew, just to get away from the men Kevlar and Pyro had seen and put more distance between themselves and the downed chopper.

They walked for about an hour before they stopped to get their bearings and take a short break.

Blink slowly lowered Josie to the ground, then turned to check on her. "You okay?"

She nodded. There was no expression on her face. It worried him.

"Here," Kevlar said, holding out a bottle of water.

Blink took it and offered it to Josie. She drank a few sips. Then his brother handed him a packet of crackers from the MRE he'd had the night before.

Glancing at it, he smiled. "Pepperoni pizza crackers," he told Josie. "Not quite the same thing as a gooey, warm pizza pie from the store, but they're still pretty good."

He held one out to her, but she didn't take it. Blink took a chance and stepped into her personal space. She could've backed away, could've shaken her head at him and he would've given her space. She didn't. She just looked up at him, now with that same worried look on her face that she'd had way too often recently.

"I wish you could tell me what you're thinking. We're okay. My brother and Pyro know what they're doing. They're pilots, yes, but they've also had extensive SERE Training, which stands for Survival, Evasion, Resistance, and Escape. They aren't SEALs, like Kevlar and me, but they're pretty damn close."

"Gee, thanks for the effusive compliment," Tate grumbled.

Blink ignored him. "You can trust them. You can trust *me*. We aren't going to let anything happen."

Josie's mouth opened and closed as if she wanted to say something. Then she closed her eyes and scowled in frustration.

Blink slowly wrapped his arms around her and pulled her close. Her forehead rested on his chest, but her arms remained limply at her sides. It seemed as if the adrenaline that had kept her going throughout their escape had finally run its course. He'd seen this time and time again. People stayed strong until they had no more to give.

He didn't say anything, they just stood like that, Blink holding her as she rested against him. After too short a time for his peace of mind, she straightened. Looking up at him, she nodded, then reached for the crackers he still had in his hand.

"Fuck, Spirit, you impress the hell out of me," he blurted.

Once again, her lips moved as if she was saying something, but no sound came out.

He led her over to where Tate and Pyro were sitting and helped her to the ground. They ate some snacks—Kevlar ate his while standing, head on a swivel, watching and listening for anything out of the ordinary—as the pilots discussed the best LZ for whoever might be coming to extract them

"I'm thinking that way," Pyro said, pointing to their west. "We don't want to find ourselves out in the open, but the peaks seem to be farther apart there. A chopper could easily slip down between them and pick us up."

"Not north?" Tate asked, looking in that direction.

"No. The last thing we want is to get too close to the

Iranian border. Iraq won't be thrilled with an extraction, but at least it won't cause an international incident."

"I'm not completely sure where we landed, but we want to stay away from any towns or cities if we can. We don't want the Taliban extending our stay in any way."

Blink snorted. *Landed.* His brother was funny. But he supposed anytime a chopper went down and they walked away relatively unscathed could be called a landing and not a crash.

"Right. How're you doing, Josie?" Pyro asked. "Your legs okay? It can be tough to be carried for long distances...feet and legs going numb and all that."

Blink looked at her, interested in her answer.

She nodded at Pyro and held up a foot, rotating it a couple of times, then shrugging.

"Good," he said. "You should eat more," he added, tossing a packet toward Blink.

He caught it instinctively, reading the slender packet before glancing at Josie. "You should feel special, the applesauce with mango and peach puree is one of the best things in these MREs. They're highly sought after."

Instead of looking happy that Pyro had obviously given her such a precious food item, she frowned and shook her head.

"Nope. Not taking it back. It's for you," he told her.

Josie looked at Blink expectantly, as if seeking his support in her need to refuse it.

"Sorry, Spirit, I agree with Pyro. At least try it. You might not like it." Blink tore the top off the squeeze tube of applesauce and handed it to her.

As she took it, he saw how dirty her hands were still, even though he'd done his best with the wet wipes the night before. He hated that for her. He wanted to be able to give her a long hot shower. But it would have to wait until they were out of there.

She kept eye contact with Blink and brought the apple-sauce up to her lips. She squeezed a bit into her mouth...and her eyes widened as the flavors hit her taste buds.

"Good, huh?" he asked with a small smile.

She nodded.

"I can't wait for you and Remi to meet," Kevlar said out of the blue. "She has that same sense of...enjoyment and appreci-ation for the little things in life."

"We should keep walking," Tate said, not giving Blink a chance to question Kevlar's bold statement. As Remi was one of his closest friends, he'd love for Josie to meet her. But he knew nothing about her life in the States and couldn't make assumptions...even if he wanted to.

She tried to hand the packet of applesauce back to Blink, but he shook his head. "You can eat while we walk," he said, turning to let her get on his back.

They were both used to him carrying her now, so they set off this time without hesitation.

They all pushed fairly hard as they headed for the moun-tain peaks Pyro had pointed out. Blink never would've chosen them as a good extraction point, but the two pilots knew what their fellow Night Stalkers could and couldn't do, and if they thought that was the best place to be picked up, he wasn't going to argue.

After several more hours of tromping through the mountains, his legs were throbbing and felt like they weighed eight hundred pounds, but he didn't utter a word of complaint. He'd learned the hard way that things could always be worse. They'd been walking all day, and while Josie wasn't a heavy burden, his body had been through hell recently and was finally protesting what he'd asked it to do.

It was late afternoon when Tate finally stopped, looked around, and said, "This'll do."

Blink didn't hesitate to lower Josie to the ground. Then he leaned over and put his hands on his thighs and closed his eyes as he did his best to work through the pain coursing through his body. He was strong. Tough. But he did have his limits, and it seemed as though he'd reached them.

Feeling a hand on his arm, Blink opened his eyes to see Josie standing next to him with a worried look on her face. She took his hand in hers and pulled. Following her, frowning at the way Josie was limping, he sat where she indicated, relieved he was off his feet.

"Forgive me for saying so, but you two look like shit," Tate said. He wasn't joking, and wasn't being mean, he was simply stating a fact.

"Feel like it," Blink told him.

Now *Tate* looked worried.

"I'm okay," he said. "Just had a difficult few days." He tried to stand again, but he froze in surprise when Josie hissed.

She was glaring at him and frowning. She stabbed a finger down at the ground a couple of times, then pointed at him.

"All right, all right. I'm staying here."

She nodded, then walked over to the pack Kevlar had just dropped to the ground. She opened and rummaged through it for a moment before pulling out an MRE. She walked back over to where Blink was sitting and joined him on the ground, where she attempted to open the tough plastic bag.

"I'm kind of scared to give her my knife," Tate murmured with a chuckle as he held it out to Blink. "If I piss her off, she might use it on me."

Josie turned her glare on Tate.

Blink simply laughed. "Here, Spirit, let me help."

She let him cut off the top of the MRE packet, then pulled it back toward herself.

"Enjoy dinner," Tate said with another laugh, before heading back over to where Pyro and Kevlar sat, opening their MREs.

Meanwhile, Josie had pulled out all the small packets inside the MRE and laid them out next to each other.

"Beef ravioli. One of my favorites," Blink told her.

He wanted to help, but at the same time, it felt good to be taken care of for once. He didn't speak as Josie figured out how to use water to heat up the ravioli. She read the packets, seeing what was inside each, before carefully opening one at a time. Before he knew it, using the empty MRE bag as a makeshift platter, she'd made a charcuterie board of sorts with the various food items. The salted caramel marshmallow crisp bar had been torn in half, the breadsticks were laid out to form a perimeter for the food, the cheddar cheese spread was in the middle, and she'd sprinkled the M&Ms in and around everything.

When she got to the fruit punch electrolyte powder, she hesitated, then gestured toward Blink's pocket. He was confused for a moment, until he remembered. He pulled out the small metal cup and handed it over. She put a bit of the powder in the cup, then poured in some water.

When the ravioli had finished heating, she put the pouch down with the other food items, then looked up at him and smiled.

Blink had honestly never been so touched in all his life. It was just an MRE. He'd eaten hundreds of them. But he'd never had someone work so hard to make it look more like a gourmet meal than this woman just had.

"Looks good," he told her.

She picked up the cup and held it out to him. For the second time, she was offering him water that she so desperately needed.

This time, Blink didn't hesitate. He took it from her and swallowed half the liquid in one gulp before handing it back. She finished it, licking the extra from her lips before turning her gaze back to the food.

She picked up an M&M and studied it with a small smile before popping it in her mouth. She chewed the little chocolate candy with her eyes shut, obviously relishing the treat.

Blink loved seeing her enjoy the candy, but she needed nutrients. He picked up the pouch of ravioli and speared one with the fork before holding it out to her. "Try this."

Her eyes opened, and she leaned forward, her mouth open.

It felt so intimate, feeding her, and even though he'd done it the evening before with the meatballs, this time felt just as satisfying deep in his soul.

They took turns eating the ravioli, and she had a couple bites of the other food. Just as before, she stopped way before he thought she could possibly be full. But then again, her stomach had probably shrunk because of the lack of food.

Feeling anger rise up within, and the need to exact revenge on the assholes who'd taken this innocent woman captive, he looked at his brother, needing a distraction. "What's next?"

Tate shrugged, seemingly unconcerned that they were camping out in the middle of the mountains in Iraq and anyone could stumble upon them at any moment. "Depends."

When he didn't elaborate, Blink asked, "On?"

"You and Kevlar. How closely do you think you guys are being monitored?"

Before his team leader could respond, a harsh snort escaped Blink's lips. "Like a parasite under a microscope."

"Then I'd say this time tomorrow, we'll be back on the naval carrier enjoying a shower and a real meal."

Josie made a noise next to him, and Blink glanced at her. Her eyes were wide in her face, and she looked both scared to death and excited at the same time.

"We made it as easy as possible for our fellow Night Stalkers," Pyro added. "This extraction point is a piece of cake. They can lower between these two peaks, and even land on the ground there if necessary."

The area of ground Pyro pointed out wasn't exactly level. It was full of boulders and actually not flat at all. And the peaks he was talking about didn't look wide enough to accommodate the rotor blades of a chopper to Blink, but then again, he wasn't an expert on choppers. If Pyro said this was the best place for an extraction, he believed him.

For the first time, he thought about what would happen

immediately after they were rescued—especially for Josie. The US government didn't make it a habit of picking up people from behind enemy lines without knowing something about them. And while he knew in his gut that Josie was no threat, the officers on the carrier didn't. Hell, he didn't even know if she was American or not. He thought she was, but without knowing anything about her other than her first name, there would be questions. Lots of them.

His belly churned. The food he'd just eaten threatened to come back up. He wanted to shield Josie from what was to come but he didn't know how.

"We need to talk," he blurted as he turned to Josie.

She tilted her head in question.

"When we're extracted, we'll be taken to a Navy ship in the gulf. There will be questions...for both of us. I'll be taken to one area to explain what happened to me, and you'll be—"

Josie didn't let him finish. She shook her head almost violently and fisted his shirt sleeve.

"It'll be okay. You'll be safe and—"

She shook her head again and made a growling sound. To Blink, she sounded terrified.

"Look at me," he ordered, reaching up to stop her from continuing to shake her head. He put his hands on either side of her face and literally held her still as he looked into her eyes. "You'll be fine. No one on the ship will hurt you."

She didn't pull out of his grip but pointed at him, then pointed at herself. She did it again. And again.

"You want to stay with me?"

She nodded as best she could in his grasp.

"I'm not sure that's possible," he said.

As soon as the words were out, Josie closed her eyes and began to shake. It was a full-body tremor. If he didn't know better, he would've thought she was having a seizure.

"Josie!" he said urgently.

But she stubbornly kept her eyes shut.

"Do you think I'm going to let anything happen to you? I'm not," he said, answering his own question. "But they aren't expecting you. The rest of my team has probably already informed the higher-ups that you were a captive in the same place I was, and that you were extricated at the same time, but they don't know anything about you. For all they know, you could be a plant. Someone who was put in that cell to gather intel about our ships. Our manpower."

She snorted and her eyes flew open. She pulled out of his grip and frantically looked around for something. Then she grabbed the plastic knife that had been in the MRE kit and crouched over an area of undisturbed ground.

For a second, Blink was afraid she was going to try to hurt herself, but instead, she started writing in the dirt.

England

"You're from the UK?" Blink asked.

She shook her head in frustration, then wrote something else.

Josie England

"That's your name?" Tate asked. He'd come closer when she'd started writing.

Josie nodded. Then wrote some more.

Las Vegas Vacation Kuwait

"You're from Las Vegas and were on vacation in Kuwait? Not exactly a hot spot for tourism," Kevlar commented. His team leader, Pyro, and Tate were all gathered around now, reading her words.

But Blink's attention was laser focused on the woman herself. She was on her knees in the dirt, already scrubbing the words away with her hand to write more. Her face was flushed, and she looked almost desperate to give them information about herself. She was terrified of being questioned when they got to the carrier, that much was obvious.

Ayden Hitson Army R&R Boat ride

"He's your boyfriend?" Tate asked.

Blink's stomach rolled again.

Was Break up after

"So you came to visit your boyfriend, who was on R&R in Kuwait, and you were going to break up with him? And you went on a boat ride?" Tate asked almost gently. "What happened? Where's Hitson?"

Shot dead Took me

"Fuck," Blink said. He stood abruptly and began to pace. He'd gathered something bad had happened in regard to a boat, considering Josie's reaction to getting into one back in Iran. But he hadn't expected *this*.

"Right. You're an American named Josie England, from Las Vegas," Kevlar summed up. "You were in Kuwait visiting the military man you were dating. You went on a boat ride, probably crossed over into Iranian waters, and your captors came after you. Ayden Hitson was killed and they took you hostage. Why?"

Blink wanted to know the answer as much as the others. But Josie didn't attempt to write anything in the dirt. She shrugged.

"There has to be a reason," Tate pushed. "Did they ask you anything? Want information about anything related to the military? Did they contact anyone for ransom?"

Josie stared at them for a beat, then once more used her hand to wipe away the last words she wrote and picked up the plastic knife.

Beaten Left alone Forgotten No food no water Didn't care

The words looked stark and ugly scratched into the ground. He couldn't wrap his mind around what she was telling them. Of course, the condition she was in gave credence to what she was saying, but it was still hard to believe.

She angrily scrubbed out the words, then began to write again.

Woman trash Not Army Not worth trouble

Blink was done. "You are not trash," he said almost angrily.

They think Not me

But Blink wasn't sure she truly believed what she'd written. He could see it in the way her shoulders slumped. How she tried to curl into herself. She'd been thrown into that cell and forgotten, like she'd said. Or maybe she wasn't forgotten, but clearly no one gave her enough thought to neither continue to torture her, nor keep her alive. She was literally *nothing* to their captors. Just like she said. And it pissed Blink way the hell off.

"You have family, Josie?" Tate asked gently. "Someone we can get in touch with to let them know you're okay? Someone has to be worried about you."

Josie stared at Blink's brother for a tense moment before

shaking her head and shrugging again. She dropped the knife and stood, pointing toward the bushes where they'd been going to pee, and slowly disappeared behind them.

"Well, shit," Pyro said.

"If she had anyone who was worried about her not returning from vacation, surely they would've contacted the authorities by now. Told them that she'd gone to Kuwait and hadn't come back. That information would've gotten to someone in our circles eventually," Kevlar stated.

Blink would've liked to think so, but he wasn't sure. If she truly didn't have anyone who'd noticed she was gone...

That was unfathomable.

Josie returned before they could discuss it further. She began to clean up their dinner, carefully putting the uneaten food back into the pouches so they could eat it later. No one felt much like talking after learning what they had about Josie's situation. So everyone simply settled in to wait. For darkness to fall. For rescue. Something.

Blink couldn't stay away from Josie if his life depended on it. Without a word, he scooted up behind her and urged her to lay on her side to rest, then spooned her. His arm went around her waist, and he held her against him, secure in the cradle of his body. He completely dwarfed her. But it felt right, as if he was protecting her from the world.

She was stiff at first but gradually relaxed. Blink shifted until his other arm was under her head, so she could use it as a pillow.

Neither of them slept, but it felt good to just lie there. With her.

CHAPTER NINE

Josie was embarrassed. She'd kind of freaked out, after doing so well in the last few weeks to feel nothing. But knowing that she'd likely be separated from Nate, and would probably never see him again, made her panic. She was no one. Nate was a Navy SEAL. He was important. And realizing the military people on the boat might think she was a traitor or a spy had made her desperate to let these men—men who seemed to actually like her a little—know who she was.

It was hard to communicate without speaking. But she'd been able to tell them some basic facts. Maybe it was enough for the people in charge on the boat not to lock her in the brig—she had no idea if that was even a thing anymore—and they'd figure out a way for her to get home.

But the thought of going back to Las Vegas, to her empty apartment, wasn't appealing. She doubted anyone even noticed she hadn't come back from vacation. Hell, they probably didn't even know she'd left. The mail carrier might've noticed, but only because she never came in to get the mail she'd put on hold.

Her life was kind of pathetic, and she wasn't eager to return to it. But where else would she go?

With a sigh, she inched slightly closer to Nate. Lying there with him felt...good. She was relieved he hadn't thought badly of her for coming to Kuwait to see a guy she was going to break up with. It had been a horrible idea, obviously, but she was thankful Nate didn't seem to think so.

Or hell, maybe he did, and he just wasn't saying anything.

Maybe he felt too sorry for her to share his opinion.

But she didn't think so. She wasn't an expert on men, but surely he wouldn't be snuggling with her if he thought she was stupid?

She was too tired to think about it anymore. Tired but not sleepy. Which made no sense. So Josie simply lay in Nate's arms, doing her best not to think about the future either. She couldn't predict what would happen. Things had been so crazy, she couldn't imagine what was up for her next.

She didn't have to wait long to find out. She felt Nate pick his head up at the same time she heard a faint drumming sound in the sky.

"They're here," Pyro suddenly announced.

Nate was up and moving in a flash. He urged her to sit up and said, "It's time, Josie. We're going home."

She kind of missed Nate calling her Spirit. She wasn't sure about the nickname at first, but she'd gotten used to it pretty quickly. She'd never been given a nickname before, and knowing why he'd called her that felt pretty darn good.

She got to her feet and stood with the others, looking up

at the sky. The sun had almost set and there was just enough light to see without tripping over any rocks. But Josie had no idea if someone flying a helicopter could see well enough to land, especially not where they were currently standing. Maybe they'd have to go up that rope thing again. It wasn't something she was looking forward to, but if it would get them out of there, she'd do whatever it took.

"Here they come," Tate said unnecessarily.

The chopper appeared over a mountain peak like a beautiful angel. It hovered for a moment, whipping up dirt all around them, before slowly lowering exactly where Pyro had said they would.

To her amazement, the helicopter managed to fit between the two mountain peaks but it didn't exactly land. One of the skids rested on a rock and the chopper actually kind of tilted downward, as if inviting them to climb aboard.

No one spoke; it wasn't as if they could be heard over the rotor blades. Josie closed her eyes against the onslaught of dirt and dust being whipped into the air.

She felt Nate grab hold of her upper arm and start walking. She trusted him to keep her upright and followed him. When the sound of the engine got louder, she squinted her eyes, wanting to see what was happening.

Pyro and Tate were already inside the helicopter and before Josie knew it, she was being handed up into their arms. She was sitting inside before she could even blink. Nate jumped in as if he hadn't just been tortured and beaten a day or so ago, Kevlar at his heels, and she felt the chopper lifting up and off the ground.

She held her breath as they got higher and higher into the air. There were mountains on either side of them and they seemed close enough to touch as they rose. As soon as they cleared the peaks, the pilots seemed to gun the engines, then they were flying over the same terrain they'd just hiked through.

Nate suddenly had a set of headphones, and he placed them over her ears. The engines were instantly muffled, and Josie let out the breath she'd been holding. Their extraction had been fast and uneventful. It was quite the change from the last time she was inside a helicopter.

Tate and Pyro placed headphones over their ears, as did Nate and Kevlar. She could hear everyone speaking to each other.

"Buck! Obi-Wan! Good to see you!" Pyro exclaimed with a laugh.

"Someone had to come and get your asses back to work after you decided to take a vacation in the mountains," one of the pilots said, glancing over his shoulder to grin at them.

"Whatever, Buck," Pyro retorted good-naturedly.

"You all good?" the other pilot asked, who Josie assumed was Obi-Wan.

"Yeah," Tate said.

"Laryn is gonna kill you," Obi-Wan said.

"I know. She worked hard to get that chopper working perfectly, then someone had to go and blow a hole in it," Tate said almost mournfully.

The conversation seemed so normal. Like friends meeting up after a long absence.

"Laryn's the head mechanic who worked on my MH-60,"

Tate said, looking at Josie. She figured he'd forgotten mentioning her earlier, so she simply nodded.

"She's a contractor, and one of the best mechanics I've ever known. Wouldn't trust anyone else with my babies. You might get to meet her. Depends on what happens when we land."

And just like that, nerves struck Josie once again.

"You good, Blink?" Buck asked. "Your team told us what they knew when we saw them on the ship. Said you had a tough time?"

"Not as tough as Josie," Nate said.

She felt six sets of eyes on her. Not knowing what else to do, she gave the two pilots a lame little wave.

Chuckles echoed in her ears.

"Right. Josie. It's nice to meet you. On behalf of the US Army, we're glad you're okay...and that we could be the ones to get you the hell out of there. Because we all know the Navy wasn't up to the task."

Josie was about to get mad on Nate and Kevlar's behalf before she realized Obi-Wan was joking. Sort of. It had to be a long-standing ribbing thing between the Army and the Navy, because Kevlar leaned forward and smacked the back of the pilot's helmet.

"Hey! Watch it! Don't mess with the pilot while he's flying," Obi-Wan complained.

"You could fly this thing with one hand tied behind your back and both eyes blinded," Nate returned.

"True. I'm that good," Obi-Wan agreed.

"Oh Lord, now you've done it. Stroked his ego. He'll be even more impossible now," Buck moaned.

Josie listened to the banter with interest but internally, she was still freaking out about what would happen when they got to the ship. Would she be in trouble? How was she going to answer any questions when her stupid voice wouldn't work? Now that she was safe, she half expected to magically be able to speak again. But of course, she had no such luck.

Soon they left the brown dirt of the desert landscape behind and there was nothing but water beneath them.

"It's okay. We're safe," Nate said, obviously seeing her discomfort.

Josie nodded but still couldn't relax.

At least not until Nate took her hand in his. Looking down, Josie should've been embarrassed at how disgusting her fingers looked. There was so much black dirt encrusted under her nails, she wasn't sure she'd ever be able to get it out. But Nate didn't seem to mind.

"There she is. Can you see her?" Buck asked, turning to look at Josie, then pointing out the front window.

Sitting up as straight as she could, Josie could just see a speck in the distance, getting closer and closer as they flew toward it.

It didn't take long before they were hovering over the deck of the huge warship. The food Josie had eaten threatened to come up when the chopper bumped as it landed.

Then something struck her, and she squeezed Nate's hand tightly.

"What? What's wrong?"

It was stupid. She didn't need it anymore, but the thought of it having been left behind made her feel panicky and sick.

She reached forward to pat Nate's pocket but felt nothing inside. A choked noise worked its way up her throat.

"Your cup? I've got it here. In my other pocket," Nate told her through the headset. "It's okay, Spirit. I've got it."

Relief hit her so hard, she felt dizzy. It was just a cup. There were probably hundreds more like it on the ship. She didn't need it anymore. And yet she still felt attached to the damn thing. It had kept her alive. Without it, she'd be nothing more than a heap of rotting flesh in that damn prison cell.

She managed to nod. The others were taking off their headsets, so Josie did the same, the noise from the outside world pressing in on her all at once. People talking, yelling orders she didn't understand back and forth, the rumble of the chopper engine.

"Come on, let's get out of here," Nate said, tugging gently on her hand.

Looking out of the helicopter, Josie saw a wave of people, all looking in their direction.

She was suddenly overwhelmed. Glancing down at herself, she realized how ridiculous she probably looked. Socks, a huge T-shirt, a pair of boxers. Not to mention she was covered in dirt, and her hair was matted and disgusting. She had no reason to be embarrassed or ashamed after everything she'd been through...but somehow, she still was.

Nate seemed to understand how she felt, because he turned and grabbed a blanket that had been folded neatly into a small cubby inside the chopper. Without letting go of her hand, he wrapped it around her shoulders, assisted by his brother. She clutched it against her chest with her free hand.

With Nate on one side of her, and Tate on the other, they stood. Kevlar hopped out then turned, holding out his hands to steady the trio as they exited the chopper. Suddenly, she was standing on the deck of the huge ship.

She heard a woman yell, "Casper! What the hell did you do to my helicopter?"

Looking over, Josie saw a woman in her mid-thirties, about five-five or so, dark hair pulled back into a neat bun, dark eyes sparking as she marched up to Tate and poked him in the chest. She wore a pair of coveralls with what looked like grease smeared down the front of her right thigh.

Tate smiled at Josie and Nate. "Good to see you, bro. Don't be a stranger. We'll get together back in the States."

Nate nodded at his brother, and Josie watched as Tate walked off with the woman right at his side. But even as she gave him grief, Josie could see the relief in her eyes that he was alive and in one piece. And Tate certainly didn't look upset by whatever she was saying. He actually looked pleased to see her.

"Guessing that was Laryn," Nate said with a small grin.

Before she could even nod, someone approached them.

"Blink!" the man exclaimed, giving him a one-armed man-hug before they'd taken more than two steps away from the helicopter.

"Good to see you, MacGyver," Nate said. Josie recognized him from the short amount of time they'd been with the man after getting out of their cells.

"Come on, the guys are waiting to see you."

"To interrogate me, you mean," Nate said with a small laugh.

"Naw, we're saving the ass-chewing for later," Kevlar piped in, and both he and MacGyver laughed.

"For now, we're just glad to see you alive and kicking," MacGyver told him.

"Sorry, but the admiral wants to talk to the two of you," an officer standing nearby interrupted, nodding at both Nate and Kevlar.

"An admiral?" Nate whistled.

"Yes. If you could follow me," the man said, gesturing toward one of the doors.

"What about Josie?" Nate asked, not moving an inch.

Without thought, Josie stepped closer to Nate. She wanted to press herself against him, beg him not to leave her, but she couldn't speak.

"Is that her name? There's a captain waiting to speak with her."

"Then what?" Nate asked.

The officer blinked. He hesitated a beat before saying, "I don't know. It depends on what's said, I suppose."

Nate shook his head. "She's coming with us," he told the man.

"I don't think—"

"Where she goes, I go," Nate repeated firmly. "She can come with me and Kevlar to talk to the admiral."

"He's not going to want to talk about what happened on a top-secret mission, or what happened after, with a civilian there," the officer warned.

"Tough. She knows just as much as I do about what happened after, and maybe more. She was a guest of the terrorists way longer than I was. Don't you think the admiral will want to hear what she knows?"

Josie had never seen this side of Nate. He sounded pissed off and more authoritative than he'd ever been. It didn't turn her off. Not at all.

"It's your ass," the officer said with a shrug before turning toward the door. "If you'll follow me."

"Impressive," Kevlar mumbled from behind them.

Nate turned to his friend. "I need you to watch out for her," he said. "If they take her away from me, don't leave her alone for a minute. You know she doesn't talk, so they're going to have to give her time to write out whatever they want to know. And she needs to eat again. And drink. And shower. She—"

"Easy, Blink," Kevlar said, putting a hand on his shoulder. "If you think anyone is going to argue with you, you're wrong. You were a POW. They're treated with kid gloves around here. No one will upset you."

"Right. Tell that to the admiral," Nate muttered.

"I'm guessing he's the one who made the order," Kevlar said, sounding unconcerned. He smiled at Josie. "Now that we're safe, and aren't hanging out of a chopper or taking a pleasure hike through the mountains...I want to thank you for taking care of this big lug. He's a pain in the ass, but he's *our* pain the ass. Even if he did take off for Iran without telling us."

"Didn't have time," Nate told him. "The commander gave me thirty minutes to get to the base before wheels up."

"I know. I'm only half giving you shit. Trust me, the

commander knows that none of us are happy with how things went down."

"Fuck. I didn't even think about the mission until now. Is the other team okay? They got away?" Nate asked.

Josie's head felt as if it was on a swivel watching the two men talk.

"They're fine. Your distraction was enough for them to slip away successfully and get to the extraction point."

"Good," Nate said with feeling.

"But I have to say, if you ever do *anything* like that shit with us, you aren't going to be happy with the consequences."

"Noted. But I don't regret it. Not for a second." Nate glanced at Josie.

She was puzzled by the conversation, not exactly sure what they were talking about. But she didn't get a chance to indicate her confusion to Nate before they were shuttled through the bowels of the huge ship.

Josie's feet slipped on the metal floors in the socks she was wearing, and she would've fallen at least twice if it wasn't for Nate's iron grip on her hand. She held the blanket around her like a shield, not thrilled with the looks she was getting from the sailors they passed.

They were led to a door where someone was standing at attention. The man saluted the officer leading them, then opened the door. The official-ness of his actions made Josie nervous. There was obviously someone important in the room. Someone who would judge her for her actions, and possibly decide she was...what? A liability? A spy? An idiot? She wasn't sure what to think anymore.

Nate didn't let go of her hand, but he did salute the man sitting at a round table with a laptop in front of him. He was wearing a white uniform that looked squeaky clean...which made Josie feel all the more grubby.

"Sit," he ordered, pointing to the chairs across from him.

Kevlar entered the room with them and took a chair on one side of her, while Nate sat on the other.

As soon as Josie sat, she immediately stood back up and looked at the chair. It had an upholstered tan seat, and the thought of contaminating it with her stinky self was abhorrent. Without any other choice, she dropped the blanket from around her shoulders and arranged it over the chair carefully, then sat again.

When she did, she saw everyone's eyes on her. Swallowing hard, she shrugged awkwardly and did her best not to hyperventilate.

"Right, so...tell me what happened, Blink. And don't leave anything out," the admiral ordered.

Without hesitation, Nate began. He talked about events Josie didn't understand, but they were obviously why he'd been in Iran in the first place. His tone was almost unemotional as he explained how he was captured and tortured. He also explained how he knew help would come—because of the tracker he wore—and that when Kevlar and his team arrived, he delayed his rescue so they could get Josie out too.

He made everything they'd been through sound so... casual. As if being held down while someone poured water over his towel-covered face was normal, and not a big deal at all. His description of being shot at while being hoisted into the helicopter, and the chopper getting hit by that missile and crashing in the mountains, was like an everyday occurrence. She was beginning to think for him, it probably was.

"And you?" the admiral asked, turning his attention to Josie.

She sat up straighter instinctively.

"I want to know how the hell you ended up in a prison cell in Iran. And why we didn't know anything about you being there."

Josie opened her mouth, but of course nothing came out. Thankfully, Nate was there to speak for her. Like his own, he made her story sound much more ordinary than it was. Even *she* knew it wasn't normal for an American to vacation in Kuwait.

"Specialist Ayden Hitson? His body was discovered the day after he went missing. You claim you were on a boat with him?"

There was so much suspicion in his tone, Josie was almost offended. Why *shouldn't* she have been with him? Did he actually doubt her story? Did he think *she* killed Ayden? Visions of sitting in another cell, this time somewhere deep inside this ship, threatened to overwhelm her.

Without thought, she pointed at his laptop and snapped her fingers impatiently.

"What?" the admiral asked.

"She wants to use your laptop," Nate said in a bright voice. It almost sounded as if he was amused, but Josie was on the verge of a nervous breakdown. She had to get this man to believe her. And she needed words in order to do that.

The admiral clicked some buttons, probably closing out sensitive documents or something, before pushing the laptop over to her.

Josie was amazed that he'd done as she asked, but she didn't hesitate. She put her fingers on the keyboard, feeling normal for the first time in ages, clicked on the Word icon, then began to type.

"Fuck," Nate said with a small chuckle as her fingers flew over the keys.

"The girl can type," Kevlar commented dryly.

Josie barely heard them. She was too busy typing out exactly how she'd ended up in that cell in Iran.

Back home, she was a caption editor. She wrote the text that appeared on TV screens during movies and shows. She was known for her accuracy and being able to caption live shows. Her typing speed worked in her favor now. In ten minutes, she had over fifteen hundred words and her entire story typed out.

She explained how she'd been talked into going to Kuwait, how Ayden dismissed her concerns about going on a boat ride, how cocky he'd been while speeding around and showing off. Then how everything happened so fast, and they hadn't even been given a chance to explain how they'd ended up in Iranian waters. She told the admiral how scared she'd been when Ayden was shot and thrown overboard, and when she'd been hauled onboard the Iranians' boat and thrown into the prison cell. Explained about getting beaten, the occasional scrap of bread she'd occasionally been given, then absolutely nothing but the water that dripped into her cell thereafter.

She told him everything as succinctly as possible, hoping against hope she'd be allowed to stay with Nate.

Kevlar and Nate both read over her shoulders while she typed, so when she finished and pushed the laptop back toward the admiral, they already knew what she had to say.

"Fuck, Josie," Nate said, resting his forehead against her temple. She closed her eyes, waiting for the admiral's judgement.

It didn't take long.

"I'm very sorry for what you went through, Ms. England. My staff will need to look into this, check with the hotel and airlines to verify your story, but I can tell by looking at you that you've been through hell, and I find no reason to doubt you. You're a very lucky young woman. Not many people have been where you have and lived to talk about it. I'm guessing you don't want the press to get a hold of your story?"

She shook her head almost violently.

"Right. We'll do our best. You're all dismissed. Kevlar, I'm sure one of your team is waiting nearby. All three of you can head to the bunk area where your team is staying. You can get cleaned up and eat. We have a psychologist available if you want to talk about what happened. Otherwise, tomorrow we'll get you all flown to Germany, and then you can catch a ride back to the States from there. Any objections?"

"No, Sir," both Nate and Kevlar said at the same time.

Josie felt almost deflated. That was it? That was all he was going to say about her appearance on his ship?

Apparently so, because Nate took her elbow and helped her stand, but not before re-wrapping the blanket around her shoulders. Then she was once again led toward the door. It was opened almost magically by the man standing outside, and then they were walking back through the ship.

"Josie?" Kevlar said, pulling her to a stop after they'd gone less than a couple dozen feet. They were standing in the middle of a walkway, blocking it entirely, but thankfully they were alone at the moment.

She looked up at him, wondering what he was going to say. Maybe tell her that she was an idiot for coming to Kuwait in the first place? Reprimand her for going on a fucking pleasure cruise with Ayden in a very volatile area of the world?

Instead, he pressed his lips together briefly before blurting, "I mentioned this before, but Remi's going to want to meet you."

Huh? Josie was confused.

"Sorry. Remi's my girlfriend. And the two of you have both been through some pretty intense trauma. And she's really great at befriending people. I just know you're someone she'd want to take under her wing. Please say you'll come to Riverton when we get back to the States."

"Kevlar," Nate said, in a tone Josie couldn't interpret.

Still confused, she glanced at Nate. He was glaring at his friend.

"I'm only doing the asking because I have no idea what's going on behind *this* guy's stoic exterior. There's a reason he's known as Blink. It's because he doesn't fucking blink when he's about to rip someone a new asshole."

Looking again at Nate, Josie had no doubt what Kevlar was saying was true.

Kevlar grinned, then said, "You *did* tell me to look after her."

Instead of replying to his friend, Nate took hold of Josie's shoulders and gently turned her to face him. "Kevlar jumped the gun on me, but yes...I'd like you to come to Riverton with us. You can't go back to Vegas, Josie. No one even fucking reported you missing. And if Ayden's mother and sister knew you were going, like your report to the admiral said, why the hell didn't *they* say anything? Especially when the Army would've notified them of Ayden's death weeks ago."

Josie had written in her report that Ayden's relatives had helped him talk her into going, so the admiral would understand why she might choose to go to Kuwait. In fact, when she'd decided to take the trip, she'd asked if they wanted her to bring anything to Ayden. And they had. Half the crap in her suitcase was stuff they'd sent for Ayden.

She'd wondered the same thing as Nate. But she also didn't know what happened when they found out about Ayden's death. It was very likely they just assumed she'd been killed too.

"But that doesn't matter. Trust me when I say the shit that happened...it can eat at you. Come out when you least expect it. Spend a few weeks in Riverton. You can stay with me. Get your bearings. Ease back into life."

She wanted to. Josie was surprised at how badly she wanted to accept. What did she have back in Vegas? Nothing. No one. Besides, the thought of being able to stay near Nate was irresistible.

She gave him a small nod.

"Yes? You'll come back to California with us?"

She nodded again.

The smile that spread across Nate's face made a warm glow move through her body.

"Good. And yeah, Remi's gonna love you. Wren too."

"Don't forget Caroline, Alabama, and the whole gang," Kevlar added.

"Can you not freak Josie out right when she's agreed to come back with us?" Nate complained, as he grabbed her hand and began walking again.

"Sorry. But seriously, this is great!"

Josie felt a little weird about how happy these men were that she'd decided to go to California. If they knew how pathetic she was, and that she literally didn't have anyone who would be glad to see her back in Nevada, they might not be so excited to have her join their little group.

They didn't get much farther before MacGyver joined up with them, leading the way. They walked down so many corridors, Josie was completely lost by the time they reached yet another hall filled with doors and MacGyver finally opened one. She recognized the men inside. They were the ones who'd gotten her and Nate out of the cells. She was relieved they were all okay, especially after the terrifying escape to the ocean they'd all endured.

"Blink!"

"Holy shit, man, good to see you!"

"You're an ass. Can't *believe* you ran off to Iran without us!"

The comments came fast and loud as Nate was pulled away from her, hugged, clapped on the back, and greeted warmly by his friends.

"Easy," Nate complained. "I already have enough bruises, don't need you assholes adding to them." He then turned and re-introduced everyone to her, which Josie appreciated. She'd forgotten who was who.

"God, you stink," one of the other guys said when he'd finished.

Nate rolled his eyes. "Thanks, Smiley. You think you'd smell any better after spending the better part of a week on a mission?"

Everyone laughed, but talk of being smelly made Josie self-conscious about her own lack of hygiene. And she'd been away for much longer than a week.

"Speaking of...we need showers. And Josie needs something to wear. And food and water," Nate announced.

"I'll go to the exchange and find something for her. Not sure if they'll have anything small enough, but I'll see what I can do," Safe said.

"And I'll head down to the canteen and get something for you both to eat," Preacher offered. "Bring it back here, so you can eat in peace. Too many people know about what happened. At least that you were in Iran and had to be extracted. Won't be comfortable to eat in public for a while."

"I'll set up a bunk for her," MacGyver offered.

"As for a shower, the women's head is just down the hall," Flash said.

Nate nodded. "Appreciate it, you guys."

"Of course."

"Any time."

"Be back soon."

Nate then turned to Josie. "Right, so, as much as I wish I could tell you that the showers onboard are luxurious, they aren't. There should be hot water, but it's not guaranteed.

And it'll have to be fast. I'm sorry. When you get to California, you can take as long as you want, but here..." His voice faded off.

Josie put her hand on his arm and mouthed, *It's okay.*

"I wish I could give you a lot of things right now, a long hot shower being one of them. But I can give you soap, a safe place to lay your head, food, and hopefully the reassurance that everything is going to be good from here on out."

She nodded at him, grateful for every single thing he'd done for her now, before, and in the future.

"Guys, you should've seen our girl type. Shit, I swear her fingers were smoking on the admiral's keys. Oh! And the way she snapped her fingers at him, and he *actually* did what she wanted?" Kevlar laughed. "If I wasn't already in love with someone, that would've done it."

MacGyver chuckled as well from behind one of the lockers, where he was grabbing blankets, presumably to make a bed for her.

"Come on, I'll show you where you can shower. I'm sure Safe will be back with some clothes for you before you're done. When he sets his mind to something, he gets it done fast," Nate said.

Looking at one of the bunks longingly—she suddenly felt as if she was about to pass out from exhaustion—Josie followed Nate out the door and back down the hall. He stopped in front of a metal door that said WOMEN in big bold letters.

"Are you going to be all right?"

She nodded.

"Okay, I'll stay out here until you're done."

Josie frowned at that and tilted her head at him in question.

"I just don't want you to be self-conscious or be bothered by anyone. They can wait until you're done."

Josie wanted to protest. Tell him she was sure it wouldn't bother her if another female entered, but by the fierce look on his face, it was obvious he was intent on letting her have some space.

She wasn't sure she wanted space, especially not from him, but she nodded anyway.

That guess was proven correct when, the second the door closed behind her, it took all of Josie's inner strength not to wrench it open again. Being alone for the first time since Nate had been dragged into the cell next to hers brought back too many bad memories.

She took a deep breath. Then another. She had to figure out how to go back to her solitary lifestyle without having a panic attack every time a door shut behind her.

She slowly walked over to the line of curtained-off showers against the wall. Just like that, the thought of being clean overrode any other emotion. She dropped the blanket, took off the socks, the shirt, the boxers, and the damn bikini, and closed the shower curtain behind her, then turned the knob. The water was a light spray from the showerhead, and it was only lukewarm, but it felt absolutely heavenly.

By the time she turned off the water—after quickly soaping herself down several times and scrubbing lightly at her scalp—Josie could barely keep her eyes open. Her hair was still a disaster, but she was too exhausted to do anything more about it now. It was enough that her body was clean.

She couldn't wash away the feeling of lying in the dirt, and she still had dark lines deep under her fingernails, but the smell of finally being clean felt amazing.

"Josie?"

She heard Nate's voice and peeked around the shower curtain, making sure she was shielded from view. He'd seen practically all of her anyway, including the way her bones protruded from her skin, but now that they weren't in the middle of an escape from a terrorist's prison cell, it felt more awkward being naked around him.

"Safe brought some clothes. I'll put them here for you. Take your time getting dressed. No one will come in until you're done."

Then he nodded at her and left her alone once more.

Josie didn't like seeing Nate's back as he walked away from her, but she'd have to get used to it. Steeling herself, she stepped out of the shower stall and walked over to the pile of things he'd left behind. There was a towel on top, which she wrapped around herself.

Safe had gotten her a T-shirt that said NAVY across the front, a pair of sweatpants with the word NAVY down one leg, a pair of underwear and a sports bra. Oh, and some socks as well.

Just seeing the clean clothes made tears well in Josie's eyes. She quickly dried herself off and donned everything. She felt like a different person, now that she had real clothes. *Clean* clothes.

She opened the door a little and saw Nate standing with his back to the door, blocking anyone from entering. There was a woman standing to the side with her arms crossed, looking irritated, but the second she saw Josie, the irritation faded away.

"Oh, you're so tiny," the woman blurted.

Josie would've laughed, as she got that a lot, but Nate filled her vision. "You okay? Everything fit?"

She nodded, feeling shy all of a sudden. It hit her then that Nate still hadn't showered. He'd just stood in the hall while she took her sweet time, getting clean. She frowned, then pointed at the door across the hall that said MEN.

Nate turned to look at where she was pointing. "Yeah, I'll clean up once you're settled back in the bunk room." Then he pushed past her into the women's room.

The sailor waiting to enter rolled her eyes as she held the door open for Nate.

Josie watched as he walked over to where she'd taken off the clothes she'd been wearing and dumped them into the trash can. Then he walked back to her and gently took her arm. "Come on, the guys should be back with something for us to eat and drink. I'll get you settled, then shower and be back before you even know I've been gone."

Josie wasn't sure about that, but she nodded anyway.

He led her back to the room with all the bunk beds, and he was right, his teammates were all there waiting on them. And they'd set up what looked like a feast. Someone had pulled a trunk out from under one of the bunks and set it up as a table. There was a ton of food piled up, but what caught Josie's attention was the fresh fruit.

She reached for a strawberry without thought—then froze, feeling terribly rude.

"Go on, Josie. Help yourself. I'll be right back." Then to

her surprise, Nate kissed her on the temple before grabbing a pile of clothes from a bunk and leaving the room.

For just a moment, she panicked, before forcing herself to take a deep breath.

"You're doing good, Josie," Kevlar told her. "The first day or so back in civilization is always hard." His hair was wet and it was obvious he'd taken a shower at the same time she had.

"If you can call this civilization," Smiley bitched.

"True," Kevlar said with a small grin. "Come on. I'll bore you with stories about my Remi, and Safe can regale you with tales of his Wren. Did Blink tell you about Caroline and Wolf? No? Well, do we have some stories to tell you! You'll fit right in with everyone...although it sucks that you had to go through what you did."

The next thing she knew, Josie was sitting cross-legged on one of the bunks, with a plate heaping with food on her lap, as all the guys took turns telling her about the people she'd meet in California. No one seemed to think it was weird that she'd be going back to Riverton with them. In fact, they seemed excited to have her.

Her head was spinning by the time Nate returned. He hadn't been gone more than fifteen minutes, but it felt as if it had been hours.

"Anything left for me?"

Josie could only stare at him. He was the same man she'd gotten to know, but he looked different now. He'd washed away the grime and had trimmed his beard. The freckles on his face stood out even more now that they weren't hidden under all the dirt and blood. He still had bruises on his face, but he looked...

Untouchable.

What the hell had she been thinking to agree to go back to California with this man? He was so out of her league it wasn't even funny. He was tall, muscular, and handsome, and she was...what was she? Short, plain, and skinny as a stick.

Her appetite disappeared in an instant.

But Nate didn't seem to notice. He sat next to her after piling his own plate with food. Then he reached over and took her hand in his, eating with the other, all while bantering with his friends. No one seemed to care that he was holding her hand. They didn't give him shit, simply went on with their conversations.

Josie's head hurt. She was confused, tired, and overwhelmed with everything that had happened in such a short time.

"We're losing her," someone said quietly.

The plate in her lap was removed, and then Nate was urging her to lie down.

"You're tired, Spirit, and it's no wonder. Close your eyes. Sleep."

A second ago, Josie had decided this man wasn't for her. But now at the thought of him leaving her side, she panicked. She grabbed his wrist when he started to stand up.

To his credit, Nate didn't pull away or ask what she was doing. He simply sat back down, then adjusted to lay next to her. "Come here," he urged, pulling her closer.

The next thing Josie knew, her head was on his shoulder and her arm was resting on his belly. His arm wrapped around her shoulders, holding her against him. "Sleep, Josie.

Tomorrow will be another long day since we'll be flying to Germany, then back to the States."

Nodding, Josie wanted to stay awake to hear more details about what would happen next. But she couldn't keep her eyes open. With the easy thumping of Nate's heart under her cheek, she fell into a deep, healing sleep, secure in the knowledge that this man wouldn't let anything happen to her while she was resting.

CHAPTER TEN

Blink slept the sleep of the dead. He'd needed it. He hadn't had a good night's sleep since before he'd been awoken in the middle of the night and told he needed to get to the base to leave for a mission to Iran within the hour.

And having Josie at his side only made his sleep all the more healing.

Looking down at the woman still sound asleep on his chest had Blink taking a relieved breath. She smelled like him. Like his soap. Her hair was still a disaster; it would take more than a crappy naval carrier shower to address it. But seeing her skin scrubbed clean, seeing the flush on her cheeks last night as she ate and drank to her heart's content...it had gone a long way toward making what he'd been through seem like small potatoes.

He still couldn't believe this woman had been rotting away in an Iranian cell, and no one knew. If he hadn't been captured, she'd still be there. It was unbelievable. Unacceptable.

He hadn't missed the way she'd tensed after seeing him freshly showered. And he thought he knew why. She'd gotten used to seeing him in soldier mode, complete with a scruffy beard and covered in days' worth of grime. But if she thought she was going to back away now, she was wrong.

She was the woman Blink had waited for his entire life, and he'd do whatever it took to prove it to her. Whatever insecurities she had about the two of them together were bullshit. He could tell by her sudden unwillingness to meet his gaze, the way her mouth had turned down last night, that she was suddenly uneasy around him.

And it cut deep. But he'd make her comfortable around him again. Somehow. He was the same man she'd gotten to know when they were fighting for their lives.

He hadn't lied, today would be long and difficult. There would be more questions, doctors would need to examine them, and then the long flight back to California. But he'd be right there by Josie's side. Whatever she needed, he'd make sure she had it, and that she was handling all the attention she'd be getting.

She stirred in his arms, and he felt the moment she became aware of her surroundings when she tensed against him.

"Shhhh," he murmured quietly against her hair. "You're good. We have a few more minutes before we have to get up. I'm sure Kevlar's alarm is going to go off here any moment. Then we'll have to deal with Flash and Smiley being bitchy, because they hate having their precious sleep interrupted.

MacGyver will be up and ready to go in seconds, which is just annoying, and Safe will be a zombie until he gets coffee, although it's not the fancy stuff he likes. Preacher will be dressed and packed and bugging us to hurry the hell up, and Kevlar will be the last one to leave, checking to make sure we didn't leave anything behind, like someone always does."

He felt Josie smile against his chest. Then she lifted her head and studied him with a quizzical look on her face.

"Me?" he asked.

She nodded.

Blink shrugged. "I go with the flow. Not bringing attention to myself, not getting in the way. Watching the others, observing. My brother is the outgoing one. I'm the kind of guy who stands back and gets the lay of the land before acting. I've learned a lot by watching."

Josie rested her chin on her hand as she continued to look into his eyes.

"You want to know what I've learned by watching you?" he asked.

Josie's brows furrowed, and she shook her head.

Blink chuckled softly. He was enjoying this moment in time. The intimacy of it. Even though they were in a room with all of his teammates, it felt as if they were in a bubble of their own. "I'm going to tell you anyway. You're like me, Spirit. You watch others. Figure out what they're all about before you interact. You did that with me. You weren't sure you could trust me. Didn't know what I might do when I found out you were there in that cell. And when you realized that I was on your side, that I wouldn't hurt you, you acted."

Josie moved so her cheek was resting on his chest once more, breaking eye contact.

"You giving me that water...it changed my life, Josie," Blink admitted in a whisper. "I know what that water meant. It was literally your lifeline. By all rights, you should've been dead. I don't know how long you'd gone without food, but any idiot could see it was a *very* long time. It took over a day and a half for that cup to fill with water. And you *gave* it to me. Not half of it, the whole cup. My teammates would give their lives for me, and I'd do the same for them, but outside those men...no one has ever shown me the kind of courage and self-lessness you did.

"I'm going to do everything in my power to return that kindness. Not because I have to. Not because I feel obligated in some way. But because if I can't find a way to keep you in my life, I'm not sure I can even keep doing what I'm doing. I've seen too much hate. Too much death. I need you in my life to balance it. Not someone *like* you—but you."

As soon as the words left his mouth, Blink suddenly wished he could take them all back. By the look on her face, he knew he was coming on too strong. Way too fucking strong. This woman had just been through hell. She had a life back in the States. And here he was, basically telling her he wasn't going to let her go. Shit, like he was a stalker or something. The thought made him want to beat his own ass.

Josie picked up her head and looked at him once more. She had tears in her eyes, and Blink panicked, his own eyes going wide at the sight. He hadn't meant to upset her! Hadn't meant to make her cry.

"Fuck," he swore.

To his great surprise, she gave him a watery smile. "You say fuck a lot."

Blink gaped at her in total shock. Her voice was a low and raspy whisper, as if her vocal cords were rusty from not having been used for so long. And she seemed just as surprised to hear it as he was.

He wanted to leap up and let out a yell of triumph. She'd spoken! To *him*! It felt like a huge victory.

He forced himself to keep his cool. "Yeah. I do. Should I apologize?" he asked.

She gave him a small shake of her head.

"It's just that the word perfectly sums up how I feel when I use it. If I'm hurting, surprised, concerned, excited...it can convey all those feelings. It's a multipurpose word that always fits the occasion." Blink brought his hand to her face and wiped away the tears on her cheeks with his thumb. "Don't cry, Josie. I can't stand it when you cry."

She gave him another wobbly smile.

Then Kevlar's alarm started pealing in the quiet room.

There were moans and groans from the men around them. Kevlar barked, "Time to get up, boys! We're going home!"

"The only reason you're excited is because you get to see Remi," Smiley bitched.

"Yup. And one day, you'll have your own woman to go home to, then *you'll* be the first one up. Getting on all of our nerves by trying to make us hurry."

"Not likely," he groaned.

"Told you," Blink said quietly to Josie. "You ready for today?"

She shrugged.

"Well, whatever happens, I'll be there. So you don't need to worry. Okay?"

Okay, she mouthed.

Blink hadn't expected her to start babbling away, now that she'd finally spoken, but he hoped she'd gain some confidence and would be able to use words more often than not. He smiled at the thought.

Josie poked his chest and tilted her head at him in question.

"I was just thinking about how I'm the verbose one in this relationship," he admitted honestly. "Which is hilarious, because I'm anything but talkative...with anyone other than you."

"He's not lying," Flash said from the bunk next to them. "Blink's a *seriously* quiet guy. You know he's thinking a mile a minute under that dead-eye stare he's got, but he never opens his mouth unless he's got something to say."

Josie gave Blink a small smile. One that went straight to his heart.

"Get up, lazy bones," Kevlar told them. "We have to grab breakfast and see the admiral, then I'm sure you want to say goodbye to your brother before we head out."

"Let's do this," Blink told Josie.

"Let's do this," she whispered back.

"Wait—did she just talk?" Preacher asked.

Safe smacked the back of his head, but Blink didn't take his gaze from Josie's. Every word from her mouth felt like a huge win, though honestly, he didn't care if she was mute or not. He seemed to be able to understand her just fine. They were connected by circumstance. They'd been through hell together and come out the other side.

* * *

Josie stood on the deck of the aircraft carrier and watched as Nate hugged his brother goodbye. He was there with five other Night Stalker pilots. She'd been introduced to the ones she hadn't met yet—Chaos and Edge—and couldn't help but smirk a little at all their call signs. Obi-Wan, Buck, Pyro, Casper...she wanted to ask how they got their nicknames. What they all meant. But she wasn't going to get the chance. They had to get on the plane that was waiting to take them to Germany.

In the meeting with the admiral that morning, he told her that a replacement passport would be waiting for her in Germany. Something about how a man named Tex had arranged it. Josie didn't know who Tex was, but she was grateful for his assistance. The thought of having to wait on the ship or in Germany while Nate and the others all went home scared the hell out of her. Not that anyone had been rude or mean to her, she just felt more comfortable around the men she already knew.

Who was she kidding? It was Nate she felt the most at ease around. He saw past the traumatized, grubby, smelly, skin-and-bones creature he'd first met to the woman underneath it all. She felt as if she was emerging from years of living in dark and dank sewers. Covered in filth, forgotten. And in a way, she was.

Technically, she was still Josie England, the same forgettable and uninteresting woman she'd been before. But Nate made her feel like...more.

His words from that morning echoed in her head.

I need you in my life...Not someone like you—but you.

They were life-changing words.

Ayden had told her early in their relationship how much he loved her. How beautiful she was. How smart. But in the end, they'd been nothing but pretty words to get her into bed. She understood that now, and he'd shown his true colors soon enough. He didn't care about *her*, just about what he could get from her.

But Nate? He saw straight to her soul, and what he saw didn't seem to turn him off. She certainly hadn't been at her best since they'd met. Either physically or mentally. But it didn't matter. That cup of water she'd given him? He might think it was a difficult decision for her to make. To give up the only thing keeping her alive. And with anyone else, it might've been. But the fact that Nate hadn't demanded she share, hadn't expected anything from her, as Ayden would have, made it all the more easy to offer it.

The truth was, she regretted not giving him the water earlier. She shouldn't have waited so long. But thankfully they'd been rescued, and in the end it didn't matter.

"He's a good man," Kevlar said to her, as they watched Nate and Tate say their goodbyes. "I owe him everything. He saved my Remi. Did what he does best, watch and observe, then acted when it was needed."

Josie looked up at him. She remembered Nate telling her about what happened with Remi, being kidnapped and almost buried alive. He'd downplayed his role in the entire fiasco, obviously.

Kevlar turned to look at her. "He's been through hell. And I'm not talking about this latest shitshow. He lost his former SEAL team. Some died. Some were hurt so bad they were medically retired. For weeks he did nothing but sit at the local bar we like to go to and stare into space. But he's literally one of the strongest men I know. We're lucky to have him, and when we heard what happened—that he was sent back into Iran where he'd lost his last team, and got himself captured so the men he was with could get away—there was no way we weren't going to be the ones to come get him. You and him...you're so much alike, it's not even funny. You both have pain you've shoved deep down inside, but you don't let it stop you from surviving. I think you're perfect for each other.

"And I realize people will be skeptical. Hell, *you* probably are. But I knew the moment I saw Remi that she was it for me. I didn't admit it to myself, but I knew all the same. He can heal you if you let him, just as you can do the same for him. Just don't hurt him, Josie. I'm not sure he can take it. Not after everything else."

Her heart broke for the man who'd quickly become everything to her. She wanted to tell Kevlar that she wasn't going to hurt Nate. But the words wouldn't come. All she could do was nod.

"Good. Glad we had this talk," Kevlar said with a small chuckle. "I've already told you that Remi's going to want to meet you, and I wasn't lying. She'll be chomping at the bit to meet Blink's woman. They have a special bond. One that I am in no way jealous of. Without him, I wouldn't have her. She might be a little protective of him, so I'm asking that you give her some grace. You two went through hell together, but so did she and Blink."

Josie nodded again.

"Thank you. I swear, Remi will be as loyal a friend as you'll ever have. She's a cartoonist. Wait until you read some of her Pecky the Traveling Taco cartoons. They're hilarious."

"Lord, are you going on about Pecky again?" Flash asked from behind them.

Josie turned to see the SEAL smiling at them.

"Yup," Kevlar said without turning around. "If I could get everyone I meet to read her stuff, I could retire from the Navy and be a house-husband."

"You can already do that," MacGyver said. "We all know she makes gads of money from that damn taco."

"Whatever," Kevlar mumbled.

Josie couldn't help but giggle at them.

"Such a sweet sound," Safe said, looking at her in surprise from the other side of Kevlar.

For some reason, Josie felt herself blushing. As Nate joined them after saying goodbye to his twin and the other Night Stalkers, she realized what a good group of men she'd ended up with. They were loyal, friendly, and kind of badass. No, not kind of—very badass. She hadn't forgotten how they'd broken her and Nate out of their prison cells, and how they'd been all...soldier-y as they'd crept through the town before all hell broke loose and they'd had to split up.

"Sorry, that took longer than I thought it would. Tate and his crew are headed to the States. Back to Norfolk, Virginia, where they're currently living. Since he lost his chopper, he'll have to be issued a new one, then work with the mechanics to get it outfitted and running the way he likes it."

"Lost it? Is that what they're going with?" Preacher asked with a snort.

Nate smiled. "Uh-huh."

He looked almost boyish when he smiled. Josie liked all his sides. Serious, intense, deadly, joking, sleepy, concerned about her...but especially this one. The teasing one.

"Let's get off this hunk of junk. I'm ready to see Wren," Safe said.

Everyone leaned down to pick up their duffle bags, and Josie felt weird that she didn't have anything other than the clothes on her back...and her little metal cup that Nate had insisted on keeping in his pocket. He'd claimed it was good luck, and he promised not to let anything happen to it.

Since Josie trusted him, she hadn't protested. It wasn't as if she had a bag of her own to put it in. And no pockets in the sweatpants she was still wearing.

They walked across the deck toward a waiting plane. She wasn't thrilled about the procedure for taking off from the moving ship, but she wasn't about to complain. The thought of being back on solid ground in the States was enough motivation for her to do whatever was asked of her.

* * *

Twenty-four hours later, Josie was done. Done with traveling. Done with being polite. Done with being patient. Done with being social. It made no sense, when it wasn't so long ago that she would've done anything to be around other people. But after the stressful trip to Germany, then being poked and prodded, and told she was malnourished and anemic—duh—by a doctor at the military hospital who'd had a tendency to talk about her as if she wasn't right there in the room with him, simply because she wasn't speaking, and then the long flight back to California with a plane full of other sailors and soldiers who were *also* on their way home, Josie longed for a bit of alone time.

She was also feeling...off. She hadn't been part of regular society for so long, just being in Nate's car as he drove them to his house was nerve-wracking. It was dark, she had no idea what time it was, but even the few cars on the road with them were freaking her out.

"Breathe, Josie. We'll be at my place in a few minutes. Then you can relax."

She wasn't surprised Nate was so in tune with her. He'd stayed right by her side throughout their travels. He'd given her the window seat on the flight to Germany, sitting in the middle even though he'd looked completely cramped in the small seat. His hand stayed on the small of her back as they walked to and from planes, and through the military hospital in Germany. He'd hadn't been allowed to stay in the room with her while she was examined, and just being away from him for that small period of time almost sent Josie over the edge.

She was tired, cranky, and almost sick with worry about what would happen next. Had she made the right decision to come to California? Maybe she should've gone back to her apartment in Vegas. Although she wasn't even sure she still had a place to live there. She'd been gone long enough that her landlord probably thought she'd left him high and dry, and who knows what had happened to her stuff.

Panic was setting in. What if all her things were gone? Sold? Trashed? It wasn't as if she had anything valuable, but the pictures, the sentimental doodads, the clothes she'd spent hours searching for that finally fit her perfectly after some alterations. She didn't want to start over. Didn't know how to even *begin* to do that. And she needed to contact her boss, make sure she still had a job.

"Josie, what'd I just say? *Breathe*," Nate ordered firmly.

Looking over at him, she could just make him out in the glow of passing cars and the streetlights they drove under.

"I know today has been trying, but we're almost home."

Josie wanted to snort. Trying. Right. That wasn't the word she would've used. But...she really shouldn't complain. No one had told her she had to fork over a credit card before she could get on any of the planes. She had a passport, and she was alive and free.

"I live in an apartment. It's nothing fancy. I want to buy a house someday, but with my job, it doesn't seem like a smart thing to do right now. Remi used to live in the same complex, but she moved in with Kevlar. When we get there, you don't have to do anything. You can just sit and acclimate. Trust me when I say that I understand how you're feeling. It's noisy here, isn't it? Cars honking, engines, thumping radios. Even though it sucked being in that cell, being around all these people seems...chaotic."

Josie did as ordered and took a deep breath. He was right. It felt as if her entire life was spinning out of control, and she prided herself on *always* being in control. She hadn't been able to control anything that happened to her for weeks, and even after she was free, she still felt as if she was being told what to do by everyone around her. She hadn't had any choices... except to come to California with Nate. Which felt right.

And just like that, she relaxed a bit.

"Here we are," he announced as he pulled into a parking lot. While the apartments seemed older, they didn't look run down. And the lot was well lit. Not that it mattered.

Josie wasn't afraid of the dark. She'd spent her time in captivity in almost total darkness, so her demons didn't stem from a lack of light. Being on the water, yes. Not having access to food or something to drink, yes. The dark, no.

Nate pulled into a space and shut off the truck's engine.

"I'll come around," he told her, opening his door.

She waited for Nate to walk around the truck without complaint. He opened her door, and a small chuckle escaped his lips. "I need to get a step stool for you so you don't break your neck getting in and out," he murmured. Looking down, Josie saw that she was pretty high off the ground. Being short had its drawbacks, and this was one of them.

The second she had the thought, she took it back when Nate's arms closed around her and he lifted her off the seat and placed her feet on the ground. Being in his embrace didn't suck.

Nate grabbed his duffle bag out of the bed of the truck and held out his hand.

Josie didn't hesitate to take it as he led them toward one of the doors on the first floor of the complex. He pulled keys from his pocket, unlocked the door, then pushed it open for her. "After you," he said.

Josie stepped inside and into the main living area while Nate flicked on a few lights. Looking around, she saw nothing out of place. The books in a bookcase against the wall were lined up perfectly. The few pictures on the walls were evenly spaced and not crooked even an inch. There was a blanket on the back of the couch that was folded perfectly. The pillows were placed just so in the two corners. The coffee table was clean, no magazines or knickknacks littering its surface.

Glancing into the kitchen, she didn't see any dirty dishes in the sink, the countertops were spotless, and the few appliances on their surfaces were pushed back toward the wall and lined up precisely.

"I'm a bit of a neat freak," Nate said from behind her. "It was drilled into us in boot camp."

Josie turned toward him and knew she was smiling like an idiot, but she couldn't help it. Her place in Vegas looked just like this. Orderly, not cluttered at all.

At seeing her expression, the worried look on Nate's face disappeared. "I take it you aren't going to run out the door complaining I'm a total anal freak?"

A sexually loaded inuendo immediately popped into Josie's mind, but she simply shook her head.

"Good. What do you want to do? Shower? Watch TV? Sit and stare into space? Sleep?"

Her belly decided at that moment to growl, embarrassing the crap out of Josie. Nate had made sure she had plenty to eat during their trip. He was constantly pulling granola bars and dried fruit out of one of his many pockets. Not to mention making sure she had access to as much water as she wanted.

"Eat it is," Blink said matter-of-factly as he dropped his bag and headed for the kitchen. It was small but had all the things a kitchen needed to be functional. He went to the pantry and looked inside for a long moment, then grabbed for something.

"I don't have anything fresh, I need to go to the store, but I've got some au gratin potatoes in a box that I can make. And some canned green beans. Oh! And some tuna. I can put together a tuna salad. It's really good with some mayo and pickled jalapenos. I usually make a sandwich out of it, but I don't have any bread. I *do* have some crackers. We can crumble those in it, or treat it as a dip."

He grabbed more things as he talked, and now he turned to her with his arms full...and for some reason, Josie wanted to cry again. They'd just gotten home, it was late, he had to be as tired as she was, and he had his own medical issues and probably psychological ones to deal with because of his time as a POW—and here he was, going out of his way to feed her.

"No, do *not* cry," he ordered, obviously seeing her distress. "We can order a pizza if you want, just don't cry."

Josie couldn't help but laugh through her tears. She was pretty sure he knew she wasn't emotional over what he'd chosen for them to eat, but was attempting to make her laugh. He'd succeeded.

"Can I help?" she asked, once more surprised at the rasp of her voice. It sounded weird to her ears, and the words popped out without any real thought on her part. Other times, when she really wanted to say something, her vocal cords wouldn't cooperate. But it seemed around Nate at least, when she felt the most comfortable, they came out without too much effort.

"Sure," he said. "If you want to grab a couple of bowls from that cabinet, then open the cans, that would be a good start."

She was glad he didn't make a big deal out of her speaking. It would've felt weird and made her self-conscious.

They worked together to make the meal, and it was ready in no time. As the potatoes finished simmering on the stove, they ate the tuna and the green beans. And while Josie still didn't eat as much as she usually did, she didn't get full as fast as she had even the day before.

"Tonight and tomorrow, we rest. Recuperate. The day after that is soon enough for both of us to get back to the real world. I know you probably have some people you need to contact, I'll need to go to the base, but we'll have at least a day to do nothing. To reacclimate. Okay?" he said at one point.

Josie nodded. Doing nothing sounded really good. Even though she'd spent the last few weeks doing exactly that, it felt very different now that she was safe, her belly was full, and she wasn't on edge, waiting for something bad to happen.

They ate the potatoes when they were finished, and to Josie, they were the best thing she'd ever had. Cheesy, creamy, and so damn good, she felt like crying again. But she didn't get the chance. There were dishes to be done and put away, counters and a table to wipe down, and then it was time for bed.

Nate led her to his spare room. It was obvious he didn't get many guests, as there were boxes, some weights, and a hodgepodge of furniture in the small space. It was the most cluttered space she'd seen in his apartment. A twin bed sat against a wall, and suddenly all Josie could think about was curling up and sleeping for hours.

"There's a bathroom in the hall. I'll put out a toothbrush you can use. Tomorrow, we'll work on your hair. Do not touch it tonight. Hear me?"

Josie looked at him in surprise.

"I mean, I know it has to be bothering you. I just don't want you reaching for a pair of scissors or doing anything drastic before you give me a chance to help you with it. I haven't had any experience with getting snarls and mats out, but I'm willing to try if you are."

She nodded shyly at him, wondering how in the world he knew she was thinking about chopping it all off and starting over. She'd always thought her long blonde hair was one of her best features, and she hated to cut it. Any help he wanted to give her, she'd gladly take.

"Good. I'm right next door. If you need anything, don't hesitate to come get me. I'll bring you some water you can keep next to the bed, and—oh! Your cup." He pulled it out of his pocket and held it up.

Here in the real world, amongst the neat and clean atmosphere of his apartment, the thing looked pathetic. It probably had some nasty germs and parasites in it as well. But Nate didn't seem turned off or haunted by seeing it. She couldn't interpret the look he had on his face, but it wasn't disgust.

"I'll just leave this here," he said quietly, placing the small cup on the table next to the bed. Then he stepped up to her and lightly brushed a finger over her cheek. "Thank you for fighting. For not giving up. For being here. For being you, Josie." Then he leaned down, kissed her forehead, and left without another word.

If Josie was anyone else, she would've called him back. Told him how grateful she was for his hospitality. Thanked him for being with her in Germany after the examination was done, and the stupid doctor was going over everything he thought was wrong with her. For sitting next to her on the planes and keeping her calm. For feeding her tonight, for making her feel normal, even though she knew she could never return to the woman she used to be before making that fateful decision to go to Kuwait...and further, getting on that boat with Ayden.

But she didn't. All she did was watch him walk away.

Instead of going to the bathroom to brush her teeth—she'd scrubbed them for fifteen minutes straight when she'd arrived in Germany—she simply turned and climbed under the covers on the small bed. She didn't bother to remove the sweats or the shirt she wore. She was suddenly too exhausted to do anything other than lie down.

Within seconds of her eyes closing, she was asleep.

CHAPTER ELEVEN

Blink wasn't sure what woke him. He lay still in his king-size bed and stared at the ceiling, trying to reorientate himself. It wasn't that long ago when he was on his back, staring up at the concrete ceiling of a prison cell in Iran. Now he was home, safe, comfortable...and suddenly on edge.

Something had disturbed him enough to wake him from a deep sleep. Then he remembered that Josie was with him. In the other room. Was she having nightmares? She hadn't had any that he knew of since they'd been rescued, or even while they'd been in the cells next to each other, but many times they wouldn't start until after getting out of whatever situation had caused psychological stress in the first place. He had firsthand knowledge of that.

Looking at the clock, he saw he'd been asleep for a few hours. It was just beginning to lighten outside, but it was definitely still early in the morning.

Sitting up, Blink flung his covers aside and stood. He

headed for the door to check on Josie when something made him turn around and look behind him.

There, on the floor at the foot of his bed, was Josie. Curled into a small ball, with the blanket from the guest room wrapped around her.

"Fuck," he muttered.

Remembering the first words Josie had spoken, about him saying that word a lot, he sighed as he headed to her side. Crouching next to her, Blink brushed a lock of matted hair off her cheek.

"Josie?" he said quietly, not wanting to startle her.

Her eyes popped open, and she stared up at him.

"It's me, Blink. Are you all right?"

"Woke up. Couldn't sleep," she said drowsily.

"Did you have a bad dream?" he asked.

She shook her head. "Just didn't see you. Got used to sleeping in your presence."

Her words made his heart skip a beat. This woman. She slayed him.

He reached out and picked her up off the floor without any effort whatsoever. It made him realize anew how far she still needed to go to get healthy. But he'd work on that. They would go to the store and he'd get all her favorite foods, making sure to follow the doctor's orders about eating lots of protein and healthy food to build her muscles back up.

He walked around the bed and placed her on the mattress, then said, "Scoot over."

She did as he asked, and soon he was in the bed with her, pulling up the covers. He wrapped an arm around Josie, so her head was once more on his chest, the way they'd slept on the Navy ship. "This is better," he said with satisfaction.

Josie nodded against him. It hadn't escaped his notice that she'd spoken when she'd been half asleep, as if she wasn't aware she was doing it. Her voice was there. She just needed to get used to using it again. Feel safe doing so.

It wasn't long before he felt Josie's breaths even out against him. One of her arms was across his belly and one of her legs had actually hitched up and over his thigh. He felt pinned down by her, even though she weighed less than a hundred pounds. She probably had no idea that she held all the power in their relationship. Blink was helpless against her...and he couldn't be more content.

When he woke up hours later, he was alone in bed. Panic set in, and Blink threw the covers back and was across the room before he thought about what he was doing. He ran into the living area and stopped in his tracks.

Josie was sitting on his couch, curled into the corner with a bottle of water on the table next to her, a book in one hand and a sleeve of crackers in the other. She looked up at him with wide eyes.

"Are you okay?" Blink barked.

She nodded quickly.

And just like that, his muscles relaxed. "I woke up and you weren't there. I thought...hell, I don't know *what* I thought."

Josie set her things down and got up off the couch and walked over to him. She was still wearing the same sweats and T-shirt she'd gotten on the ship. Blink made a mental note to prioritize getting her some more clothes.

She walked right into his personal space until her cheek

was resting on his chest. Wrapping his arms around her, Blink immediately felt better.

Josie hugged him hard. Then lifted her head and tilted it back to look at him. "I got hungry."

"Right. Of course you did. How about you let me make you something a little better than some yucky old crackers?" he told her.

She smiled. "Are you going to get dressed first?"

The fact that she was talking to him felt so good, even if he didn't have anything to do with it. "Oh, yeah. Probably should do that, huh?" he asked, looking down at himself. He had on a pair of boxers and that was it. He usually slept in the nude, but he'd made an exception last night since Josie was there.

To his surprise, she put her head back on his chest and tightened her arms around him once more.

Blink would've stood there forever if that's what she wanted, but eventually, she lowered her arms and took a step back.

"Right. Going. I'll be right back," he said, backing away from her slowly. As he went, he could've sworn he saw desire in her eyes. But he was probably projecting what he wanted to see, rather than what was really there.

He showered, brushed his teeth, and got dressed in record time, and was back in the living room in less than ten minutes. Josie had settled back on the couch and smiled up at him when he returned.

"I put a fresh T-shirt in the bathroom for you. And another pair of sweats. They'll be too big, but after we eat, I'll work on getting you more appropriate clothes."

The moment the last word was out of his mouth, there was a knock on his door.

Frowning, Blink went to answer it.

Remi and Wren were standing outside with huge smiles on their faces. Kevlar and Safe were standing by their cars in the parking lot, also smiling. Assholes knew Blink would've cussed them out for disturbing him and Josie but wouldn't say a word to the women.

"Hi!" Remi said. "We heard about Josie and went to the store this morning to get her some stuff. Because of *course* you don't have the things she probably needs."

"Bo said you probably didn't want to be bothered yet, but we literally couldn't stay away," Wren told him. "I already called Julie, you know, from My Sister's Closet? She was so great about finding me some awesome stuff, and when she gets in, she's going to see what she has in Josie's sizes. Bo says she's tiny, so Julie isn't sure what she has, but she'll let you know when she goes through her inventory."

"Is she up? Can we meet her?" Remi asked.

"We won't stay long," Wren added.

Blink looked back at his friends. They both gave him a chin lift and didn't look inclined to join their women.

He opened the door with a sigh, and Remi and Wren filed past him, each carrying several bags. They put them down in the foyer and walked into his living area. Blink left the door open behind him and followed.

Josie was standing now, looking unsure. He hated that she obviously felt so uneasy.

"Hi! I'm Remi. And this is Wren. You probably heard, but we bought you some things. After hearing all about you from our guys last night, we bugged them to take us to the store this morning. We got all sorts of soaps and lotion, and some shampoo and conditioner that smells awesome. Blink's great and all, but he's also a guy, so he probably thinks Irish Spring is perfectly acceptable for a woman to use when she showers."

Blink almost missed the way Josie's lips twitched, but it was enough for him to relax a fraction.

"And we got you some other things that every woman needs. Leggings, shirts, thick socks...and chocolate. Lots and lots of chocolate," Wren added.

Josie smiled outright at the two women at that. It was a more relaxed expression, more real.

"I know this is your day off—Vincent already told me that we shouldn't bug you—but I wanted to make sure you know how amazing Blink is. He's my second-favorite person in the entire world...no offense, Wren."

"None taken," the other woman said easily.

"Anyway, he'll take really good care of you," Remi finished.

"Who takes care of *him*?" Josie asked.

Blink was shocked yet again. This was the first time she'd said anything to anyone other than him.

"Good question," Remi said. "I guess all of us. But you're here now. You can do it."

"I can take care of myself," Blink felt obligated to point out.

To his amusement, both Remi and Wren rolled their eyes.

"*Anyway*. We guessed that you guys probably don't have anything fresh to eat, seeing as how Blink's been gone a while, so Remi and I put in a huge order at the grocery store. It should be delivered within the hour. Got a ton of fresh fruit and veggies, and while we tried to control ourselves and only get healthy stuff, we couldn't resist throwing in some things that any self-respecting doctor would frown over but we consider vital," Wren said with a smile.

"Like Cheetos. Blink is addicted to the things," Remi said.

He would've protested, but she wasn't wrong.

Remi took a step toward the couch but didn't encroach on Josie's personal space. "I'm really sorry about what happened to you. It's so awful...but you're here now. Anything you need, Blink will help you with, and if he can't, we'll all step up."

"Yeah, and Bo has already been in touch with Cookie. He's a retired SEAL that he's close with. His wife, Fiona, went through something similar as you. She was a captive for a long time. Cookie said she's more than willing to talk to you, but only if you want. She had some PTSD for a while, but she's good now. Happy." Wren glanced at Remi with a frown. "Shoot, I'm overstepping, aren't I? I meant to keep this upbeat and welcoming, and instead I had to go and bring up what had to be bad memories."

She looked back at Josie. "I'm sorry. All I meant was... we're all here for you if you want to talk, or just sit and listen to us babble on about nothing. We're kind of good at that. And I'm already getting the impression that you're a lot like Blink. You like to listen rather than talk. Which is cool."

"I'd like that," Josie told her.

"Oh! Good. Talking to Fiona or hanging with us?" Wren asked.

Josie just nodded.

Wren and Remi both beamed. "Great! Awesome. Okay. Blink, maybe you can bring her to Aces. It's this cool bar that all the guys go to. It's super safe, and I bet Jessyka would be willing to open early so we can all hang out there without any of the other patrons. You know, so you can get to know us without worrying about anyone else around. Not that you would. Worry about anyone, I mean. Because there's no one to worry about, but, you know...without the pressure."

"She knows what you mean," Blink said, taking pity on the obviously nervous and babbling Wren.

Josie nodded again, backing him up.

"Okay. Great. Well, um...we'll just be going now," Wren said.

"Yeah. It was great meeting you. Thank you for taking care of Blink over there. He's important to me...to all of us. We'll be in touch. And please let us know if there's anything else you need. We're happy to get it for you. Blink has our numbers, and he can call or text. Enjoy the stuff we brought and the food delivery. I'm looking forward to getting to know you, Josie."

Blink walked the women out, giving Kevlar and Safe a chin lift before shutting the door.

He let out a long breath of air, then turned to Josie. "They're talkers," he said unnecessarily.

She giggled. The sound went through him like a bolt of electricity. He liked seeing her happy. Wanted to keep her that way for the rest of her life.

"Shall we see what they brought?"

Josie nodded and walked over to where he was standing by the bags. The two of them carried everything to the kitchen table and began to unpack.

Blink shook his head when it was all laid out in front of them. "They went a little overboard," he said.

That was an understatement. There was enough chocolate candy to last for months, three different kinds of shampoos and conditioners, lotions, makeup—what looked like half the beauty aisle. They'd also picked up several different colors of leggings and a plethora of shirts and other lounging clothes.

He turned to look at Josie, and saw her staring at the gifts spread out all over the table with tears in her eyes. He instantly panicked. "It's too much, isn't it? We can take it all back, anything you don't like or want. Don't cry, Spirit, please. I can't stand it!"

She turned to him, and her lips quirked upward even as two tears fell. "It's wonderful," she said quietly.

Blink tried to relax. "Oh...okay."

Josie picked up a bottle of spray detangler, then looked back at him and gestured to her hair.

"Yes, we can get to work on that. You want to shower first? And when I say shower, you can stay in there as long as you want. I'm not sure how long the hot water will last, but I've got a decent tank. I'll carry this stuff into the bathroom for you and you can try it all out...but I have to say, there's nothing wrong with Irish Spring."

She huffed out a laugh, and wiped her cheeks with her shoulders.

Blink loved that he could make her smile. "While you're showering and going over your clothing options, I'll see if I can make some room in my pantry. Because I'm sure those two bought out the damn grocery store. I'm expecting a huge truck to back up to the door to unload it all."

She smiled at him again, and Blink realized how content he was. He hadn't felt like this since...well, never. After his previous team was ambushed, he fell into a spiral of depression. It hadn't been easy to pull himself out of it, but with the help of Remi and his new team, he had. But despite clicking so well with his teammates...he'd still just been going through the motions of life.

Even after all he'd been through in the last week or so, he felt happier now than he could remember being even before losing his friends and teammates.

He had a new mission in life...Josie.

It took them three trips to get everything Remi and Wren had bought into his little guest bathroom, and there wasn't much room on the counter after everything was transferred. It occurred to Blink that his en suite bathroom had a lot more counter space, but he wasn't going there. It was too fast. But that didn't make the thought go away.

He opened his mouth, but before he could say anything, there was another knock at the door. "That had better be the groceries, and not the rest of the guys," he muttered.

Josie giggled again, and Blink smiled. "Enjoy your shower. Don't bother too much with your hair, I'll take care of it for you when you get out. Just enjoy the hot water and being clean."

Then he leaned forward and kissed her gently on the lips.

He didn't plan it, just did what felt right and normal. And he was instantly ready to apologize, until he realized that Josie didn't look upset or taken aback. Instead, she gave him that familiar shy smile.

Blink forced himself to back out of the room before he

did something *really* stupid—like pick Josie up, set her ass on the counter, and kiss her the way his heart was demanding.

"Food," he muttered to himself.

When he opened the front door, he saw that indeed, Remi and Wren had definitely gone overboard with groceries too. But at least he and Josie wouldn't have to leave the house today, after all. They certainly had everything they needed in order to make some hearty, healthy meals.

CHAPTER TWELVE

Josie's lips tingled. Even after standing in the hot shower for twenty minutes. The various soaps Remi and Wren had bought her smelled heavenly. She'd tried all four of them. It was extremely difficult to get out of that wonderful shower and get dressed, but she was hungry. And she wanted to see Nate.

That kiss. It had surprised her, but she wasn't upset about it. Not in the least. In fact, she wanted more. She'd been physically attracted to him from the first moment, even bloody and beaten in that cell. Of course, she wasn't interested in doing anything but getting out of the hell she'd found herself in back then. But now?

Bringing a hand to her lips, she traced them with her finger. She was safe. Away from terrorists, and beatings, and from the threat of starving to death. Now she wanted to *live*.

Josie had figured Nate saw her as someone who needed

taking care of. More like a sister than anything else. But that kiss changed things. At least for her.

Maybe he didn't mean it? Maybe it was a spontaneous thing that he now regretted. Looking down at herself, Josie wrinkled her nose. She wasn't exactly a cover model. Too skinny, too short, too...quiet. She'd surprised herself with the ability to speak to others today. True, she hadn't exactly been a chatterbox, but words were coming easier now.

Staring into the mirror, she continued to study herself... and frown. She wasn't the kind of woman who men fell all over themselves for. Especially after what had happened to her. Everything about her was plain. Her best feature used to be her hair, and even though Nate said he'd help her with that, the urge to cut it all off was strong. She didn't quite have dreadlocks, but it was close.

Lowering her head, Josie braced herself on the counter and closed her eyes.

What was she thinking? Even stoic, Nate was larger than life compared to her. He needed someone who was outgoing to balance his introverted side, good in social situations, and who didn't look as if she lived out of her car or something.

"Josie?"

Her name on Nate's lips scared her so badly, she jerked away from the sound and almost tripped over the small throw rug in the bathroom.

But Nate was there, his arm around her waist, saving her from falling on her ass.

"Fuck! I'm sorry. I didn't mean to scare you. I thought you heard the door open."

Josie shook her head as she looked up at him.

"What's wrong?"

How could she explain what she was thinking? That she was pretty sure she was falling in love with him, but she didn't think there was any way he could ever feel that way about her? That she wasn't good enough for him. That she dreaded going back to her lonely life in Las Vegas.

But as usual, Nate seemed to understand how on edge she was. He pulled her close, and she gladly buried her nose in his chest and clung to him.

"You smell good," he murmured.

Josie wanted to snort. Of course she did. She'd used four different soaps and wasn't wearing the same stupid beach cover-up she'd worn for weeks and wasn't wallowing in the dirt anymore.

"Vanilla with hints of peach and some kind of flower," Nate said with a chuckle.

Josie looked up at him with a small smile on her face.

"And the clothes look like they fit pretty well. Much better than my huge shirt and sweats."

She liked wearing his clothes. It made her feel as if she was constantly being hugged by him.

"But I have to admit, I liked you in my clothes," Nate went on, as if he could read her mind. "Come here," he said, even as he was turning her in his arms and stepping in front of the sink. Then he put a finger under her chin and forced her to look at their image reflected in the mirror. "I bet you were in here cataloguing everything you think is a flaw."

Josie's surprised gaze went to his own.

"I've been where you are now, Spirit. I can't tell you how long I spent staring at myself in the mirror after my team was killed and injured. Questioning my very existence. You want to know what I see when I look at you?"

She didn't. Not really.

But apparently it was a rhetorical question, because he didn't even give her time to respond before he continued speaking.

"I see strength. Stubbornness. A resiliency that I rarely see these days. Not many people would've been able to survive what you did. Society is pampered. If someone doesn't get their half-caf, triple-shot, caramel, mocha, soy, no-foam, extra-whip, extra-hot, upside-down, caramel drizzle with seven pumps of mocha syrup double-blended Frappuccino, they have to go to bed for two days because they don't feel well. And that's not a surprise, because all that sugar has probably clogged their arteries and made them unable to think about anything for more than two seconds at a time."

Josie couldn't help but snicker at that.

He smiled back at her and ran one of his large hands over her hair. Then he leaned into her, tucking his chin on her shoulder and wrapping his arm around her. "But you, Spirit. You did what you had to do to survive. You didn't give up. Even when you had every right to. You fought to stay alive. Rationing water, staying calm. Waiting for fate to bring me to your side."

Okay, she was going to cry if he didn't stop.

He didn't.

"If you think anything about you makes me want to turn up my nose, or repulses me, you're so far off it's not even funny. I like you, Josie England. A lot. I've never felt as comfortable with someone as I do with you. You don't make me feel as if I should be anyone other than who I am. Which makes no sense, because we haven't really had much of a chance to sit down and really get to know each other. But there it is.

"I want that...to get to know you. I want to know *everything* there is to know. About where you grew up, if you had a good childhood, more about your job, your friends, your life. I want to know what you like to eat, and your favorite things to do for entertainment. I want to sit in the same room as you and not speak at all, but look up and feel content simply because you're there, occupying the same place as I am.

"And yes, I'm physically attracted to you as well. I've always been attracted to petite women, but you..." He swallowed hard. "There's something about you that draws me in like no one ever has before. I shouldn't be saying all this. Not after the trauma you've experienced. I should be getting you to a psychologist so you can talk through—or write about—what happened. But knowing all that doesn't stop me from wanting to hold you. Touch you. Kiss you. And of course, take care of you. I want to make sure you're fed. Make sure you're getting enough to drink. Wanna keep you safe from anyone or anything that might hurt you, ever again."

The tingles Josie felt earlier when he kissed her had started up again, but this time throughout her entire body. She couldn't tear her gaze from the man standing behind her. Holding her. Seeing herself through his eyes was enlightening, and it only made her want him more.

"Fuck. I'm saying too much again. This is why I usually keep my fool mouth shut and observe rather than talk."

But Josie shook her head, then turned in his arms. She felt

small around most people, but in Nate's arms, she felt especially tiny. But also stronger. More confident. Moving a hand to the back of his neck, she went up on her tiptoes and tried to bring his head down to hers. She wanted to kiss him. *Needed* to kiss him.

He resisted for a moment. "Are you sure?"

Sure she wanted to kiss him? Yes. A hundred times *yes*.

"Yes," she said firmly.

As if her consent was all he'd been waiting for, Nate's head dropped and his lips were on hers.

They both moaned as passion flared between them.

Josie usually felt self-conscious the first time she was intimate with a man. But with Nate, kissing felt right. Natural. His arm banded around her and he straightened, taking her with him. Her feet left the floor but Josie barely noticed. She couldn't seem to get enough of this man. Their tongues dueled as they fought for dominance over the kiss. He tasted like strawberries. She wanted more. So much more.

Wrapping her legs around him, Josie threaded the fingers of one hand through his hair and clutched him to her with the other. She felt Nate walking, but with her eyes closed and their mouths still fused together, she didn't care much where he was taking her.

She opened her eyes and pulled back a fraction when she felt him lower himself onto a soft surface. The couch. She shifted until her knees were on the cushion on either side of his thighs. She liked this. Felt as if they were on a more even level. She could look into his eyes without having to strain her neck.

"Hi," she blurted like a complete dork.

He smiled. "Hi," he returned.

Up close like this, his freckles stood out even more. And Josie had the urge to count every single one. But it would take too long. He had too many.

One of Nate's hands was at her back, almost spanning it from one side to the other, and his other hand was at the nape of her neck, stroking the sensitive skin there with one of his thumbs.

"I have the stuff ready to work on your hair."

It wasn't what she'd expected him to say—and it was as if someone had thrown a bucket of cold water over her. Josie was suddenly embarrassed by her actions. He'd been telling her how impressed he was with the way she'd handled the situation she'd found herself in, and then she'd gone and thrown herself at him.

She shifted her body weight so she was leaning away from him, but he scowled, tightening his hold on the back of her neck.

"What? What did I say? You don't want me to touch your hair? Okay, I'll talk to Caroline, see if she knows someone who will come to the apartment. Or maybe Remi or Wren know someone. Maybe they can help."

He sounded panicked. Josie shook her head.

"No? You don't want them to help? You don't want to do anything with your hair? No *what*, Spirit?"

"I didn't mean to maul you," she blurted out.

Nate stared at her for a moment, then inhaled deeply as he closed his eyes. But he immediately opened them. "In case you missed it, Josie, I was just as into that as you were. Christ, I've thought about almost nothing but kissing you from the moment you sacrificed your water for me in that hellhole—and felt like shit as a result. You were hurting, traumatized, and all I wanted to do was feel your lips on mine."

Josie was genuinely shocked. Not by what he said, but that he'd felt the same pull toward her as she had for him.

"With that said, I'm also not dumb enough to haul you to my bed right this second."

She frowned.

"Not that I don't want to, but I don't want whatever this is between us to be a one-and-done kind of thing. I wasn't lying when I said I want to get to know you. I want to know what makes you tick before taking you to bed. Because when I get you there, I'm going to want to *keep* you there. Hell, I already do. Sleeping next to you since leaving those cells has been...incredible. I just don't want to rush us." He then chuckled and shook his head. "As if I haven't already done that. But seriously."

Josie was embarrassed to discover that she *wanted* to be rushed. She wanted to know what it was like to be with this man. To have all his attention. To have his hands on her body. To have him *inside* her body. Her nipples tightened at the thought, and her position over him made her pussy clench. She was straddling him. She could reach down and undo his pants and take him into her mouth. Show him how badly she wanted him.

"Fuck. You're so beautiful," Nate said reverently, his gaze running down her body.

Josie couldn't help but squirm a little.

"We have time," he told her. "Time to get to know each

other. Time to explore this attraction we have for each other."

In response, Josie placed her hand on his chest and ran it all the way down to just above his waistband, then back up.

She could hardly believe she was acting this way. This wasn't like her. She was the shy one. The one who always questioned whether she should or shouldn't take a relationship to the next level. She second-guessed everything. But after her brush with death, she was going to go after what she wanted. *Him*.

Nate caught her hand with his and brought it up to his mouth, kissing her palm. "You're going to be a handful, aren't you?" he asked.

Josie gave him a huge smile.

"Right. You're stubborn—but so am I," he told her. "And right now, I want to get my hands on that hair of yours." Then he picked her up and turned her on his lap before placing her on the floor in front of the couch.

He moved her so easily. In the past, Josie would've been offended if someone had done what he just had, but since it was Nate, she was more turned on by his strength than anything else. She couldn't help but think about how he could move her around in bed, to any and every position he wanted to take her in.

Her libido had roared to life, and it made her feel *really* alive for the first time in weeks. But Josie took a deep breath. He was right. She didn't want a one-night stand either. She wanted Nate, sexually, but she wanted him by her side as a partner, boyfriend, whatever, even more.

Maybe she was just feeling this way because of what

happened. Because he'd been her knight in shining armor. Because he'd saved her.

But she mentally shook her head. That wasn't it. Yes, she was thankful he was there when she needed someone the most, but she was old enough to know what she was feeling was real. Not a result of some savior complex.

Then something else suddenly occurred to her.

She turned her head and blurted, "I'm thirty."

Nate was holding a wide-toothed comb and the bottle of detangler, giving her a confused look. "Okay?"

"I had my birthday while I was in that cell."

Understanding dawned. "*Fuck*."

Was it stupid that she'd gotten used to hearing him say that? And that she loved it? Probably. "I forgot until just now," she told him.

"Well, Happy Birthday, Spirit."

She grinned at him, then turned around and brought her knees up. She clasped them against her as she felt the first spray of detangler against her scalp.

Was she upset that her thirtieth birthday was in that hellhole? Not really. It wasn't as if she would've celebrated all that much if she'd been in Vegas. Even though she lived in Sin City, she didn't go to the Strip that often. To her, it was gross and dirty. She understood the draw for tourists, but the glitz and glamour did nothing for her.

When she'd been a little girl, she'd always assumed by the time she was thirty, she'd be married and have a couple of kids. Thirty seemed so old to her back then. But now? She felt as if she was just figuring out who she was and what she wanted out of life.

Josie went into a kind of trance as Nate worked on getting the snarls and mats out of her hair. The tugging didn't hurt, and the way he ran his hand over her head again and again felt amazing. She loved being touched, hadn't had a lot of opportunity to experience it much in her life.

And while he worked on her hair, Nate talked. Told her all about his SEAL teammates who had died and been injured. Spoke more about his current team. About his brother and some of the shenanigans they got into when they were little. More about his dad, who sounded like a man she really wanted to meet.

He told her about boot camp, and training to be a SEAL. How he'd almost quit a few times, but obviously stuck it out.

Listening to his deep voice was comforting. Soothing. By the time Josie realized he was running the comb through her hair from her scalp all the way to the ends, over and over, she was a pile of mush leaning back against the couch, his thighs cocooning her, making her feel safe and cared for.

"I don't think I've ever talked so much in my life," Nate said. "But there's something about you that makes me feel comfortable spilling my guts."

Josie tilted her head back and looked up at him. "I love the sound of your voice."

"And I love that you're finding yours," he returned. Then he leaned forward and kissed her. The angle was weird, and feeling his nose on her chin made her giggle.

He straightened, and she loved the grin on his face. "Your hair is amazing," he told her. "So long and silky. And I had no idea it was so blonde!"

Josie wasn't surprised. It had been thoroughly coated with

dirt and grime. Her white-blonde hair had looked almost brown the entire time he'd known her.

She licked her lips, wanting Nate to kiss her again, but her stomach chose that moment to let out a loud growl.

"I need to feed you," Nate said, sounding concerned. "Come on. Up you go. Wren and Remi totally went nuts and sent what looks like the entire store. I cut up some strawberries, you can munch on those while I see what I can whip up real quick."

Before she knew it, Josie was sitting at the table with a bowl of strawberries in front of her, while Nate puttered around his kitchen, muttering about the fact it was closer to lunch than breakfast now as he pulled things out of the pantry and fridge. Being waited on was a new experience, so she decided to enjoy it. Tomorrow, she'd insist on pulling her own weight, but at the moment she was still feeling kind of floaty after having Nate's hands on her for so long.

She couldn't stop herself from reaching up and running her fingers through her now detangled hair. It felt so soft, and she smiled as she stared at Nate.

He turned then, catching her looking at him. He returned her smile, and the electricity that had been arcing between them flared for a moment. She thought he was going to stalk over to her and kiss the hell out of her, but she underestimated his self-control.

Nate took a deep breath, then turned his attention back to the lunch he was preparing.

Twenty minutes later, he put a plate as big as her head in front of her, filled to overflowing. He'd used an air fryer to cook some strips of chicken, then smothered it with salsa and sour cream. He'd added garlic toast, a salad, and some instant mashed potatoes.

It looked and smelled delicious.

"It's too much," Josie said.

But Nate simply shrugged. "Eat what you can. We'll box up the rest and you can either eat it later or tomorrow."

To her surprise, Josie was able to eat almost everything on her plate. She was stuffed but felt absolutely amazing. She'd forgotten what it felt like to be so full. She'd never take food for granted again. Not after going without it for so long.

"Go sit," Nate ordered. "I'll clean up and join you when I'm done."

But Josie was done being lazy. She ignored him and picked up her almost-empty plate and brought it into the kitchen. "Do you want to do dishes or pack up the leftovers?" she asked, trying to sound firm.

Nate grinned. "I can't decide if I liked it better when you didn't talk and did what I asked, or this new bossy Josie."

She lifted a brow at him.

"Fine. I'll pack up the leftovers."

Happy she'd gotten her way, that he was letting her help, Josie turned on the water in the sink and got to work rinsing everything off before putting plates and utensils in the dishwasher.

Working together, they got the kitchen cleaned up in no time. Nate led her back to the couch and sat, pulling her down next to him. He settled her under a blanket, against his side, before turning on the TV with the remote.

"Anything you want to watch?"

Josie shook her head. She'd never been much of a TV

watcher, and she had no idea what was even popular after so much time away.

Her eyes felt heavy as the eventful morning caught up to her. The hot shower, his hands in her hair, the full belly. She was suddenly exhausted.

"Sleep, Spirit. I've got you."

That was all it took. She relaxed completely, secure that the man she was using as a pillow would keep her safe.

CHAPTER THIRTEEN

Blink was having a hard time remembering that he and Josie hadn't known each other all that long. She fit into his life like she'd always been there. He was completely comfortable around her, which wasn't something he could say about many people. She was easy to live with, easy to please, and he found himself wanting to be around her every second of every day.

The other night, when she'd fallen asleep against him on the couch just the way she had earlier that same morning, he couldn't stop thinking about ending *every* day that way for the rest of his life.

The next day had been another lazy one for them both, though he'd done laundry and reorganized and repacked his go-bag. Then they'd worked together to make a feast for dinner.

He had to stay a *little* busy, otherwise he couldn't stop looking at Josie. With her hair now sleek and shiny, she looked completely different from the woman he'd first seen in that cell, feral and terrified, huddling in the corner. She was blossoming, and he was becoming very attached to her already.

He could read her emotions without her needing to say a word. Like the relief she'd felt after emailing her landlord in Vegas and finding out that, while he'd rented her apartment to someone else, he hadn't thrown out her belongings. Since she'd always been a good tenant, and he liked her, he'd packed up her belongings and placed them in an empty apartment he used for storage.

She hadn't been nearly as happy after receiving an email back from Ayden's mother. Apparently, Millie Hitson wasn't thrilled to hear that Josie was safe and sound in California. Josie hadn't let Blink read the email, but he knew without her having to share anything that whatever the woman had to say, it cut deep. He was determined to read it eventually, so he could counter whatever the woman said.

An idea had also been brewing in his head for a couple days, and whatever Ayden's mother had said put Josie in such a funk, he'd started the wheels in motion while working out with his team that morning. His friends thought it was a great idea and had volunteered to do whatever was necessary to help make it happen.

But for now, he was rushing to get home. That afternoon, Kevlar had dropped Remi at Blink's apartment during his lunch break, to keep Josie company while they were at work. He'd worried about how Josie was doing alone. Of course, now he was worried about how she and Remi were getting along.

Blink had a soft spot in his heart for Remi. The two of

them had been through a horrible experience together, and it had bonded them in an unbreakable way. But as outgoing as she'd become, she could still be a little introverted around people she didn't know well. And Josie was hardly a chatterbox. So without Remi having a way home, Blink worried that things could have gotten awkward for the women, since he and Kevlar had been held up at work longer than he'd expected.

Kevlar pulled in behind him when he reached the parking lot of his complex, and they both walked quickly to his door.

The scent that hit him when he stepped inside the apartment made Blink's mouth water. Italian. He had no idea what the women had made, but it smelled absolutely delicious.

Walking inside with Kevlar on his heels, Blink saw Josie and Remi sitting on opposite sides of his kitchen table. Josie had his laptop open, and she was typing furiously with a pair of headphones over her ears, while Remi had a sketchbook in front of her, with her *own* set of headphones on.

It looked as if the women were in their own worlds, which concerned him.

Josie saw them first. Her fingers paused on the keyboard, and she smiled as she reached up to take off her headphones.

Kevlar went up behind Remi and touched her shoulders, leaning in to kiss her temple. She jumped a little but immediately smiled up at him.

"You're back!" she exclaimed a little too loudly, since she was still wearing the headphones.

Kevlar chuckled and removed them. "We're back," he agreed.

"Josie and I had the *best* day!" Remi exclaimed. "We talked

—okay, I talked mostly, she listened—while reorganizing the pantry, watched a couple episodes of *Big Brother*, made Crock-Pot lasagna for you guys for dinner, then decided we probably needed to get some work done. Josie heard back from her boss, and he was excited to have her return to work and gave her a new caption job on the spot. So she's been working on that, and I've been drawing my next Pecky cartoon. Pecky gets taco-napped and is about to be eaten when he's saved by the big bad Enchilanator...you know, like the terminator." Remi grinned up at the two men.

Blink's tense muscles relaxed. "Sounds like you had a good day," he said.

"We had a *great* day! Didn't we, Josie?"

She smiled, nodding enthusiastically.

"Can we do it again?" Remi asked her. "I mean, I know you probably have a lot to do, what with getting your stuff in Vegas, and your job and all, but being around you is so *calming*. I got so many ideas today, and while I don't mind being by myself all day, I think I enjoy being around you more. Oh! And maybe next time, Wren can come too? She can work on her PR stuff for her dad's company, and we can do our thing. Maybe we can even go to her and Safe's house. I think it's a little bigger, and Safe has that huge TV—"

"Breathe, Remi," Kevlar scolded.

"Sorry," she said with a little blush. "I just...today has been fun."

Seeing the usually somewhat shy Remi be so effusive was a little surprising, but Blink wasn't all that shocked she'd come out of her shell around Josie. There was something about his Spirit that brought out a different side of people. Maybe because she didn't talk much, but looked at you as if you were the most important thing in her world at that moment.

"I didn't know you were feeling cooped up," Kevlar said with a little frown.

"Oh! I'm not! Not at all. I love being in our apartment. It's just...sometimes it's nice to have some female company."

"I agree," Josie said quietly.

"See! She agrees," Remi said. Then she skirted the table to where Josie had stood next to her chair and hugged her. "I just want to put you in my pocket and take you home," Remi said with a huge smile.

Josie rolled her eyes, but it was obvious she wasn't offended by her new friend's comment.

"And here I was afraid you two might not get along," Blink said.

"What? Why wouldn't we? Josie's awesome. And so smart. You should see how fast she can type. I swear it's inhuman."

"I've seen," Blink told her.

"Right, of course you have. It's impressive. I have an idea to make Pecky take a typing class where he's hunting and pecking for each letter, but his teacher is this amazing, tiny little burrito, and when they get shoved into an oven by the big baddie, the burrito saves the day by being able to tell the fire-fighters where they are by texting with her fast little fingers."

"You seem a little obsessed with putting Pecky in situations where he's kidnapped or in danger," Kevlar said with a little frown.

But Remi shrugged off his concern. "It's a phase. Considering what my friends and I have been through, I want to show Pecky going through tough situations but being able to bounce back with the help of the brave characters who save him, and also with the help and support of his friends. It's a kind of therapy for me. Whatever."

"As long as you're okay," Kevlar said, pulling Remi against him and kissing her temple once more.

"I'm okay," she promised. "Do you think we can stop for tacos on the way home? For some reason, I'm in the mood."

"You aren't staying for dinner?" Blink asked in surprise. He was standing in the entrance to the living area, giving Josie some room. What he really wanted to do was go over to where she was standing and give her a huge hug, but he was trying not to overwhelm her or pressure her too much. It sucked, frankly.

"Nope. We made the lasagna for you two. Josie told me how much you and your twin liked your dad's lasagna, so we wanted to attempt to make something like it," Remi said.

"See you tomorrow," Kevlar said as Remi packed up her drawing supplies. "I'll let you know what Benny and Jessyka say after I talk to them tonight."

Blink nodded.

"What they say about what?" Remi asked after she'd gathered her things.

"I'll tell you on the way home," Kevlar said.

"Thanks again for the great day," Remi told Josie. "I'll text you with details on our next get-together. With Wren this time. Okay?"

Josie nodded with a smile.

The door shut, and then it was just Blink and Josie.

"Whew. Remi isn't usually such a...hurricane," he said with a smile.

Josie chuckled.

He couldn't stay away from her any longer. Drawn to her as if she were a magnet, Blink crossed the room to her side. Without thought, he leaned in and kissed her lips. It was a short, welcoming kind of kiss, but electricity still shot straight to his cock at the feel of her lips against his. Thankfully, his camouflage uniform pants somewhat hid his reaction.

"Hi," he said after straightening. "It smells absolutely wonderful in here. You didn't have to make dinner. I would've figured something out when I got home."

Josie rolled her eyes. "You worked all day. It was the least I could do."

"You apparently worked too. You got your captioning job back? That's awesome."

She sighed. "It's a relief."

"I bet." Remi also said something about Josie going to get her things in Vegas, but Blink wasn't sure he wanted to bring that up. Because he didn't want her to tell him she was going to find a new apartment and move back to Nevada.

"And I have to go get my stuff. My ex-landlord says he needs the space."

Blink nodded. It was uncanny how they were always on the same wavelength. "No problem. The weekend is coming up. We can drive up there and figure out what to do with it all."

Josie bit her lip and dropped her gaze from his, looking anywhere but at him. He hated that whatever she was thinking was making her uncomfortable. He put a finger under her chin and lifted her gaze to his. "What? What's wrong?"

She shrugged. Then huffed out a breath and pulled his laptop closer. Blink let her go, and she sat down and started typing something fast and furious. When she was done, she turned the computer toward him.

He said most of my stuff is boxed but he didn't have a place to store my furniture. So he left it in my apartment for the guy who moved in. He said he'd pay me for it, which is fine. But I need to figure out what to do with the boxes of my things. I could rent another apartment there, but I don't know that I want to live in Vegas anymore. Never really liked it, and since Millie and Gen are there, and aren't very happy with me, I'm not sure I should stay in Nevada anyway. I like it here, but don't want you to feel obligated in any way. I'm sure I can find an apartment here in Riverton. Now that I have my job back and will get some money from my landlord for my furniture, I could probably afford the security deposit and first month's rent.

Blink understood why she'd wanted to write out those thoughts. While Josie was talking again, it was in short bursts. "No," he said with a shake of his head. "You don't need an apartment, you can stay here."

Josie stared at him with a worried frown on her face. "I can't stay here forever."

The first thing that sprang to Blink's mind was, "Why not?" But instead, he said, "Maybe, maybe not, but you don't need to worry about finding a place to live right away. Give yourself some slack, you just got back from something traumatic. Let me help you, Josie. We'll go to Vegas and pick up your things, and if we need to, we can find a storage place here. But I'm sure Safe has space in his garage or something. How much are we talking about?"

Josie shrugged. "Depends on how he packed everything. Maybe twenty boxes or so?"

"Right. So I'll rent a little trailer, just in case. We can go through the boxes, and you can take out what you want and need in the short term and bring it to the apartment. We can play renting a storage unit or talking with Safe by ear. Now... what's this about Millie and Gen? They're still giving you a hard time? More than that email you got from Millie?"

Josie looked away once more, telling Blink all he needed to know.

"Did you get another email?" he pressed.

She nodded.

"Let me see it."

This time, Josie shook her head.

"Why not?"

"Because. They're upset. Millie lost her son. She didn't mean what she said."

"What did she say?" Blink asked.

Josie simply stared at him.

Blink sighed. "Please, Josie. I know you feel awful about what happened, but it wasn't your fault. Bad decisions were made, on your part and on his. It's part of being human. If you're being harassed, that's *wrong*. You were a prisoner. The fact that either of them feel it's okay to harass you about Ayden's death is totally fucked up. Do we need to take out a restraining order?"

Josie shook her head urgently.

"Please let me read the email," he said, putting his hand on Josie's thigh. She felt fragile under his touch, but he knew better. This woman was made of steel. Anyone else would be a shell of a human after what she'd been through. And she not only seemed to be coping well, now that she was safe, she was blossoming.

With a sigh, she clicked a few things on the computer, then turned it back to him.

It didn't take long to read the email. It was short and to the point...and absolutely vile.

You killed my son. I knew from the moment I met you that you were the devil. And you led my Ayden to his death! If it wasn't for you, he'd still be here. He didn't even want you to go to Kuwait, only asked out of pity. He was dating that woman in his platoon. She was his soul mate, and you wouldn't get your claws out of him. I hope you suffered, but even if you did, it wasn't nearly enough. It should've been you, bitch. It should've been you!

The email wasn't signed, but the address had Millie's first and last name in it, so it wasn't hard to figure out who it was from.

The words on the screen were hateful and nasty, and it made Blink's heart hurt to read them. How could one human being wish such awful things on another? Without thought, he closed the laptop and pulled Josie onto his lap. She didn't struggle, just turned into him. Her legs hung off one side of his lap and he tightened his arms around her.

"She's wrong," he murmured into her hair. Today, she

smelled like lilacs. He wasn't sure if it was lotion or shampoo or perfume. All he knew was that he wanted to rub himself against her so he could smell her on his skin long after she was off his lap. "You didn't kill Ayden. And if he was seeing someone else, he should've had the balls to tell you, to break off your relationship. He sounds like an ass," Blink couldn't stop himself from saying. He didn't like talking shit about someone who wasn't there to defend himself, who shouldn't have died the way he did, but the more he learned about her ex, the more disgusted he became.

"*He* made the stupid decision to rent that boat. To show off by taking you out too far. Yes, you went to Kuwait when you probably shouldn't have, but that mistake doesn't condone what happened to you."

They sat like that, cuddled together on one of his dining room chairs for several minutes. Josie wasn't crying, which Blink was grateful for, but she was obviously still feeling a lot of emotions.

Eventually, she lifted her head to meet his gaze. "I emailed her because I thought she would want to know what happened. I didn't know what the Army had told her. I knew she wasn't my biggest fan, but I didn't realize she hated me so much."

"Some people are just like that, Spirit. They hold more hate in their hearts than kindness."

"I wanted to fix things after her first email. Told her I was in California, that I wanted to talk to her in person. Explain further. I told her I'd be coming to Vegas to get my things. That's when she sent this last email."

"Well, you won't be seeing her, that's for sure," Blink said, the very thought making his head want to explode. "I won't let her talk to you like that. We can block her email so you don't have to read her shit anymore. If the need arises, we'll take out a restraining order so she can't get within three hundred feet of you."

Josie nodded.

Knowing he needed to change the subject, for her peace of mind and his, Blink said, "So, you and Remi had a good day, huh?"

She smiled and nodded again.

"You aren't just saying that because you know we're close, are you?"

"No. She's fun. And Pecky is awesome."

"Pecky the Traveling Taco *is* awesome," Blink agreed. "And I'm guessing so is that lasagna that's making my stomach growl. I can make us a salad to go with it."

"Done."

"Bread?" he asked.

"Done," Josie repeated with a small smile. "Well, it's ready to go in the oven."

"Great. Then if you'll let me up, I'll get on that, because if I don't get that Italian goodness in my belly in the next ten minutes, I won't be responsible for my actions."

Josie giggled. "You were the one who hauled me onto your lap."

"You object?"

Instead of the teasing response he expected, Josie offered her shy smile. "I like when you put me where you want me."

And just like that, Blink had a vision of picking her up and pressing her down onto his rock-hard cock, holding her above him as he fucked her hard and fast. His dick liked that thought, and it hardened under her ass.

He was about to apologize, when he felt Josie shift, as if wanting to feel more of him.

"Fuck," he muttered, earning him a small giggle from the woman in his lap.

"Dinner," he said under his breath, as he picked up Josie and placed her on her feet next to his chair. He stood, not able to stop himself from reaching down to adjust his erection to a more comfortable position before heading into the kitchen. He found the loaf of bread on the counter, already cut and loaded up with butter and garlic. He turned on the oven, practically threw the bread in, and turned without a word toward his room.

"Gonna get a quick shower. I'll be right back," he told Josie.

He thought he heard another giggle behind him, but he was too focused on getting to his room. His clothes were on the floor of the bathroom in seconds, and then Blink was under the hot spray of his shower, cock in hand, furiously pumping as visions of Josie riding him hard and fast flew through his mind.

It didn't take long for him to orgasm. Ropes of come dripped down his shower wall as Blink sagged against the tile. His cock was still half hard, even though he'd just come harder than he could remember doing so in a long time. This didn't bode well for being able to control himself around his houseguest. He wanted Josie. With every fiber of his being. She was his, he knew it as well as he knew his name.

But the last thing he wanted to do was scare the crap out

of her with his need. He had to stay cool. So he quickly soaped himself up, rinsed off, and got out of the shower. He shoved his dick into a clean pair of boxers and put on a pair of jeans and a shirt.

When he got back into the living area, he saw that Josie had served them both up some lasagna, put the salad in bowls, and the bread was in the middle of the table. She gave him a smile as she stood next to a chair.

"This looks amazing. I can't wait to tell Dad that he's got competition for his cooking now. He'll be thrilled. He's been telling me to find someone who can cook as well as he can for years now. Sit."

They both sat, and from the first forkful, Blink was more sure than ever that Josie was the woman for him. She really *did* cook better than his dad. She also turned him on more than any other woman had, and she soothed him in a way he thought he'd never experience. After all he'd seen and done, that was a big deal. In the past, he constantly thought about what he should've done differently on missions, how he might prevent any of his teammates from getting hurt in the future. But with Josie, he'd found he wasn't stuck in his head. He could just...be. And he hoped it was the same for her, as well.

They ate without speaking, but it wasn't an uncomfortable silence. Working together as they had each night, they cleaned up after their meal and settled on the couch.

Holding Josie against him always felt like coming home.

"Tonight...after I fall asleep...can I..." Her voice trailed off.

"What, Spirit? Can you what?" Blink would let her do anything she wanted. Anything.

"Can I sleep with you?" she asked. "You always carry me to

the guest room, and it's nice in there, but," she looked up at him, "I want to be with you."

Blink's heart stopped beating for a moment. He swallowed hard, wanting nothing more than to pick her up right that second and carry her to his bed.

"Sorry. That's weird, right? I just—"

"No! It's not weird." He'd paused too long and she felt uncomfortable. That was unacceptable. "I want you there. Always. I just don't want to do anything that would make you think I was taking advantage of your situation."

"You aren't. I...I like you, Nate. A lot."

There she went again, making his heart skip a beat. "Good. Because I like you too."

"Will you kiss me again?"

"With pleasure."

It took every ounce of strength Blink had not to strip off all of Josie's clothes and take her right there on the couch. But he was enjoying their not-so-innocent making out too much to do anything that might change her mind about liking him. He loved having her hands on him. Loved the feel of her body against his own. Loved even more seeing how much their kisses affected her. The fast beating of her heart, her quick breaths, the way her eyes got glassy and her nipples pebbled under her shirt.

When they finally settled in to watch a movie, Josie quickly fell asleep in his arms, as usual. Blink lived for this moment. For holding her. Watching her sleep. Knowing that she trusted him enough to completely let down her guard.

Later that night, when he got up to go to bed, instead of taking her to the guest room as usual, he felt deep satisfaction well inside him as he opened his bedroom door and gently placed her on his mattress. She'd slept there before, when he'd woken up and found her on his floor that first night. But tonight felt like a new beginning. She wasn't coming to him because she was uncomfortable and needed the reassurance of knowing he was close. She was there because she wanted to be with him. And because he wanted her there, as well.

Blink stripped down to his boxers and climbed under the covers. It felt as natural as if they'd done it every night for the last ten years or more for her to snuggle up against him and use his shoulder as a pillow. Her gorgeous blonde hair draped over his chest, and he inhaled deeply, loving how feminine she smelled.

But he wouldn't have cared if she was still covered in dirt and muck from that damn cell. Just having her in his arms was perfection.

CHAPTER FOURTEEN

The last week had been like a dream come true for Josie. She'd never felt so at peace. Of course, she still had plenty of things to stress about...her belongings, Millie and Gen, getting back into the swing of things with her job...but the good far outweighed the bad.

Nate was at the top of that good list. He was everything she'd ever wanted in a guy. He wasn't perfect, but then again, neither was she. But things between them were fun...and exciting, intimate, comforting, and promising. She felt more at home with Nate in the short time she'd known him than she did with Ayden or anyone else she'd ever dated.

And the more time she spent with both Remi and Wren, the more at home in Riverton she felt. With friends like them, and a man like Nate to spend time with after he got home from work, Josie was falling into a rhythm.

That's why she wasn't thrilled with their plans. She and Nate were going to Vegas to pick up the things her landlord had stored. Somehow, she felt as if going to Vegas was going to burst the happy little bubble she'd been in since she'd been rescued. Which was stupid, but she still dreaded it.

Millie and Gen hadn't let up on the emails. She'd blocked them both, but all they did was create new email accounts to use to harass her. She'd block those too, but the next morning, she'd have *another* email from one or both of them, telling her what a horrible person she was, how she'd regret killing Ayden.

She hadn't told Nate about their harassment because it upset him so much. And there wasn't anything he could do about it anyway. She just had to ignore them until they got tired of their juvenile games and left her alone.

Still, even being in the same city with them made her uneasy. It wasn't as if they knew she was going this weekend, but returning to the place where she'd met Ayden, where she'd lived before making that fateful decision to fly to Kuwait, felt as if she was entering the lion's den. Like she'd somehow get sucked in and wouldn't be able to leave.

"Breathe, Josie. This'll be fine."

Josie smiled at Nate. She wanted to believe him, but she couldn't shake the feeling of dread.

"Did you see Remi's latest cartoon?" he asked as he put an overnight bag in the back of his truck. They were driving up to Las Vegas today, spending the night in a fancy hotel on the Strip, then going to her old apartment complex tomorrow morning, loading up the trailer he'd rented, and coming back to Riverton. She would've preferred they do it all in one day, but since he'd be doing most of the heavy lifting, literally, and it was at least a five-hour drive, she didn't him want to overdo it.

Josie nodded. Remi's latest Pecky the Traveling Taco featured Pecky at a night club. He was so exuberant on the dance floor that he lost most of his filling, leaving him feeling naked with only the meat in his shell. But then Latrice the Lettuce Leaf came forward and enveloped him in a big hug, covering him up.

It was a nod to Wren, and what happened to her at Aces Bar and Grill. Josie had been appalled to learn that she'd been drugged by a blind date, and everything that had happened after that, but happy that everything had worked out, especially between her and Safe.

"Are you worried about the drive?" Nate asked, turning to her.

Wishing she was better able to hide her trepidation, Josie shook her head.

"Your stuff? We have no idea what your landlord actually kept or how he packed."

She shook her head again.

"I don't ask you this very often, but...talk to me, Josie. Tell me what I can do to make you feel more at ease. You want me to call Preacher and see if he can go with me instead? You can stay here. I'm sure Remi or Wren would be happy to come over and keep you company."

"I'm just not a fan of the city. I don't like the person I was there." It wasn't the best explanation, but it was all she had at the moment.

"I can understand that. But you aren't the same person you were before. What you've been through has changed you.

You're stronger, maybe more cautious, and much more in tune with what you want out of life. You're amazing, Josie. And I'm proud to know you."

That felt good. Really good.

She walked toward him and put a hand on his chest to steady herself as she went up on her tiptoes. Thankfully, Nate understood what she wanted and obliged, bending down so she could reach his lips.

"Thank you for driving. I packed extra Cheetos, just in case."

He chuckled. "A woman who knows what I like. Every man's dream," he teased.

Josie blushed. She wasn't sure about that, but yes, she did know what Nate liked. Fast showers, her lilac lotion, the really bad-for-you cheesy snacks, fresh strawberries, thriller books and movies, and he had a weakness for Italian food.

She also knew he didn't like to sleep with many clothes on, and that he always stuck a leg out of the covers in the middle of the night. And when she rolled away from him, he always cuddled up against her back, spooning her. He hated alarms in the morning and usually woke up before it went off. He had an aversion to being late, and he was an exceptionally loyal friend. He didn't say much around them, letting others do more than their fair share of holding up the conversation, but at home with her, he was a chatterbox.

Yes, it was safe to say that she knew what Nate liked. Except when it came to intimacy. She wanted to know that stuff too. So badly it almost hurt. But she was afraid to make the first move. It would destroy her to be rebuffed.

Even though she was pretty sure he wouldn't turn her

down. Not if the way they made out every night was any indication. But he was still holding back, and that confused Josie.
Made her think there must be a good reason why he wasn't
moving their physical relationship forward, beyond his insis-
tence he didn't want to rush her. It was enough to make her
second-guess her role in his life.

"What are you thinking about so hard?" he asked.

Josie felt herself blush. If only he knew. "Nothing much.
The trip," she lied.

"It's going to be fine. Safe said anything we didn't want to
keep here, he'll store for you. And it's actually better that
your landlord gave away your furniture, because then we really
would've had to rent a storage unit or deal with selling it
ourselves."

He spoke as if her living with him was a permanent thing.
Josie wished with all her heart that was the case.

After helping her into his truck—he still hadn't gotten a
step stool for her, not that she wanted one; she wasn't a kid,
even though she was as small as one—he got behind the
wheel of his truck and they headed out of the parking lot
toward the interstate.

Secretly, she liked that Nate manhandled her into his vehicle. Was glad that he still could. During her short couple of
weeks in California, Josie had already gained back a lot of the
weight she'd lost. It felt good to be able to look down at
herself and not see her ribs or hip bones sticking out. She'd
never been a big person and didn't plan on becoming one now,
but she'd needed to put on some weight, and she felt healthy.
Strong.

They'd been driving for thirty minutes and were out of the

worst of the traffic when Nate asked, "Will you tell me more about yourself? Your mom, your life before we met?"

Josie looked out the window at the scenery going by and sighed. It wasn't as if she didn't want to tell Nate about her family, it was just painful.

Better to get it out fast. Like taking off a Band-Aid. Thankfully it was more and more easy to talk every day. To Nate, at least. She still got tongue-tied around others, but with him, she had no problem talking anymore.

"My mom was great. Single mother, worked hard to give me anything I needed. My senior year of high school, she got sick. Thyroid cancer. She fought hard, but it spread too fast. She died a month before I graduated. There was no money for me to go to college, so I started doing what I was good at...typing. I did a bunch of random jobs, along with waitressing a little, and managed to get an apartment. I worked from home a lot, so I found it hard to make friends. I went out with some of the other waitresses now and then, and met a few men here and there, who I had relationships with. They never lasted though.

"Then I met Ayden. He was with some buddies on the Strip when we met. He was stationed at Fort Irwin, just across the California state line, but his family lived there in Vegas. I really liked him, and I thought he liked me too. Things got serious fast. He emailed a lot, told me things I wanted to believe...I think because I was lonely. He came to Vegas to see me as much as he could.

"Eventually though, it felt as if he was just using me for a place to stay when he came to town to party with his friends, because he didn't want to stay with his mom or sister. I started to question whether he really liked me or if I was just convenient for him. When he was deployed this last time, he told me how much he'd miss me, and he kept emailing, saying all the right things. But by then, I was pretty much done. Especially when I got an email from someone in his platoon... warning me that he was screwing a woman they worked with. You know the rest."

Nate was frowning, and he held out his hand, palm up. Josie took it.

"He was an idiot," he said firmly. "And I'm sorry about your mom."

For some reason, those six simple words coming from Nate meant more than all the other sympathies she'd received in the years since she'd passed.

They sat like that as they continued northeast through the state on I-15. Gradually the landscape turned barren and brown, but that had its own sense of beauty. They passed Barstow, then Baker, which boasted what it proclaimed was the world's largest thermometer. The traffic got a little clogged up outside the Nevada state line but cleared again not too long after that.

The five-hour trip had gone by fairly quickly, and even though she and Nate didn't talk about anything heavy after her story about her mom and Ayden, Josie still felt as if she'd somehow gotten to know him a little better anyway.

Maybe it was watching him down Cheetos like a toddler, or threatening to wipe his cheesy fingers on her, or smiling as a little girl in a car they passed waved at them. He was so easy to be around, which made Josie relax. She also had complete confidence in his ability to get them to their destination safely. Hell, he'd gotten them out of that prison cell and into the chopper, and through the mountains of Iraq, and back to California. Why wouldn't she trust him behind the wheel of a vehicle?

He pulled into the parking garage of the hotel where they were staying and turned to her with an apologetic look. "I would've valeted, but with the trailer, I'm thinking that wasn't the best option."

"It's fine," Josie told him.

"Stay put, I'll come around," he told her, as he always did when they drove somewhere together. Josie had stopped trying to convince him that she could get out of the truck without his help, since she loved having his hands on her, so she waited until he walked around the truck and opened the door. Like always, she gripped his forearms as he lifted her out of the truck. But he didn't immediately let go as he stared at her.

"I would never take advantage of your giving nature," he said seriously. "I love how you take care of me. Coming home to you at the end of the day is something I never thought I'd have. But you aren't in my house because I want someone to cook or clean for me. It's because I want you there. And I'm falling for you, Josie England. If that scares you, or if it isn't something you want, you need to tell me now...and I'll do my best to back off."

She shook her head immediately. "No."

"No, that's not what you want?" he asked.

"No. It doesn't scare me, because I've already fallen for *you*, Nate Davis." For a split second, she wondered if confessing was the right thing. The worry about what people would say, would think, that they were moving too fast, sprang to mind...but when she saw the smile on Nate's lips, she pushed those thoughts away. They *weren't* moving too fast. She knew this man, as well as he knew her.

"Good."

Good? That was his only response?

Josie watched as he reached into the bed of the truck and grabbed the bag he'd thrown there before they'd left. He'd insisted on putting her things in with his, saying that since they were only going to be staying one night, it was silly to bring two bags. Then he wrapped his arm around her shoulders and pulled her against his side as he started walking through the parking garage.

Josie had questions. Lots of them. But she just put her arm around his waist for now. Questions could wait. With Nate by her side, it was enough that she felt as if she could slay any demons that might rear their ugly heads here in the city she'd dreaded returning to.

* * *

Blink wanted to pick Josie up, throw her over his shoulder, carry her off to their room, lock the door, and not come out for days. But he forced himself to act as normal as possible.

She'd fallen for him. That's all he needed to hear.

Josie would be his tonight. She already felt as if she was his, but he wanted to show her with his body how much he revered her. How amazed he was that she'd chosen him. There were better men out there, of that he had no doubt. But they wouldn't love her like he could.

Love.

He should be freaked out by that word. But after observing Kevlar and Safe with their women, he wasn't afraid of the emotion. Not anymore. Not after he and Josie had survived something horrific together.

Blink wanted to show her without words how much she meant to him. How she was the most important person in his life now. More than his SEAL team. More than his father. More than his twin. Tate would understand. Would probably be jealous. But he'd also be thrilled for them both.

They stood in line to check in, and Blink wrapped his arms around Josie from behind and urged her to lean against him as they waited. When it was their turn, he quickly got them checked in and took the key from the woman behind the counter. Getting to their room was a little complicated, and Blink winced as they walked through the loud, smoky casino to get to the elevator that would take them up to their room.

He felt Josie sidle a little closer as they passed a group of men who were obviously drunk and laughing a bit too loudly.

"Almost there," he reassured her, steering her into an elevator.

"Everything seems so...busy," she mumbled against him as they rode up to the twenty-second floor.

"That's because it is," Blink agreed. "At least here in Vegas."

The hallway was empty when they got off the elevator, and Blink got them into their room without any issues. It was a generic hotel room, nothing too flashy. Two queen beds, TV, small table in the corner.

Blink went over to the window and opened the curtain, letting in the bright Vegas sunlight. They were facing the Strip, and he was glad to see they had blackout curtains, since the lights being on all night would certainly be a detriment to sleeping.

He turned around to make a joke about the lights outside, when he saw Josie standing near the door, looking uncertain.

"What? What's wrong?" Blink asked, striding back toward her.

Thankfully, she didn't try to prevaricate. "Two beds?" she asked.

He relaxed a fraction. "I didn't want to presume anything."

"But...we've been sleeping in the same bed at your place. Do you not like that?"

"No!" Blink said so fiercely, she jumped. He took her face in his hands and tilted her head up so he could look into her eyes. "I mean, *yes*, I love sleeping with you. I've been sleeping better than I ever have. I just didn't want to pressure you into doing something you might not want to do. Lately things have been a little out of your control, and I wanted to make sure you know you're in control here. With us."

"I want to sleep with you," she said firmly.

"Then one bed it is," Blink reassured her.

But she shook her head as well as she could within his grasp. "No, I want to *sleep* with you," she repeated.

Blink's heart began beating overtime. He didn't disrespect her by asking if she was certain and pointing out that she'd been through something traumatic, or telling her they should wait a little longer. Josie knew her own mind. And the truth was, he'd already decided he was making this woman his tonight; her words only made him more eager to show her exactly how much he cared about her.

"Are you hungry?" he asked.

She looked confused, but shook her head.

"You want to walk around? Check out the hotel?"

"No."

"Gamble?"

She took a step closer, making her have to crane her head back farther to hold eye contact. Blink moved his hands to her hips.

"No. I want *you*, Nate. There's something about you that called to me from the first time I saw you dragged into that cell next to mine. I feel safe with you. Content. Happy."

Blink couldn't even put into words how she was making him feel. As if he was on top of the world. She'd chosen him. *Him*. If she'd seen the man he was even just a few months ago, she probably would've stayed as far away as she could get. He'd been broken in ways he never thought he'd be able to come back from.

But then again, Remi hadn't been turned off by the shields he'd put up. He had a feeling Josie would've seen right through him as well.

"No going back once we do this," he warned.

"Good," she answered firmly.

So many things ran through Blink's mind. How he wanted to take her for the first time. How he wanted to rip all her clothes off and throw her on the bed. But he didn't want to scare her. Didn't want to do anything that might remind her of the violence and horror she'd been through.

Grasping her hand, he led her to the end of the closest bed, then turned to face her...and slowly began to strip. He wanted to reassure her. Use loving words. But it felt as if his body was on fire and all his words had turned to ash.

Without a word, she mimicked his actions, pulling her T-shirt up and over her head, shoving her jeans off her hips.

Blink finished undressing before she did and felt not one ounce of discomfort as he stood in front of her without a stitch of clothing on. His mouth watered as more and more of her body was revealed to him. He'd seen her in nothing but a bikini and the see-through cover-up before, but this was way different.

She'd filled out in the short time she'd been in California. Blink had done his best to provide her with lots of protein and nutritious food, to try to help her put on some of the weight she'd lost while in captivity.

Now she stood before him in her bra and panties, and looked up at him uncertainly.

That was unacceptable. His woman should never feel anything but sexy and desirable when she was around him.

His hands went to her hips, and he looked her in the eye as he said, "You are literally the most beautiful woman I've ever seen in my life."

She scoffed.

"I'm not lying."

"My hip bones still stick out a bit. And my boobs are still flat as a board."

But Blink shook his head in denial. "Your body is the epitome of strength. If you were any other shape, you might not have survived what you did."

As his words sank in, he slipped his hands under the elastic band of her panties. "May I?" he asked softly.

She gave him a small nod, and Blink held his breath as he slid her underwear down her legs. Then he reached around her and unfastened the clasp of her bra. When they were both naked, Blink took in the woman in front of him, from her head to the tips of her toes and back again. Her nipples tightened as he watched, and the sight was so erotic, it was all he could do not to come right then and there.

Excited as he was, seeing her naked made him worry for the first time. She was tiny, and he was...not. His cock was jutting from between his legs, eager and ready to bury itself inside her body, but he realized that he would have to make *very* sure she could take him without pain. Which wasn't going to be a hardship.

Blink reached out, grabbed her around the waist, and picked her up. Then without thought, he did what he'd been wanting to do since they'd walked into the room—threw her onto the mattress.

For a moment he was pissed at himself, but Josie just giggled. That small sound went straight to his dick, making a bead of precome leak out of the slit.

Lifting a knee, he started to crawl onto the bed, until Josie began to push at the comforter.

"What are you doing?" he asked, worried she was trying to cover herself up.

"These things are gross. I have no idea who's been doing what on top of it. At least we know the sheets are clean."

Blink chuckled. He couldn't disagree with her. He helped

push the comforter down to the floor, then joined her on the mattress.

Without preamble, he pushed her legs apart and lowered himself between them. He could smell her arousal, and it ramped up his own need tenfold. Seeing her slick folds, the evidence that she wanted this as much as he did, went a long way toward calming Blink's nerves. He couldn't screw this up. It was too important. *She* was too important.

Then he was licking her. Over and over. The first burst of her musky flavor on his tongue wasn't enough. Not *nearly* enough. He went at her like he was a starving man, and she was the only sustenance that could sustain him.

He heard Josie squeak, felt her hands in his hair, but he didn't look up. Didn't look away from her pink pussy laid out before him. Blink was so into eating her out, lapping up as much of her juices as he could get, that he barely heard the grunts and groans he was making. He was in heaven, and he wanted more. Needed more.

With rough hands, he grabbed her hips and manhandled Josie until she was on her knees, right over his face when he rolled to his back, his legs hanging off the end of the bed.

Neither spoke as he feasted between her legs. He sucked, licked, slurped...and it still wasn't enough. Would *never* be enough. He needed this woman's essence like he needed air to breathe. He wanted her branded on his soul.

His hands gripped her hips tightly as he ate her out. It was messy, uncivilized, and he loved every second. He'd never been this...unrestrained before. He'd gone down on women in the past, but it never felt like this. As if he would explode if he didn't feel her orgasm on his tongue.

As soon as he had the thought, he felt tremors start in Josie's thighs. "Yes," he mumbled against her. "Come all over my face. I want to taste you on me for hours."

His words were crude, and not exactly loving, but he couldn't help it.

Josie began to rock against him, making Blink want to pound his chest like a caveman. He was bringing her pleasure. His lips, his tongue. *Him*.

He latched onto her clit and sucked. Hard. And was rewarded by a gush of her release. Moving downward, he lapped at her as fast as his tongue could move.

"Nate!" she cried.

Afraid he'd scared the crap out of her, he looked up, past her tiny belly, her tits, to see her looking down at him. But instead of looking freaked out or disgusted by his lack of restraint, she licked her lips and said, "More."

She wanted more?

He'd give his woman *everything*.

Blink lifted his head and began working her clit once again. Josie jerked in his grasp, and he tightened his fingers around her waist. Holding her steady as he brought her to orgasm a second time. His cheeks were wet with her juices, and Blink eagerly licked his lips, loving her taste.

It wasn't hard to pick her up and physically move her yet again, her arousal painting his chest as he eased her down his body. It felt primitive, as if she was leaving her mark on him. At the last minute, right before bringing her down onto his cock, he paused.

"Fuck," he mumbled.

He heard, and felt, a chuckle move through Josie's body.

"Condom," he choked out. Everything within him was screaming to take her. To pull her onto his dick and fuck her hard. But he wouldn't do that to her, or any woman. He wanted to protect her at all costs.

"Where?" she asked.

"The back pocket of my jeans," he said between clenched teeth.

He should move. Get up and get the condom he'd stashed there before leaving his apartment. But he couldn't. His dick hurt so much if he moved even an inch, he'd lose it. Explode. He was on a hair trigger.

Blink forced himself to let go of Josie, and he watched as she got up on all fours to crawl to the end of the bed. The sight made another spurt of precome ooze out of the tip of his cock. He grabbed the base of his dick to stop himself from coming. Josie's ass was perfect. Small, round, and he wanted nothing more than to take her from behind. Drape himself over her back, surround her with his much larger body, show off his dominant side.

He had to close his eyes, concentrate on anything but the woman in his bed. The taste of her on his tongue made that impossible.

The bed dipped as she crawled back toward him, but Blink didn't open his eyes. Couldn't.

When Josie's small hand wrapped around his dick, his eyes popped open on their own. She was kneeling between *his* legs now, her gaze fixed on his cock. He watched in hungry disbelief as she licked her lips and lowered her head.

* * *

Josie enjoyed sex with the men she'd been with in the past. But nothing had *ever* felt like it did with Nate. The way he went down on her with such abandon was the biggest turn-on. He acted like he couldn't get enough of her. His hands held her tightly, not letting her squirm away from him. And when he'd turned and lifted her over him, she'd never felt so feminine.

With any other guy, she might've felt overpowered; with Nate, she simply felt...cherished.

After she'd gotten the condom out of his jeans pocket, she'd turned around and swallowed hard at the sight in front of her. Nate in all his beautifully naked glory—she loved that he had freckles all over his body, not just on his face—with his hand around his dick. His eyes were closed and it looked as if he was in pain.

Even as she watched, a bead of precome dripped from the head of his cock, slowly moving down his thick length and onto his fingers. She had the sudden need to taste him.

Reaching out, she wrapped her hand above his own, but her thumb and index finger didn't meet, he was that thick. Her gaze fixed on another bead of precome at the slit, she leaned down. Eager to taste him, as he'd done to her. Sticking her tongue out, she licked up his essence. Immediately, another bead of precome replaced the one she'd stolen.

So she licked him again.

Nate moaned, and Josie looked up at him even as she lapped at his slit a third time.

"Fuck."

Hearing Nate swear like that felt like coming home.

Which was stupid, but the first word she'd ever heard him say was fuck, so it was appropriate.

Josie loved the feeling of power that she had in that moment. For so long, her power had been stripped from her. And having Nate on his back, with her between his legs, made her feel as if she could do anything. She'd tamed this larger-than-life Navy SEAL. She could conquer the world.

Just as she lowered her mouth to take the entire tip of his cock into her mouth, he moved. Sitting up and grabbing her around the waist, pulling her up and over him until she was straddling his belly.

"Condom," Nate ordered, holding out his hand. His teeth were clenched, and he sounded as if he was in pain.

Without protest, Josie handed him the small foil packet. He did a little sit up, she felt his abs contract beneath her, and his hands went behind her. She felt him rolling the condom down his length, impressed at how easily he was able to work around her.

Then he lay back down and lifted her to her knees. Using one hand, he held his cock upright, running the mushroom head through her folds, making sure he was good and lubricated. But instead of immediately bringing her down on top of him, he used his cock as a kind of toy, playing with her clit.

It wasn't long before Josie was undulating her hips, trying to get him where she wanted him the most...inside her.

"You want this?" he asked, sounding a little smug.

"Yes."

"Whose cock is about to be inside you?"

Josie could only moan.

"Tell me, Spirit. Whose dick are you about to ride?"

"Yours," she managed to get out.

"My name. Say my name," he ordered.

"*Nate*. Please. I need you."

The words were barely out of her mouth before he slammed her down on him at the same time he thrust upward.

It should've hurt. Nate wasn't a small man—anywhere. But all Josie felt was satisfaction as he filled her. She wiggled her hips, and he slipped inside her a little deeper.

"Look at me," Nate told her.

She met his gaze.

"You're mine," he growled bossily. "And I'm yours. Fuck your man, Spirit. Show me how much you want this."

Josie didn't need to be told a second time. She immediately began to move up and down on him. He felt amazing. Thick and long, he hit places inside her that no man ever had before. But he wasn't content to just lie under her. His hands roamed her body, caressing, pinching, playing. She felt sexy, and some of the fear and pain she'd been carrying around since she'd been captured faded away.

"That's it," Nate urged. "Fuck me."

Even his dirty talk turned her on. And Josie had never really been comfortable with that kind of thing in the bedroom. But being with Nate lowered all her inhibitions. Nothing felt awkward or weird with him.

Eventually she realized that Nate had gripped her waist and was moving her up and down with his strong arms. She relaxed into his grip, giving him her body weight, letting him move her how he wanted.

It was obvious he liked her submission, because he smiled, a satisfied, sexy smirk that touched the core of Josie.

Then he effortlessly moved them both once more, rolling until she was on her back beneath him. His cock moved in and out of her in a lazy rhythm.

"You feel so good. So petite, so fragile. But you aren't, are you?" he asked. "Fragile, that is. You're strong as steel. Refusing to bend even under the harshest pressure. It's sexy as hell. I want to give you more. Tell me you can take it. Take *me*."

Josie was practically panting. "Give me all of you," she replied, scoring her fingernails down his chest.

She felt Nate take a deep breath, then he lifted one of her legs and hooked it in the crook of his elbow. He did the same to her other leg, so she was spread-eagle under him. When he pushed inside her, it almost hurt, he was so deep.

But Josie simply moaned. She loved that he was taking her like this. Not treating her as if she were a delicate piece of glass. She might be small, but she could take whatever he gave her. Now and forever.

"Yes," she hissed.

"I dreamed of this," Nate said as his cock moved in and out of her body. "Before I met you, I dreamed of finding a woman who could take me as I am. Flaws and all. And there you were. In a fucking stinking Iranian prison cell. Looking feral but beautiful as hell. *Mine.* I knew it then, and I know it now. I'm claiming you, Josie. All of you. This pussy is mine. This body is mine. Your heart is mine."

He was pounding into her now. In time with every word.

"And you're mine. Your cock, every freckle, your heart. If

someone ever dares to try to take you away from me, I'll fight like the feral woman I was in that cell!" Josie didn't know where the words were coming from, just that it felt right to say them. They stared into each other's eyes as he continued to fuck her hard and deep.

"One day soon, I want to fill you with my come. Fill this pussy so full, you're dripping with it."

Josie's internal muscles spasmed at his words.

He grinned. "I felt that. You like that thought, huh? You want me to come inside you, Josie?"

"Yes," she whispered.

"*Fuck*," he swore.

Josie smiled. But the grin faded as he stared down at her. Neither spoke again. Just staring into his eyes felt more intimate than the sex they were having. Then he stopped moving, and Josie moaned in complaint as she curled her fingernails into his back.

He smiled but still didn't speak. He lifted his hips, leaving only the tip of his cock inside her. She tried to press her hips upward, to take his cock back, but he refused to give her what she wanted.

Then his fingers found her clit. Like with his tongue, he didn't tease, but immediately began to stroke her hard and fast. She gasped from the part pain, part pleasure he was wringing from her, but he didn't slow down or stop. He simply continued to stare into her eyes as he flung her over the edge.

"Again," Nate ordered.

Josie wanted to protest but couldn't get a word out of her suddenly closed throat. This was...the most amazing sexual experience of her life. And he'd ruined her for anyone else.

As she began to convulse once more, Nate thrust inside her, hard and deep.

A small scream left Josie's mouth. If she thought her orgasms had been intense before, it was nothing compared to how it felt with him powering through her fluttering muscles with his cock as she came.

He pressed as deep as he could get and held still as he orgasmed.

A sudden regret about the condom he was wearing hit Josie. It was stupid, she should be happy he'd protected her; instead, she felt resentment for the piece of rubber that separated her from taking all he had to give.

Nate collapsed, but he didn't crush her. Instead, he rolled once more, almost dumping them off the side of the bed. Josie laughed, then buried her nose in the crook of his neck and inhaled. He smelled like sweat and sex. And it was glorious.

She smiled. She'd had a few doubts that she'd be able to please this incredible man in the bedroom, but all her fears had been assuaged.

His large hand ran up and down her spine, holding her against him. She felt his cock soften inside her, but with the way she was lying on top of him, he didn't slip out. Josie's inner thighs were soaked, and she felt boneless.

"Are you okay?" Nate asked, in a tone completely different from the one he'd used moments ago. It was tentative, unsure.

"I'm perfect," Josie reassured him with a long sigh. She felt his muscles relax under her.

"Good. Because I was a little intense there."

That was an understatement. She hummed under her breath, too wrung out to do much of anything else. She felt more than heard a chuckle reverberate through his chest.

"You should know..." he said, then paused.

Josie forced herself to lift her head to look at him.

The second she met his gaze, he said, "That was life-changing."

Josie agreed wholeheartedly. She nodded.

"You tired?" he asked.

She nodded again.

"You want a bath? Or shower? Or to lie here?"

"Lie here," she said without hesitation. "Then a bath...later."

He nodded, and Josie lowered her head again. Several moments later, she mumbled against his skin, "Are you cold?"

He laughed. "What?"

"We aren't under the covers. I was just thinking that you might be cold."

"I'm good," he reassured her.

"Shouldn't you...I don't know...be removing that condom?"

"Probably."

But again, he didn't make a move to get up. Mentally, Josie shrugged. She knew if a condom was left on after a guy lost his erection, it could leak or slip off. But she wasn't worried about pregnancy. She had an implant to protect herself. She hadn't mentioned it to Nate because he seemed so hell-bent on wearing the condom.

SUSAN STOKER

She dozed then, lying on top of Nate as if he were a body pillow. She only woke when she was jostled. Nate had picked her up and was carrying her into the bathroom as if she were a princess or something.

"Can you stand?" he asked.

Josie nodded, but Nate kept his hands at her waist until he was sure she was steady on her feet. Then he casually removed the condom without a lick of embarrassment, leaned over, and turned on the water in the tub. "Stay right there," he ordered. Before Josie could say anything, he walked out of the bathroom.

He returned less than ten seconds later with a bottle in his hand. He held it up and said, "I brought some bubble bath."

Josie was confused. "You did? Why?"

"Because if the chance arose, I wanted to pamper you."

Seriously. He was too good to be true. If this was happening to anyone else, Josie would've rolled her eyes and said it was completely cheesy. But since this was Nate, and it was actually happening to her, she felt all gooey inside.

For some reason, she didn't feel self-conscious being naked around this man. Maybe because he seemed completely unconcerned with his own lack of clothes. Of course, he was a beautiful specimen of a man. His bruises were almost entirely gone, and she assumed his ribs didn't hurt, especially after the way he'd hauled her around in bed and out of it.

Smiling, Josie stepped toward him as the tub filled. She ran a finger down his chest, over the copious amounts of freckles. "I love these," she told him, then leaned forward and kissed one. Then another. She would've kissed every single one of the small spots, but Nate put a finger under her chin

220

and tilted her face up to his. He leaned down and kissed her. Long, slow, and deep. Then he took her hand and gestured to the tub.

"It's ready."

Looking down, Josie saw the tub was filled to the brim with bubbles. She also didn't miss the way his cock was once again hard.

"You want to join me?" she asked.

He chuckled. "Nope. We won't fit."

"But..." She gestured to his groin with her chin.

With a smile, he said, "It's always going to be like that around you. I took you hard, you're probably sore. I can wait."

This man. Jeez.

Josie stepped into the tub and settled into the hot water with a sigh. After going so long without being clean, baths were her new favorite thing. And Nate clearly hadn't missed how many she took back at his apartment.

He braced himself on the edge of the tub and leaned over, kissing her forehead. "Take your time. I'll just be watching TV."

She felt bad that he hadn't been able to clean up first. Blushing a little as she spoke, Josie told him as much.

But Nate simply shrugged. "I love smelling like you," he replied, before straightening and leaving her alone in the bathroom.

Josie closed her eyes as she soaked in the fruity-smelling bubbles. Nate had literally changed her life. And she couldn't imagine him not being in it. She hoped she wouldn't do anything to mess things up between them.

CHAPTER FIFTEEN

Blink slept hard that night. Probably a combination of holding Josie and the exhaustion of the amazing sex they'd had. He'd never been with someone more compatible. He'd surprised himself with some of the things he'd said and done.

But since Josie didn't recoil or seem repulsed by his sudden dominant streak, he tried not to worry about it too much. He'd simply done what felt right at the time. Had told her what he'd been thinking deep in his soul.

This morning they'd slept in and cuddled. Did Blink want to make love to her again? Yes, of course. But he'd taken her hard yesterday, and he wasn't a small man. And even though she fit him perfectly, she was still tiny. There was no way he'd do anything that would hurt her, so he pushed his need down and simply held her.

And it was awesome. Having his woman lay against his chest as they talked about her mom, about his childhood, about some of his missions—without details, of course. Blink felt more at home than he had since he'd moved out of his dad's house.

And now they were in his truck and on the way to her former apartment complex. She'd called her landlord yesterday, and they'd arranged for a time to meet so she could get her belongings.

Blink was both grateful and pissed at her landlord. Relieved he hadn't simply thrown away Josie's stuff, but not thrilled at how quickly he'd re-rented her apartment in the first place, after she hadn't come home from her vacation.

Pulling up to the lot, he saw the complex didn't look super expensive, but it wasn't run down either. The neighborhood seemed to be fairly middle class. Average.

He and Josie knocked on the office door and a man around Blink's height answered. He looked clean-cut and businesslike. He greeted Josie and led them to the building next door, where he opened an apartment door. "Sorry, but you're going to have to figure out which boxes are yours. I just kind of shove everything in here when people leave. When it gets too full, I eventually take it all to Goodwill or other charity shops."

Blink frowned in annoyance. But his Josie was as gracious as ever.

"It's okay. I appreciate you holding onto my things for as long as you did."

The man nodded, then pulled a check out of his pocket and held it out. "For your furniture."

Josie took it and put it away without looking to see how much it was for.

After an awkward pause, the man said, "Glad you're okay.

I wondered what happened. Take your time in here. When you're done, just lock the door behind you."

When he left, Josie turned to Blink. "It's okay, Nate."

"It's not okay," he said with a shake of his head. "He sold your furniture, probably ripped you off in the process, then dumped all your things in here with the crap people just leave behind when they go."

Josie put her hand on his arm. "But they're here. That's all I care about."

Blink nodded, but he still wasn't happy. "I can't really help you look through boxes, because I don't know what's yours and what isn't, but I can carry everything to the trailer."

And with that, they began the daunting task. There were a lot of boxes in the empty apartment. Apparently the manager was lazy and only brought things to the thrift shops once in a blue moon.

After working their way through the sea of boxes, Josie found what seemed to be her belongings against a far wall, under a bunch of other boxes. Josie opened each one, checking to make sure the items inside were her own, while Blink acted as courier, carrying them from the apartment to the trailer he'd rented.

He was walking toward his truck in the parking lot for the tenth time or so, when he heard a commotion behind him. Turning, he saw two women standing in front of the apartment where Josie was working. And they were yelling at the top of their lungs.

Blink put the box down right where he was standing on the sidewalk and quickly ran toward the women. A few people were starting to gather, watching the spectacle. It wasn't until Blink heard what they were saying that his anger spiked.

"...wouldn't be dead if it wasn't for you, bitch! You led him on, treated him like shit! All he wanted was to be loved, and you shit all over that."

"It should've been *you* with a bullet in your head! You're going to pay for what you did to Ayden!"

Blink wasn't normally a violent person. And he wasn't the kind of man to put his hands on a woman, but without a second thought, he shoved the younger woman aside, away from the door, so he could get between the hate the two women were spewing and his woman.

"What the *fuck?*" he asked, as soon as he was inside the apartment. Josie was standing in the corner, surrounded by boxes, while the two women harangued her from the entry-way, blocking her from going anywhere, from getting away from their hateful words. She looked a little shellshocked and a lot freaked out.

"Who the hell are you?" the older woman asked.

"I'd ask who the fuck *you* are, but I already know. Millie and Genevieve Hitson, I presume," he drawled.

"That's right. But who the hell are *you?*" Gen, the younger woman, repeated.

"I'm Nate Davis, and I'm Josie's man. You need to turn around and leave. Right now."

"No," Millie said, crossing her arms over her chest. "This is a free country, and I'm allowed to go where I want, and say what I want, to *whoever* I want."

"Not to Josie, you aren't. How the hell did you even know she was here?"

"Unlike *her*, we have friends here," Gen told him.

"So you had people spying for you. Awesome," Blink sneered.

"She killed my son!" Millie said angrily. "She needs to answer for that."

"Josie had *nothing* to do with your son dying. He was the idiot who rented a boat and took it into notoriously dangerous waters. As a soldier, he damn well should've known better. He crossed into Iran illegally and was killed as a result. What *I* want to know is, why didn't you tell the authorities about Josie? You both knew she went to Kuwait to visit him."

"We figured she died too," Gen said, a little too defensively.

"*She* should've been the one who was shot!" Millie shouted, obviously not ashamed in the least by the hate she was spewing.

"So you would've preferred for your son to be thrown into an Iranian cell and tortured?" Blink asked. He shouldn't be trying to reason with these women, but he needed them to understand exactly what Josie had been through.

"The government would've gotten him out!" Millie yelled. "She should've rotted to death in that cell. Paid for her sins. For killing my son!"

Blink was done. There was clearly no arguing with Ayden's mother. "Get out," he said, taking a step toward them.

"No," Gen said, straightening. "What are you going to do? Make us? There are witnesses. You touch us and you'll go to jail for assault. Do it. I dare you!"

Frustration ate at Blink. He wanted nothing more than to shove the two women out the door and slam it in their faces.

But they'd probably just lurk outside until they exited again. And it wasn't as if they could hang out in this apartment forever. He wanted to go home. Get Josie away from this place so she'd never have to come back.

"Let's just go," Josie said softly from behind him. But there was no way Blink was leaving without Josie's stuff. And he wasn't going to put up with either of them being harassed while they packed.

Without another word, he pulled out his phone and dialed 9-1-1.

"Who are you calling?" Millie asked.

Blink ignored her. "Yes, I'd like to report an altercation at the Bayview Apartment Complex."

"You called the cops? Pansy-ass loser!" Gen said.

"Two women, Millie and Genevieve Hitson, are harassing my girlfriend. Threatening her. Yes...we need assistance immediately. All right."

"You asshole!" Gen shouted.

"Figures a bitch like her would be with someone like you. You're going to regret messing with me!" Millie told Josie, looking her dead in the eyes.

"Millie," Josie said softly, a worried look on her face, obviously still hoping to smooth things over with her ex's family.

But Blink was done. That was a clear threat. "No one's messing with you," Blink said as calmly as he could, aware the 9-1-1 dispatcher was listening. "You were the ones who came here to yell at Josie. All we're doing is trying to pack her things and get out of here."

"Running away like the scared little nobody you are," Millie sneered. "No backbone. You were never good enough for my Ayden. He felt *sorry* for you—no friends, no real career, pathetic orphan."

Blink stepped toward the women and this time didn't stop until he was towering over them both. "Step back," he growled.

"Make me," Millie countered, lifting her hands and shoving Blink. Hard.

He didn't move an inch, which seemed to frustrate the older woman. She shoved him again, but he merely shifted his body weight to absorb the impact.

"Freak," Gen muttered under her breath.

Thankfully, the sound of sirens wailed close by.

"Don't come near her again. Stop sending her emails. Your son is gone. I'm sorry for that, but it wasn't Josie's fault. You need to move on with your life and let Josie do the same."

"Not a chance in hell," Millie hissed. "She destroyed my son, and I'm going to do whatever it fucking takes to destroy *her*!"

A police car pulled into the lot and two officers quickly got out and walked up the sidewalk, to where Blink was blocking the entrance to the apartment.

"Step back, ladies," one said.

To Blink's relief, they did as ordered.

"We weren't doing nothin'," Gen whined. "*They* started it. That guy, the big one, he was threatening us!"

"That's not what the dispatcher says," the first officer retorted.

"This is public property," Millie said defiantly. "We aren't breaking any laws."

"She put her hands on him," someone in the growing crowd said.

"Yeah, I have it all on video," another said.

"Do you want to press charges?" one of the officers asked Blink.

He opened his mouth to say yes, he most definitely did, but Josie put her hand on the small of his back and leaned around him.

"No. We just want to finish loading my stuff and leave," Josie said.

Blink sighed. He'd do whatever Josie wanted—but that didn't mean he'd leave her vulnerable. "We *do* want to file an order of protection against them."

"I'll get your information so we can send you a copy of the incident report from today, which you'll need to file. You can download the application for protection online."

Blink nodded.

"I'll send you the video I took if you give me your number," the bystander told him.

"Appreciate it."

Millie turned to walk away, but the officer who wasn't talking to Blink reached out and grabbed her arm. "Ma'am, we need some information from you."

With that, Millie began to fight—hard. To Blink's surprise, it took both officers to subdue her. Throughout the altercation, Gen yelled for them to stop, that they were hurting her mother. It was bedlam, and all Blink could do was wrap his arm around Josie and hold her against him as they watched everything unfold. It took a while, but finally Millie was taken away in the back of the police car, while Gen followed behind in her vehicle.

The people standing around wandered away...but Blink couldn't help but wonder which one had called Ayden's relatives, letting them know Josie was there in the first place.

Trying to shove the unsettling thought to the back of his mind, Blink turned to Josie. "Did you find everything?"

"I don't know. I still need to go through some more boxes."

"Well, go ahead and do that so we can get the fuck out of here."

To his amazement, she giggled softly.

He was blown away by her all over again. He brought his hand to her nape and leaned down to put his forehead against hers. "You're amazing, Spirit. You have every reason to be freaked out right now, and yet, you're standing tall."

"They're upset. I get it. Their brother and son died. I was going to break up with Ayden, but I didn't want him to die."

"I know you didn't, sweetheart. You *do* know it wasn't your fault, right?" Blink asked, afraid that she was taking those bitches' words to heart.

"Yeah. I told him I didn't want to go on that boat," she admitted in a whisper. "At first, all he said was that he had a surprise for me, and I should wear my swimsuit and cover-up. When we got to the dock and I saw the boat, I didn't want to board. I'd thought we were going to a pool or beach or something. He insisted that it would be fine. Fun. I said it was too dangerous. That's when he started belittling me, like usual. I didn't want to irritate him further. I should've refused, but just because I didn't stand my ground, that doesn't mean what happened was my fault. It wasn't even his, really. He was just being too cocky."

Blink closed his eyes briefly. She was being a lot kinder than he would've been in the same situation. "I still want you to submit that order of protection."

To his relief, she nodded. "Okay."

"Okay," he agreed, then straightened. "Find the rest of your stuff so we can go home."

"Home," she whispered. "How is it that I've been in your apartment for so little time, but it already feels like a safe haven?"

Blink was speechless. His apartment wasn't anything special. It was pretty average. But for her to feel safe there made him all the more determined to make sure she always felt that way.

"Thank you for being here with me," Josie said. "For helping me."

"Always," Blink replied, then kissed her briefly before heading to the door. He needed to put some space between them, otherwise, he'd end up taking her right then and there.

Checking to make sure the coast was clear, Blink hurried toward the box he'd dropped on the sidewalk earlier, when he'd heard Millie and Gen's awful words. He packed it into the trailer then went back to the apartment.

To Josie.

CHAPTER SIXTEEN

Josie woke up next to Nate and smiled. Even now, three days after their trip to Vegas, when she thought about how he hadn't hesitated to get between her and Ayden's relatives, she felt tingly inside.

Or maybe that was because of the way he'd made love to her the night before. Their first time had been fast, hard, and a little desperate. But last night, Nate had been loving and gentle. It was wonderful...and eventually, a little frustrating. She'd loved the domineering and bossy man he'd been at the hotel in Vegas. And when she'd told him that, she'd felt the change come over him.

It was obvious he thought he'd been too rough. Too hard with her. But the reality was, she felt feminine and beautiful when he put her where he wanted her, when he took his pleasure from her not with pain, but with force.

She was sore that morning between her legs, but in a good way.

"Morning," Nate said. "How do you feel?"

Josie's smile widened. "Amazing."

"Not sore?"

Her smile didn't fade in the least. "A little."

"Good."

His answer surprised her.

"Because I want you to feel me between your legs all day. Think of me while I'm at work and you're sitting at our table, typing like the wind."

Josie liked that idea too.

"And will you be thinking of me in return?" she asked.

In response, he brought her hand to his cock, which was already half-hard. "It feels like this is my permanent state now. I'm always thinking of you, and this is the result."

It was a good answer. The feeling of possessiveness that hit Josie was unusual. But she loved it.

"You like that," Nate said. It wasn't a question.

Josie nodded.

"I'm yours," he said easily. "Hook, line, and sinker. What are your plans for today?"

It should've felt like an awkward change of topic, but actually, it felt...domestic. "I have two movies I need to type captions for, then at two, I have a live news conference. On that missing person's case up in Modesto. They have more details to share."

"Don't forget, I'm taking you to Aces tonight for dinner," Nate said.

Josie nodded. She hadn't forgotten. She was nervous, but also kind of excited to meet the women who Remi and Wren kept telling her about. Caroline, Alabama, Fiona, Summer,

Cheyenne, Jesskya, and Julie. They sounded like people who'd be amazing friends to have, and she could sure use more.

She hadn't had many close friends in her life, and the closer she got to Remi and Wren, the more friends she wanted who were just like them.

"You want to shower while I make you a bagel?" Nate asked.

"I'm feeling too lazy to shower right now. I'll take one later, after the news conference. How about I get up and make *you* breakfast while you shower?"

"Deal."

Nate rolled until she was caged under him. "I love having you here. Waking up with you in the morning, eating meals with you, watching TV at night, being inside you and falling asleep with you in my arms. I didn't know when I opened my eyes in that cell that you would be the woman I'd wished for all my life, but I knew you'd change my life in one way or another."

Josie's eyes filled with tears.

"No! Don't cry," Nate ordered. "I didn't mean to make you cry."

"Then you shouldn't be so sweet," she told him.

"You want me to be a jerk?" he asked with a grin.

Josie shook her head.

"I can be, you know," he admitted, suddenly very serious.

She put a hand on his cheek and made sure she was looking into his eyes as she said, "But not to me."

"Never," Nate vowed. Then he kissed her hard and threw the covers back. He was naked, as was she. As he strode toward the bathroom, she eyed his ass. He even had freckles there, which was somehow both cute and sexy at the same time.

Nate turned at the entrance to the bathroom. "Are you checking out my ass?" he asked with a laugh.

She smiled. "Yup." The admission wasn't embarrassing in the least.

"Good. Glad my woman likes her man's ass."

"Who said I liked it?" she sassed.

She heard his chuckle as he moved out of her sight, into the bathroom.

Josie stretched, feeling like a contented cat. The twinge between her legs reminded her again of what they'd done the night before, and her smile grew. She would definitely be thinking of Nate all day.

* * *

"You seem nervous, is everything okay?" Josie asked Nate later that afternoon.

He'd checked in with her a few times over the course of the day, as was his routine. His texts, along with Remi and Wren's, made Josie feel loved.

She'd spent so much of her time completely alone in her apartment working, never talking to anyone, that it felt strange at first to have so many people checking on her, or texting her simply to tell her something that was on their minds. They weren't asking her to do anything, they just wanted to connect.

Which felt awesome.

After Nate arrived home, however, he seemed...off. Distracted. He'd been getting and sending a lot of texts.

"If you don't want to go out to eat, it's fine. I can make us something."

"No!" Nate said, a little too loudly. He took a deep breath. "Sorry, no, I want to go to Aces. And you've been looking forward to meeting everyone. We've just been going over some pretty intense stuff at work."

That didn't really make Josie feel much better, but she did her best to push her worry aside. Nate and his teammates were good at what they did. She'd seen that firsthand. She trusted that if they were sent on a mission, they'd be all right.

She'd even had a little talk with Remi and Wren about the exact topic. About how they felt when the team was deployed. They'd validated her feelings and reassured her that when the SEAL team was sent off, they knew what they were doing.

"Okay," she said a little belatedly.

The drive to Aces was taken in silence, but not an uncomfortable one. The lot was packed when they arrived but surprisingly, there was an open spot pretty close to the front door.

"It's cute," Josie said, as she studied the building. The bar wasn't in a run-down part of the city and the logo—a poker chip with the word Aces across the front, in cursive—was eye-catching and appealing. The parking lot was clean and well-lit.

"There are cameras covering every inch of the lot," Nate said, obviously watching her eye her surroundings. "Jessyka takes the safety of the people who come here very seriously. Especially after what happened to Wren. She even installed cameras looking up and down the street, in case someone doesn't park in the main lot, as the asshole who tried to assault Wren did."

Josie nodded. She'd heard the entire story about Wren's situation, and was impressed with the way Jessyka, the owner of the bar, had stepped up to try to make sure it never happened again at her establishment.

"Ready?" Nate asked after he'd lifted her out of his truck.

"Ready," Josie said firmly. And she was. Excitement was winning out over her nerves at this point. She wanted to meet the people who'd been so good to Nate. Who'd helped him get over the death of his SEAL teammates. His friends.

Nate pushed open the door and gestured for her to precede him inside. The feel of his hand on the small of her back was warm and comforting.

"Surprise!"

Josie jerked at the sound of so many people yelling at the same time. The bar was lit with bright lights that someone had turned on the moment she'd stepped inside. There was a huge "Happy Birthday" banner stretched behind the bar, and dozens of people were staring at her and Nate with huge smiles on their faces.

She turned to look up at Nate. "Is it your birthday?" she asked in shock. Surely he would've told her if that was the case.

"No," he said with a soft smile. "We're celebrating yours. You said you missed your thirtieth birthday, and I didn't want such an important milestone to go unacknowledged."

Josie swallowed hard. She could hear all the people talking

and laughing behind her...but she only had eyes for the man she'd fallen deeply and madly in love with.

"You are *so* getting some tonight," she blurted.

Nate threw back his head and laughed, and Josie had never wanted a man more than she wanted him at that moment.

"We'll see how you feel," he said, when he had control over himself.

"How I feel?" she asked.

"I'm thinking the girls want to celebrate with you in style," he told her, nodding his head at something or someone behind her.

Remi and Wren were standing there, along with half a dozen other women. They all had huge smiles on their faces. Remi handed her a giant glass filled with some sort of slushy drink.

"To Josie!" Wren exclaimed.

"To Josie!" everyone echoed.

"Drink up, woman! We have a lot of celebrating to do!" Remi told her.

Josie smiled at her over the rim of the glass and took a sip. The alcohol burned going down her throat.

"Have fun," Nate whispered in her ear as he leaned into her. His hand rested on her waist as he spoke. "I'll be over there with the guys. You're safe here, Spirit. Let loose. Enjoy."

Josie turned to him, feeling overwhelmed with love for this man. He was letting her have a good time, while making sure she was safe in the process.

"Later," he told her, as if he could read her mind, could see how much she needed him. "Thirty spanks for the birthday girl."

Her pussy spasmed at his words.

Smirking—because he knew exactly how much she liked when he smacked her ass during sex—Nate strode off toward a group of hot-looking badass men who could only be the retired Navy SEALs he'd told her so much about.

"Girl! That look on your face," one of the older women said with a smile.

"I recognize that look!" another said.

"I'm thinking Josie's gonna get lucky tonight," someone else said.

"No, *Blink* is," Wren countered.

Everyone laughed.

"Come on, we have cake to eat, presents to open, and drinks to consume," Remi said in a bossy tone, pulling on Josie's arm.

"Presents?" Josie asked in a daze.

"It's not a birthday party without presents! I'm Caroline, by the way, and you're adorable. Tiny. Pint-sized. Perfect for Blink."

Josie couldn't argue with the woman. She *was* all those things. But most importantly, she felt as if she finally belonged somewhere. She'd found her tribe—and it felt incredible.

* * *

Blink couldn't take his gaze off of Josie. She was marvelous. In her element. She'd had a smile on her face all night, and he loved seeing it. She was so far from the near-feral, trauma-tized woman he'd first seen in the dark cell next to his, it wasn't even funny.

And she was drunk.

Hammered.

Sloshed.

He didn't mind. She deserved this. To completely relax, to let her guard down. She'd only turn thirty once, and he hated that it happened while she'd been a prisoner. He loved being able to give her this. Blink had worked hard to keep it a secret and get everyone together. And his plans had gone off without a hitch.

Now it was getting late, and some people had left, needing to get home to their families. Wren and Remi, as drunk as Josie, dragged Safe and Kevlar home minutes ago.

Surprisingly, Preacher, MacGyver, Flash, and Smiley hadn't called it a night yet. Preacher was currently sitting at a table with Josie, Wolf, and Dude. Blink had thought Josie might feel intimidated being surrounded by the huge men, but from her body language, she seemed perfectly comfortable.

Caroline and Cheyenne were chatting at a nearby table, as they waited for their men.

Blink approached Josie's table, and she turned to him. Her cheeks were flushed and she was smiling huge.

"Nate! This is Wolf and Dude! Aren't those cool names? Dude is a bombadeer. You know, one of those bomb guys who keeps them from going boom! And that's how he met Cheyenne! She had a bomb strapped to her chest! Her *chest*!" she exclaimed with a small frown. "And Wolf...every time I hear his name I wanna start singing that Duran Duran song. Preacher won't tell me how he got *his* name."

"Don't give me that pout," Preacher told her with a laugh, relaxing in his chair. "Won't work on me."

"Um, you do know that's not what a *bombardier* is, right?" Blink asked Josie with a smile.

She waved her hand in the air as if swatting away his words. "Close enough."

"Should we tell her what it really means?" Preacher asked.

"No."

"Yes!"

Josie and Blink spoke at the same time. She leaned toward Preacher. "Tell me!"

"Well, it's kind of hard to explain. It's been used as a kind of alert from one guy to another. To let him know that something's happening that caused him to get a spontaneous woody. Kind of an early warning system."

Josie threw her head back and laughed. Blink could only stare at her in awe. She was so beautiful when her inhibitions were down. Though, if he was being honest with himself, she was beautiful anytime.

"Are you serious? You're kidding, right?"

"Nope," Preacher said with a smirk. "Right, guys?"

"No clue. I've never heard of that word, and I would never use it to talk about my cock," Dude said, completely straight-faced.

"Must be a youngster's word," Wolf agreed.

That set Josie off again. She laughed as if Wolf and Dude had said the funniest thing she'd ever heard. She waved her hand again, this time sort of indicating the men around her as she looked up at Blink. "I *love* them. They're awesome! I mean, not as much as I love you, but close!"

Blink stilled. She was drunk, didn't know what she was saying, but damn...hearing those words on her lips felt amazing.

"You ready to go home?" he blurted, needing to get her alone.

"Yup!" she said without hesitation. "I just need to say bye to Caroline and Cheyenne. They're great. Told me all sorts of stuff tonight about being with a SEAL. The Navy kind and not the animal." Josie giggled at her own joke.

"Oh! And I want to thank Bert...he made me the best drink tonight. Oh! And I see Smiley, Flash, and MacGyver are still here. I want to say bye to them too..." Josie got up and hugged Dude from behind, her arms barely going all the way around his shoulders. "Bye, Dude!" Then she did the same to Wolf. "Bye, Wolf. It was so nice meeting you!"

She approached Preacher's chair, but he turned, giving her a proper hug. She was so small, their heads were on the same level, even with him sitting. Then she skipped off to say her goodbyes to everyone else.

"I like her," Dude said with a smile.

"You did good," Wolf agreed with a nod.

He had. Blink was relieved his friends liked Josie, but honestly, it wouldn't have mattered if they hadn't clicked right off the bat. He had no doubt that eventually, she would've won them over.

The men all stood, and Wolf and Dude went over to collect their women before heading out the door.

Josie was talking with the rest of Blink's teammates when Preacher stood and said, "She needed this."

Blink glanced at his friend. "What do you mean?"

"This. Relaxing. Making friends. She told us she's never had anyone do something like this before. Throw her a surprise party. Got all teared up about it too. It's hard to believe a woman like her doesn't already have a dozen best friends who would bend over backward for her. To know she was in that cell, and not *one* person wondered where she was... no one alerted the authorities that she was missing... It's a goddamn crime. Because she's the sweetest, most generous, and kindest woman I've met."

Even though the words were complimenting Josie, Blink felt them down to his toes. His friend wasn't wrong.

He was honored to be the one to throw her a party. It wasn't about the cake Jessyka had brought out from the kitchen, making her blow out thirty candles. It wasn't about the presents her new friends had given her, trinkets and fun little items that weren't terribly expensive, but Blink could tell meant the world to Josie.

It was about feeling seen. Being a part of a group. Feeling as if, should anything ever happen again, she wouldn't be forgotten.

"Before Kevlar left, he told me to tell you not to come to PT in the morning. That he'd see you at our first meeting at ten. Josie's probably gonna be a little hungover, he thought you might want to be there to take care of her."

Kevlar wasn't wrong, and Blink was grateful for his team leader's generosity.

"Thanks. Think I'll see if I can wrangle her home. Thanks for getting all her things to my truck."

"Of course." Preacher slapped Blink on the shoulder. "It's good to see you happy, Blink. For a while there, we weren't sure you'd be able to climb out of that mental pit you were in."

Blink looked his friend in the eye and said, "Me either. But Remi helped with that. As did all of you. None of you looked down on me for feeling the way I did. I'll always appreciate it."

Preacher snorted. "If I lost any of you guys, like what happened to your first team, I'm not sure I'd ever be able to get over it. You told Safe earlier tonight that you're in awe of Josie's strength, but you're a perfect match for her. You're *both* strong as hell. Take her home. I'll see you tomorrow."

Blink hadn't ever really thought of himself like that. He simply did what needed to be done, when it needed doing. And he certainly hadn't felt strong when he'd been lost in his head after his friends were killed and injured. But sometimes being strong was putting one foot in front of the other day after day, when all you wanted to do instead was curl into a ball and fade into nothingness.

Josie was talking animatedly to Smiley and Flash when Blink approached. He wrapped an arm around her chest diagonally from behind. "Ready to go?" he asked, interrupting the story she was telling his friends about a possum named Pete. He had no idea what the hell she was talking about—it was amazing how quickly her words returned when she felt safe and happy—but when she tilted her head up and smiled up at him, Blink knew he'd stand there and let her babble for hours, if that's what she wanted to do.

"Ready," she said instead.

Shifting, Blink took her hand in his and gave his friends a chin lift and headed for the door, before Josie could get side-tracked again.

She paused before walking through and waved at the bar, not at anyone in particular, and said, "Bye Aces! I'm out!"

People chuckled and called out their goodbyes as Blink pulled her through the door to the parking lot with a smile on his face.

"Hey, wait...did everyone save this parking spot for us?" she asked, as Blink led her to his truck.

"Yup."

"That's awesome!" she exclaimed.

Lots of things had been "awesome" for her tonight, and Blink thought it was adorable as hell.

He opened her door and lifted her into the passenger seat with ease. She let him snap her seat belt into place, but stopped him before he could step back and close the door. "Nate?"

She sounded serious for the first time in hours. "Yeah, hon?"

"No one has ever done anything like this for me. The party. Thank you."

"You should've had this kind of thing all your life before now. And I'm going to do my best to spoil you and make sure you know how much you're loved from here on out."

A smile formed on her lips. "I repeat, you are *so* getting some when we get home."

Blink chuckled. He wasn't sure she'd be able to stay awake for the drive home, forget about doing more when they got there.

"Okay, Spirit."

"I've decided that I like that nickname," she informed him.

"Good. Watch your arm, I'm shutting the door."

She leaned left, and Blink got the door closed. He jogged around to the driver's side and climbed in. Before long, they were headed home. He kept looking over at Josie, only to see her gaze glued on him every time.

"What?" he finally asked when they were halfway home.

"I love your freckles. And your hair. I've always wanted red-haired babies."

Blink gaped. But she went on as if she hadn't just rocked his world.

"And twins. I know they're more work, but since you're a twin, they probably run in your family. I wanted a brother or sister so bad when I was growing up, but of course Mom was single, so that wasn't happening, or so she told me. I think three."

"Three what?" Blink asked when she didn't continue.

"Kids."

"You want three kids?" Blink asked.

"Uh-huh. I just said that."

Blink wanted to stop the truck right there and get to work on giving her exactly what she wanted. But he controlled himself. Barely.

"Nate?"

"Right here, Josie," he said with a small smile. She really was an adorable drunk.

"Your people are awesome."

"They're your people now too."

When she didn't respond, he looked over at her, and he couldn't interpret the look on her face. "What?"

"I have people," she whispered, sounding awed. "I've never had people before. Wanted them. Thought something was wrong with me when it didn't happen."

"Nothing's wrong with you, Josie," Blink said, a little harsher than he intended.

She snorted. "There's lots wrong with me. But when I'm with you, I forget all those things. Did you see tonight?"

Blink's heart felt as if it was going to beat out of his chest. This woman. She made him feel ten feet tall. He wanted to always be her safe place. "Did I see what?"

"My voice. It didn't go away," she said matter-of-factly. "It went away when I was in that cell, and you brought it back. It still feels rusty sometimes. But tonight, it was totally back."

Blink definitely noticed that she hadn't had any trouble speaking with others. "I saw," he told her.

"Nate?"

Lord, she was so damn cute. "Still right here, Josie."

"I think I only had a week or so left before I died, when you showed up."

Any warm feelings inside Blink dissipated in an explosion of a thousand stars. It was his turn to have no voice. He had no idea what to say to that.

"I was bad off. So hungry. So skinny. But then you came... and I couldn't give up."

Thankfully, Blink turned into the parking lot of his apartment complex. He pulled into a spot, turned off the engine, then looked at Josie. He undid her seat belt and said, "Come here."

She didn't even hesitate, crawling over to him and straddling his lap. It wasn't even a tight fit. The feel of her tiny body against his own made Blink feel the size of a mountain. She snuggled into him as if she'd done it every day of her life. She fit perfectly.

Blink held her to him with one hand on the back of her head and the other wrapped around her waist. "You were meant to be mine," he told her softly. "From the moment I saw you in that cell, I knew you'd change my life. And you have. For the better."

"Mmmmmmm," she hummed against his neck.

Blink shifted, wanting to get her inside. He opened his door and without effort, stepped out with Josie still clinging to him. She giggled a little but didn't drop her legs. In fact, she tightened them around him.

"What about my presents?" she asked as he shut the door and headed for his apartment.

"I'll get them tomorrow."

"M'kay."

Blink carried Josie inside, toward his bedroom, then straight into his bathroom. She finally lowered her legs and stood, looking up at him.

"Do your thing in here, then come to bed."

She gave him a satisfied smile. "Okay."

He left while he still had the strength to do so. He was

walking back into the bedroom after using the bathroom in the hall—and stopped in his tracks.

Josie was standing next to his bed, completely naked, a trail of her clothes leading from the bathroom to the bed.

"Hi," she said with a crooked grin.

He didn't remember taking off his clothes, but the next thing Blink knew, he was holding Josie against his own naked body.

She giggled, and his cock got even harder, which he didn't think was possible.

He picked her up and not so gently dropped her on the bed, then crawled over her, caging her in. "How do you feel?"

"Great!" she chirped.

"Not dizzy? Or nauseous?"

"Nope."

"Good. How do you want this to go?"

"This?"

"Sex. You want it slow and easy, or fast and hard?"

"Um...both?" she asked with a grin.

"I can do that," Blink said, not sure he could do slow and easy right now, especially not with her words ringing in his head about red-haired babies.

"Wait!" she exclaimed.

Blink froze as he stared down at her.

"I wanna be on top. And I want my thirty birthday spanks."

Damn, this woman. She was gonna be the death of him.

Blink rolled off her onto his back, putting his hands behind his head. "I'm all yours," he quipped.

"All mine," Josie whispered reverently. "All I've ever

wanted is a man for myself. Who loves me for me. Who sees through my weirdness to the person underneath."

"I see you, Spirit. I've always seen you," Blink assured her.

Then she moved, quicker than he would've thought she could while drunk. She threw a leg over his stomach and grinned down at him. "Thank you for my birthday party, Nate."

"You're welcome."

She scooted down his body, keeping eye contact as she went. Then she lowered her head and took his cock into her mouth, surprising the hell out of Blink. There was no buildup, no teasing, she squeezed him with her hand and immediately started giving him the best blowjob he'd ever had in his life.

It was all he could do not to explode right then and there. To avoid doing just that, Blink sat up, grabbed Josie around the waist, and hauled her up his body so she was straddling his face.

"Nate! I wasn't done!" she complained, even as she began to rock over his mouth as he ate her out just as desperately as she'd taken him down her throat.

In response, Blink smacked her ass. She squealed, then giggled. He felt a rush of wetness coat his tongue. She loved that.

He grinned. This was going to be fun.

By the time Josie had gotten her thirty birthday spankings, she'd orgasmed three times, and he'd filled her pussy to overflowing with his own pleasure.

She was lying bonelessly on top of him now, his cock still deep inside her. It was one of Blink's favorite places to be.

"Happy Birthday, Spirit."
"Best birthday ever," she mumbled against him.

CHAPTER SEVENTEEN

When Josie thought about her birthday, and the sex she and Nate had when they'd gotten home, and how sweetly he'd taken care of her when she'd woken up with a monster hangover, she couldn't help but grin.

She wasn't a big drinker, but that night had been incredible. She'd felt so loved, so much a part of something. Not like an outsider, as she'd felt for most of her life.

Remi and Wren were the best. Funny, welcoming, and Josie felt as if she'd known them for years rather than weeks. But even better, the older SEAL women—Caroline, Cheyenne, and the others—were just as welcoming.

Josie had received more texts on the new phone Nate had helped her buy than she'd probably ever gotten in her life. Her phone was constantly dinging with incoming text messages from her new friends. So much so that she'd had to silence it while she was working, otherwise she'd get too distracted.

And it wasn't just the women either. Wolf, Dude, Benny, and the other former SEALs also randomly texted her to check in when she was home by herself. At first, she wondered if Nate had told them something about her that concerned them, but he'd reassured her that, no, that's just the kind of men they were.

Things were going so well, Josie couldn't help but worry that something would happen to destroy her newfound happiness. It was a pessimistic thought, but in her experience, just when things were going well for her, the shit usually hit the fan.

But she was determined to try to live in the moment more often. Not to let what *might* happen destroy her happiness in the present. And Josie had a lot to be happy about. She had her job back, new friends, Nate.

He was the partner she'd always wanted. Supportive, kind, brave. Men like him existed in the romance stories she sometimes read, but they were fiction. She knew better than most people that reality usually fell way short of what was portrayed in movies and books.

But somehow, here she was. Starring in her own romance book. Complete with a hero who was head over heels for her, kind, badass when he needed to be, and on top of it all... outstanding in bed.

Smiling, Josie looked over at Nate. He was in the kitchen, wearing his blue camouflage uniform and making them both some eggs over easy before he left for the naval base.

As if he sensed her looking at him, he turned. "What?" he asked with a small smile.

"Nothing. I just...I'm happy," Josie blurted. "After what happened, I wasn't sure I'd ever feel this way again."

To her surprise, Nate put down the spatula and turned off the burner. He stalked toward her. When he reached where she was sitting at the table, Josie tilted her head up to look at him. He had a serious look on his face, and he turned her chair with ease, then leaned over so he was caging her in with his hands on the arms of the chair.

"I love you."

Josie blinked in surprise.

"I just wanted to make sure you knew that. This isn't a casual dating thing for me. I love everything about you. Your heart, your resilience, your strength, your body, the way you look at me with those big eyes like you're doing right now, as if you don't believe you're loveable."

Josie bit her lip and tried hard not to burst into tears.

Nate chuckled and caressed her cheek with the backs of his fingers. "Don't cry," he ordered. "You know I can't stand it."

"I love you too," Josie blurted, reaching up and latching onto his wrist with her hand.

He smiled tenderly down at her. "I know."

Josie frowned at that. "How do you know?" she asked.

"Because I see it in your eyes every morning when I wake up. And when I come home from work. And when I'm so deep inside your body, I don't know where you end and I begin. You're the first person I think of when I hear a funny joke, because I want to share it with you. You're the one I want to call when I get good news or bad. You're the center of my world, Josie England, and I can't ever imagine you *not* in my life, loving me back."

"Nate," Josie whispered, overwhelmed with emotion.

He leaned down and kissed her tenderly. A sweet kiss that she felt down to her toes. This moment felt like the beginning of the rest of her life. As if she was shrugging off the old Josie, the one who'd felt so alone in that prison cell, the awkward woman who preferred to stay at home because she had no one to go out with to lunch or dinner.

"What time will you be home tonight?" she asked.

Nate looked a little perplexed, but he answered anyway. "The usual. Probably around five-thirty or so."

"Good. Because Wren convinced me to order a negligee and it's supposed to come in today. I thought maybe you could help me figure out if it fits properly or not," Josie teased with a shy smile.

"Damn, woman. I'm thinking I can probably talk to Kevlar and get off early."

"That's what he said," Josie blurted.

It took a second for her words to sink in, then Nate threw his head back as he laughed.

"Seriously, I love you," he said, when he had himself under control once more.

"I love you too," Josie returned.

"I wish I had time to throw you over my shoulder and take you back to bed," he sighed. "But you have that live press conference in an hour, and I need to throw away the eggs I started and make new ones, then get to work. But tonight? When I get home..."

His words trailed off, and Josie's imagination went into overdrive.

Nate kissed her once more, hard and deep, before standing up, adjusting his cock in his pants, then heading back to the stove.

Josie watched with a dreamy look on her face as he washed his hands, threw the now-ruined eggs into the trash, and cracked two new eggs into the pan.

They lingered over their goodbyes that morning. After telling each other how they felt, it was as if they were embarking on a brand-new part of their journey as a couple. And she supposed they were.

With Nate, she didn't feel as if she was less than other women, something she'd always experienced before. She'd always been the odd man out, so to speak. The one without close girlfriends, without a ton of experience when it came to men. The woman who hadn't traveled much or done anything interesting.

And now she was a member of the I'm-part-of-a-couple club. It felt fantastic. More so because it was Nate who she was with. She didn't worry that he'd cheat on her, or talk trash about her to his buddies. He was who he was—a no-nonsense, tell-it-like-it-is, considerate partner.

Later, after the press conference she'd transcribed, and after she'd made herself a sandwich for lunch, Josie was sitting at the table, returning texts from Remi and Wren about the special package she'd retrieved from the mail room in the apartment complex, and advising Caroline on the best hotel on the Vegas Strip to take Wolf to for an impromptu mini-vacation, when there was a knock at the apartment door.

Surprised because she wasn't expecting anyone, Josie put her phone down on the table next to her computer—and the very skimpy, very see-through, white, could barely call it a piece of clothing that had been delivered—and walked to the door.

Looking through the peephole, Josie saw someone standing a respectable distance away. She always got annoyed when people stood so close, they were almost touching the door. The person had their back turned, and she didn't recognize the short-haired blonde.

Keeping the chain on, she opened the door. "Hello?"

In a move so fast, Josie wasn't able to back up, the person turned and kicked the door as hard as they could.

The chain broke and the door flew backward, hitting Josie in the face. She let out a surprised *oof* and stumbled, tripping over her feet and falling on her butt to the floor.

Looking up, Josie stared into the barrel of a gun.

She froze. Every muscle in her body just refused to work. She should be running, screaming, *something*. But terror held her immobile.

"Get up," the woman ordered.

Now that Josie could see the person's face, she recognized her immediately.

Genevieve. Ayden's sister. She was wearing a blonde wig and a pair of oversized sweatpants that made her look as if she weighed fifty pounds more than she did. And she was holding a pistol, aiming it right between Josie's eyes.

"I said, *get up*," Gen snarled. "Unless you want me to put a bullet in your brain right this second. Because I will. I don't give a shit if you die right here. But my mom has plans for you and wants you alive. So get the fuck up. Now!"

All the words that had returned since her rescue were once more stuck in her throat. It enraged Josie that when she was scared, her ability to speak deserted her.

Moving quickly, she got to her feet, only to have Gen grab her upper arm and give her a hard shake. All the while, keeping the barrel of the gun pointed at her face. "Don't try anything," she warned. "We're going to walk to my car, calm and easy. If you scream or do anything to draw attention to yourself, I'll happily shoot you. Understand?"

Josie nodded. The last thing she should do is get into a car with Gen, but she also believed the woman when she said she'd blow her head off. And Josie did *not* want Nate to come home to see her brain matter in the parking lot or splattered in the foyer of his apartment.

She, more than anyone, knew that as long as she was breathing, she had a chance of rescue. Nate and his friends would come for her. And it was that thought that gave her the strength to walk alongside Gen without struggling.

She let the woman lead her to a four-door sedan that Josie had never seen before. She got in on the driver's side and scooted over to the passenger seat. She stared straight ahead, and her ex-boyfriend's sister started the engine and pulled out of the parking lot.

Bile formed in Josie's throat, but she swallowed it down.

Nate would come for her. He would. They loved each other, and he would do whatever it took to find her. This wasn't like before, she wasn't going to be forgotten. She had people who would look for her, who would report her missing. She wouldn't be left to rot in a cell like last time. She believed that deep in her soul.

It was the only thing keeping her from panicking as Gen drove them out of Riverton.

* * *

Blink frowned as he drove toward his apartment. It was four o'clock, and he was anxious to get home. Not only because he wanted to see what Josie had bought; the thought of her in a sexy piece of lingerie had kept his dick half hard all day.

But more than that, he was worried.

He'd texted her several times and received no answer. When he'd tried to call her, the phone rang, then went to voicemail. It was unusual, and in his line of work, unusual wasn't a good thing.

When Blink had expressed his concern to Kevlar, his team leader hadn't hesitated to tell him to go home to check on her. All his teammates had a soft spot for Josie. Not only because of what she'd been through, but because of her size. She was tiny, especially compared to them, and they all looked at her kind of like a little sister.

Blink pulled into his usual spot in the lot, right in front of his apartment, and hopped out of his truck. He strode toward his door—and his blood ran cold as he approached.

The door was shut but, to his trained eye, obviously tampered with. There was a large footprint in the middle of the door, clearly outlined in the light layer of dust that covered the surface.

Using his elbow, so as not to contaminate any fingerprints or other evidence that might exist, Blink pushed.

The door swung open with no resistance.

"Fuck," he muttered, seeing the broken safety chain on the floor. Whoever had kicked in the door hadn't bothered to make sure it was latched behind him when he left.

"Josie?" Blink called out, a little louder than he intended.

Silence greeted him, and panic instantly set in. Blink raced through the apartment and found what he expected—nothing. Josie wasn't there. Her laptop was on the kitchen table, along with her phone, and a pile of lace and string on top of a bubble envelope.

For a second, Blink didn't know what to do. His thoughts were scattered.

Josie was gone. Missing. How could this happen?

He didn't for one second believe she was visiting a friend. Or had decided she didn't want to be with him anymore. They'd exchanged I-love-yous that morning. And she wouldn't leave without her phone. Besides, she didn't even have a car.

No, his Josie hadn't left him. The piece of lingerie was proof of that. As were her plans for the two of them when he returned home from work. And the damn broken safety chain and the footprint on his door. It didn't take a genius to figure out that something had happened. Someone had forced their way into his apartment and taken Josie.

Teeth clenched together, Blink pulled out his phone. There was only one person to call right now.

Tex.

He'd get a hold of Kevlar and the rest of his team, Wolf,

and his commander and the cops, but he needed to get Tex on this *now*. Josie didn't have a tracker, but if anyone could find her, it was the ex-SEAL.

The phone rang once. "Blink, what's up?" Tex asked in lieu of a greeting.

"It's Josie. She's gone."

"What do you mean, gone?" Tex asked in a no-nonsense tone.

"Gone. I came home from work and there's a damn footprint in the middle of my door, the safety chain is broken, her phone and mail are on the table, and she's not here."

"Any blood?"

Blink swallowed hard as he looked around. The apartment was as clean as it always was. No dirty dishes in the sink, no snacks left out on the table. Just her computer, phone, the scrap of cloth he'd had such high hopes of seeing on her, and a chair pushed partway out from the table. "No."

"All right. So she's not hurt. That's good. Can you take a picture of that footprint and send it to me?"

"Yeah."

"You call Kevlar yet?"

"No," Blink said. He realized he was talking in monosyllables, but he could barely speak at all through the panic and adrenaline coursing through his body.

"Do that. And have him call Cookie and the others. You and your team can handle the search when I have info for you, and Wolf's team can hold down things at the apartment and with the women."

Blink nodded.

"Blink? Did you hear me?" Tex asked in a demanding tone.

"Yeah," he managed to say.

"I'll be in touch. Call Kevlar. Out."

Blink clicked off the connection and stood motionless in his apartment, feeling utterly lost. It was as if all the air had been sucked out of the room. All the life. Without Josie, it seemed...empty. Blink wanted to sink deep inside himself, as he'd done after that horrible mission with his previous team. Going to that place where life didn't hurt so much.

But he couldn't. Not now. Not when Josie needed him.

He took a deep breath. Then another. Nothing could happen to her. Not when they'd just found each other. Not when they had a beautiful life ahead of them after so much heartbreak. Fate wouldn't be so cruel as to show him everything he'd ever wanted in life, only to rip it away ruthlessly.

He clicked on Kevlar's name and brought the phone back up to his ear.

"Kevlar here."

"She's gone," Blink said succinctly. "I need you and the team."

"Are you at your apartment?" Kevlar asked.

"Yes."

"I'm on my way. I'll call the others. Have you called the police?"

Blink shook his head, feeling as if he was in a long, dark tunnel.

"Blink?"

"No," he whispered.

"Okay. Hang on, buddy. We're comin'."

He nodded and clicked off the phone without saying goodbye.

Blink was *terrified*. He didn't know what to do. All he knew was that Josie was missing, she was probably scared out of her mind, and she was relying on him to find her. Except he didn't have a clue where to start. Where to look.

This feeling of helplessness was all too familiar. He'd felt the same way when watching his teammates dying and moaning in pain in Iran, and there was nothing he could do except attempt to give them cover from enemy fire.

But this felt way worse. Because Josie hadn't volunteered for this. And she'd already been through hell. It wasn't fair!

Closing his eyes, he took another deep breath. He had to get himself together. He'd be no good to Josie like this. Her scent filled his nose. The soap she used. The lotion she liked. The slight scent of eggs from that morning, still lingering in the air.

Opening his eyes, Blink felt more in control. More determined than ever to find Josie and give her the beautiful life he envisioned for them both.

Looking down at his phone, he clicked some buttons for the third time.

"Nine-one-one, what's your emergency?"

"My girlfriend's been kidnapped. I need a detective. Immediately."

* * *

The trip to Las Vegas was surreal. Gen spent the ride alternating between being completely silent and ripping into Josie for "killing" her little brother. She held the gun the whole time, using it to punctuate her words now and then.

Josie didn't dare do anything to distract her or make her lose control of the vehicle. Though Gen wasn't speeding, wasn't doing anything to bring attention to their car. At one point, she pulled over on the side of the interstate and took a small dirt road that veered off into the desert. She drove about half a mile, out of sight of any cars that might be going by, then forced Josie to get out.

She'd thought that was it. That Gen was going to shoot her in the head and leave her body to rot out there in the desert.

Instead, she told her to open the trunk. Inside was a can of gasoline. While holding her at gunpoint, Gen ordered her to put the gas into the tank. After she complied, Gen told her to toss the empty can on the ground and get back into the car. They returned to I-15 and continued their trip east toward Vegas.

Josie was going to beg her to stop so she could use the bathroom. But since she didn't seem to be able to get any words past the huge lump in her throat, and the whole desert detour made it pretty clear Gen had no plans to stop for gas, she didn't bother even trying to make her needs known. Since gas stations were obviously out, she still hoped Gen herself might need a rest area soon.

Until, at one point, Gen glanced at her with a creepy smile and said, "I'm wearing a diaper."

Josie frowned in confusion.

"An adult diaper. So I don't have to stop. I don't want to be on any cameras anywhere. Which is why I brought gas with me. And I can piss in the diaper. We've worked it all out. We watch crime shows, we know the things they look for.

We're smarter than *everyone*, even that dumb asshole you're with. They can look into us all they want, but we have alibis. Mom's probably using my phone right now, texting herself to prove I'm still in Vegas." She smiled triumphantly. "No one will ever know it was me who kidnapped you. You're *fucked*, Josie. Just like you fucked Ayden. Just like you fucked Mom and me."

Then she laughed. A maniacal laugh that made the hair on the back of Josie's neck stand up. It seemed as if she and her batshit crazy mother had planned this kidnapping carefully. Which made despair threaten to overwhelm her. But Josie pushed it back.

They weren't smarter than Nate. He and his friends would figure out where she was. They had to.

The skyline of Vegas came into view, and with every mile they traveled, Josie's hopes sank further and further. She recognized the neighborhood Gen turned into as being where Millie's house was located. She'd been there once with Ayden, shortly after they'd started dating. It was the most awkward dinner ever, and she'd managed to avoid doing that a second time.

Gen pulled up to the house and the garage door opened. She pulled in, and the door shut behind them. Then Millie was at the door on Josie's side, yanking it open.

"Out, bitch," she said.

Josie didn't want to. Wanted to stay right where she was, but with Millie now pointing a second gun at her head, she had no choice. She slowly stepped out and stood, stumbling when Millie shoved her toward the door to the house.

The two women followed and herded her inside. There

were piles and piles of stuff throughout the house. Way more than had been there when she and Ayden had come over for dinner. She'd realized then that Millie was a hoarder, and instantly understood why Ayden always wanted to stay at her place. But it seemed to have gotten exponentially worse since she'd seen the house last. There were boxes everywhere, along with piles of clothes, trash bags, and crap that hadn't been touched in what looked like years. The house was an assault to Josie's eyes and nose. It smelled...old. Funky. Disgusting.

She didn't have time to figure out exactly *what* she was smelling when Gen pushed past Josie and opened a door just off the kitchen, and gestured for her to go down a set of stairs.

She was surprised. Most houses in Vegas didn't have basements, something about the kind of rock in the desert soil making them hard to excavate. This one was small and claustrophobic. And it too was filled from corner to corner with boxes and other junk.

"Over there," Millie said, jamming the barrel of the pistol into the middle of Josie's back.

She stumbled again, struggling to adjust to the low light in the room. There was a path through the boxes that had been cleared, leading to a small door.

For the first time, Josie hesitated. This room reminded her way too much of the cell she'd been shoved into. She couldn't do it again. Couldn't be shut away like a forgotten piece of trash.

But just like on the other side of the world, she didn't have a choice here. Gen shoved her hard, making Josie fall to her knees. She felt the barrel of a gun being pressed into the back of her head.

"Don't shoot!" Millie exclaimed, and Josie broke out into a cold sweat. She closed her eyes, sure she was about to die. Her only regret was that Nate would never know what happened to her. These women would take her body out into the desert where she'd never be found. It would be as if she'd never existed.

She found her arm being wrenched upward, behind her back. "Get up, bitch! And get in there. You'll be gone soon, but we can't have you in our way while we finalize arrangements for your *future*. So get in," Millie ordered, as she opened the small door with a flourish.

Gen shoved her forward, and Josie landed on her hands and knees. She had no choice but to crawl into the small closet-like space as Gen kicked her in the ass, propelling her toward it. The tiny room was only big enough for her to sit on her butt and barely turn around. Amazingly, Josie missed what now seemed like her spacious cell in comparison.

She opened her mouth to plead with the women, to beg them to let her go, to take whatever blame they wanted to heap on her head for Ayden's death, but her voice still wasn't working. And she didn't have the chance anyway before the door slammed shut. The snick of a padlock sounded like a bomb going off in the dark space.

Then there was nothing. Silence. It was as if she'd entered an alternate dimension.

Trapped. *Again!* Only this time, there was no *drip drip drip* of lifesaving water in the corner. No small metal cup to catch the liquid.

Whatever Millie and Gen had in store for her couldn't be good.

Josie just had to hope that Nate would get to her before whatever plans the women had devised could be put into motion. She had a feeling once they were, she really *would* disappear, as so many other people in the world did, without a trace. Like a puff of smoke.

CHAPTER EIGHTEEN

"They didn't leave Vegas," Tex said. "I get what you're saying, Blink, but there's no evidence to support that they were the ones who did this."

Blink paced his living room. Back and forth. Back and forth. He couldn't sit still. Couldn't eat. Couldn't think about anything other than finding Josie.

His little apartment was full. All his teammates were there, as were Wolf and Cookie. The police had come and gone, taking a missing person's report and saying they'd be in touch, that since it hadn't been twenty-four hours, and since Josie was an adult, there wasn't much they could do, she'd probably be back of her own accord soon, etcetera. It wasn't illegal for an adult to take off.

For some reason, they didn't seem too concerned about the broken chain and footprint on the door.

It was bullshit, but nothing unexpected. The police were inundated with missing person's reports, and nine times out of ten, the person wasn't actually missing. Their phone died, or they needed a break from their life, or they just forgot to tell someone where they were going.

But Blink knew for certain none of those were the case with Josie. She'd had plans for them that night. They'd just shared their feelings for each other. She had no reason to take off and every reason to stay.

So while the police might not be looking for Josie, Blink and his friends were.

"It's *them*," Blink told Tex in agitation. "There's no one else it could be. Josie doesn't have enemies. She hasn't even met anyone here in Riverton except for our SEAL family."

"I hear you. If it's them, they've covered their tracks, because I've pinged both Gen and Millie's phones, and they're both in Vegas at the mother's house. Have been all day. And all yesterday. In fact, they've been sending texts back and forth since this morning. The GPS units in their vehicles show they haven't left the house all day either," Tex said in a calm voice that grated on Blink's nerves. Any other time, he'd be glad for the composure he was showing, but now? He wanted to reach through the phone and shake the man.

"Also, their credit and debit cards show no use. No gas stations, no food. Nothing," Tex added.

"They could've hired someone to do their dirty work, right?" Preacher asked.

"Yeah, but that shoeprint Blink sent me is honestly too small to be a man's."

"It wouldn't take much to overpower her," Smiley said. "She's tiny."

"You aren't helping," Safe told his friend in a low tone.

"If it's not the mother, or a man, who is it?" MacGyver asked no one in particular. "Could they have hired a woman to come get her?"

"It's her. Or them. There's literally no one else who hates Josie. They blame her for her ex's death," Blink insisted.

"Wait—why are they texting each other if they're in the same house?" Kevlar asked.

"Yeah. That makes no sense," MacGyver said.

"It does if they're trying to make it look like they're both in Vegas, but one of them was actually here in Riverton," Preacher growled.

"What about traffic cameras?" Flash asked Tex.

"I'm working on it. But if they aren't in their own vehicles —which I'm guessing they aren't, since I already checked the GPS data—it's like finding a needle in a needlestack to follow every car that drove by any of the roads around Blink's apartment complex."

"What about checking the car rental companies in Vegas?" Cookie asked.

"Already did that. Didn't get any hits on either woman," Tex said.

Every word out of the computer genius's mouth pointed toward someone other than either Millie or Genevieve Hitson being the person who broke into his apartment and took Josie, and yet Blink knew without a doubt that one or both were behind her disappearance. Kevlar was right, it made no sense that the women were texting each other all day, while in the same house. To be fair, occasionally he'd send Josie a text while they were both sitting on his couch, just for fun...but not repeatedly.

"It's her," Blink said firmly, forcing himself to concentrate on the here and now.

"Right. So I just need to find proof," Tex said. "I'll go and see what I can do. I'll be in touch." The line went silent.

"I'm going to Vegas," Blink announced. "No matter what Tex did or didn't find, or might find in the next few hours, I know down to my soul that's where she is."

"I don't want to be the one to say it...but they could've done something to her already. She might not be there," Kevlar said, the sorrow and unease easy to hear in his tone.

Blink wanted to lash out at his team leader. Shout that he didn't know what the hell he was talking about. But Kevlar didn't say anything Blink hadn't already thought. The image of Josie's broken and bleeding body being discarded somewhere in the vast desert between Riverton and Las Vegas made him want to throw up.

"I know. And don't think I haven't already thought about that. But you guys didn't hear the mother. The hatred in her tone was all-consuming. I don't think she'd want to simply shoot Josie. That would be too easy. No, I think she has something more sinister in mind. She wants her to suffer." Blink felt dirty just saying the words.

"So, while Tex does his thing, and the police are waiting for some arbitrary period of time to go by before they decide Josie is truly missing, who's going to Vegas with Blink?" Wolf asked.

"Kevlar and Safe have to stay here with Remi and Wren. They'd be worried sick about them otherwise, and on the remote chance this isn't the Hitsons, and has something to do with our jobs instead, I want them protected," Blink said firmly.

Kevlar opened his mouth to protest, but Preacher beat him to it. "I'll go. And Smiley will too. MacGyver and Flash, you guys stay here and see what else you can dig up. Talk to the neighbors, be Tex's eyes and ears here if he needs anything, and you can liaise with the cops."

Everyone nodded.

"I'm not sure it's a good idea for just the three of you to go to Vegas," Cookie said with a small frown.

"As much as I hate those bitches, I can't go in there balls-out," Blink said. "I'll do whatever I need to do in order to make sure Josie is all right. And if all seven of us show up, it will put them on the defensive. Maybe if it's just me and a couple friends, they'll screw up and boast about what they did. If there's the smallest chance she's still alive, that they haven't killed her, I'll take it. Do whatever I have to do. Sell my soul to find her."

"All right," Cookie said with a nod. "We'll rally the girls. Josie will need the support of her friends when she gets home."

The faith he had made Blink want to cry. Wolf, Cookie, and the rest of their team were legends in SEAL circles. They'd seen and done more things than most teams had combined. To hear him talk about Josie coming home with such certainty made his confidence rise.

"Right. Who's driving?" Preacher asked.

"I am," Smiley said decidedly. "We'll take Blink's truck, in case we need to go off-road. We can leave right now."

It took everything within Blink not to race for his front

door. "I need to pack a bag for Josie. She might need a change of clothes. And we'll want a first-aid kit...just in case."

Wolf put a hand on Blink's arm, while Kevlar's landed heavy on his shoulder.

"You'll find her," Kevlar said.

"She might be tiny, but she's tougher than nails," Wolf said. "I'm sure she has no doubt you're coming for her. Just as my Caroline did when those assholes who took her threw her in the ocean. Women like her and Josie, they're survivors. Call us when you're on your way back."

Blink swallowed hard and nodded.

Then he strode toward his bedroom to pack a bag. For a moment, he stood there, trying to find his equilibrium. Josie disappearing had shaken him to his core. He wouldn't let her down. The alternative was unthinkable. He loved Josie, and she loved him. He wasn't losing her now. No way.

Time had no meaning in the pitch darkness of the tiny closet Josie had been forced into. She strained to hear something, anything, but all she heard was the sound of her own heartbeat.

Her thoughts turned to Nate.

What was he doing right now? Surely he'd discovered she was gone. He would've called Kevlar and the others. They'd be brainstorming where she might be. Probably had called the police. Everyone would be searching.

But remembering the steps Gen had taken to stay under the radar worried Josie. Wearing an adult diaper so she didn't have to stop and use the bathroom was...crazy...and smart. And the gas. Leaving her phone in Vegas. The car Josie didn't recognize. And it hadn't escaped her that Millie was the one they'd filed the protective order against, because she was the one who'd come right out and threatened her.

If Gen was questioned, she'd claim she was here in Vegas the entire time, that she couldn't possibly be the one who'd kidnapped her, and all the evidence would support her claim. But Nate and the rest of the guys wouldn't just assume that since her phone didn't show her in California, that didn't mean she wasn't actually there.

But for the first time, worry began to creep in. Would they figure things out in time? Whatever Millie and Gen were going to do with her, Josie had a feeling it was more elaborate than simply killing her and dumping her body somewhere. That wouldn't be enough vengeance for the two women.

Millie had spoiled her only son, and Gen had always been overly protective of her little brother. His death had clearly broken them, pushed them both to do things they otherwise wouldn't have. Josie had no doubt of that.

Were they actually able to kill her? Maybe, maybe not.

But have someone *else* do something horrible, and exact their revenge so they didn't have to get their hands dirty? Yeah, she could see them doing that.

Josie shivered. It wasn't cold in the closet, but she could feel a clock ticking. And much faster than it had when she was overseas. She instinctively knew she didn't have a lot of time before Millie and Gen put whatever plan they had in mind into effect.

Hurry, Nate. I need you to find me!

* * *

Hours later, in the dark of night, Smiley turned down the street where Millie Hitson lived. Tex had sent the woman's address to them while they were on their way toward Vegas. He'd said he was still searching for any cars that showed up both near Blink's apartment, as well as on traffic cams on the route out of Riverton, but it was such a colossal task, he hadn't made much headway. He reassured them that he'd stay on it, and he'd even called in a friend to help him, a woman named Ryleigh who lived in New Mexico. But even with two of them working feverishly to hack into cameras, they all knew it would be slow going.

But Blink didn't need verification for what he felt in his heart. The Hitsons had his Josie, and he was going to get her back if it was the last thing he did.

"Don't do anything rash," Preacher said, as if he could read Blink's mind.

He didn't respond. He was beyond speaking at this point. He'd gone over and over in his head all the bad things that could've happened to Josie in the last few hours...and he wasn't up for coherent speech.

"Remember, let me talk," Smiley said as all three of them got out of the truck.

Blink had no problem with that. It was going to take all his control to not grab one of the women and shake them until they told him where Josie was.

They strode up to the door and before they even had to knock, it opened. Genevieve stood there—and for a moment she looked shocked to see them.

"Who were you expecting?" Smiley asked in a hard tone that would've had most people quaking in their shoes.

Not this bitch. She put one hand on her hip, leaned against the doorjamb and glared at all three of them. "What do you want?"

"Josie. Where is she?"

"How the hell should I know? Did she up and disappear again? Shame."

Blink's hands fisted at his sides.

She smirked at him and said, "Guess these are your super-soldier friends? I'm not impressed. Piss off."

"We aren't leaving," Smiley said. "Not without Josie."

"So, what? You're just going to camp out on our lawn? Because she's not here. And if you were smart," she told Blink, "you'd get the hell away from her, because she'll probably manage to kill you too, eventually."

"If *you* were smart, you'd quit talking out your ass and go get Josie."

"Look, you might think you're hot shit, but you soldier assholes are all the same. Cocky, conceited, and you think you're God's gift to women. News flash—you aren't. I don't know where that fucking bitch is, and I don't care. If I ever saw her again, I wouldn't lift a finger to help her. She could be drowning right in front of me and I'd stand here and watch. She's. Not. Here. Now go away."

"No," Blink said in a guttural growl.

"Oh, it speaks," Gen said with a roll of her eyes.

"Let them in." Millie had come up behind her daughter and entered the conversation.

"What? No, Mom," Gen protested.

"Yeah, Gen, let us in," Smiley echoed.

"We have nothing to hide. They won't find Josie here. If it'll make them leave, let them look. The faster they understand she isn't here, the faster they'll get the hell off my doorstep."

Gen sighed dramatically, then whirled and stomped back into the house.

"I'm allowing this because I want you gone," Millie informed them. She looked at Blink. "I hate her. She ruined my life. But I didn't do anything to the little bitch. Gen and I have been here for the last twelve hours at least."

Blink stared at the woman. She was protesting too much. No one had asked where she'd been since this morning. Only where Josie was.

Smiley stepped through the door, with Blink and Preacher on his heels.

The house was a mess. It was obvious Millie Hitson was a hoarder. There wasn't an empty spot on any of the tables in the house. They walked through the living area, sticking to a narrow path between stacks of boxes and miscellaneous crap, heading toward the kitchen. Piles and piles of clothes were on the couches, with only two spots open, obviously where Millie and Gen sat. The entire house had a kind of rank stench, a mixture of old food and possibly rotting rodents. But Blink wasn't there to judge the way Millie lived. He simply wanted Josie.

Without talking about it, the men split up. Millie and Gen sat in their places on the couch as if they were unconcerned the men were there and what they might find.

For the first time, Blink wondered if he was wrong. Would they be so relaxed if Josie was here? He wasn't sure.

It was difficult to search the house because of all the junk piled up literally everywhere. Opening closets was impossible, as they were blocked by who knew how many years of stuff being collected.

Preacher forced open a door near the kitchen and yelled, "Basement!"

Blink was surprised, since this part of the country wasn't known for having basements, but his adrenaline spiked. Josie had to be down there. She *had* to be.

It was treacherous going down the stairs, because they were broken and uneven, and there were things stacked up on each step. Looking around, Blink's optimism sank. It smelled even worse down here, and there wasn't even a path through the crap. He had no idea how to start making his way through the piles and piles of junk that had been stashed in the cramped space.

"Shit," Smiley swore from behind him.

"Josie?" Preacher called out.

"What the hell? You think she's tied up under the piles of crap down here?" Smiley asked.

"I don't know. But I'm not sure how we'll even start a search through all this junk."

Blink tuned out his friends and methodically catalogued the room. It wasn't large, but he didn't see any place where anyone could hide or be hidden. He leaned down and picked up a box and threw it to the side, not caring what was in it or where it landed. But under that box was another. And another.

Sighing in frustration, he looked around the room again. He had no idea what he was searching for, but nothing stood out as being suspicious.

"Blink?" Preacher asked.

"I don't know," he said, shaking his head. "My heart is telling me she's here, that there's nowhere else she *can* be. But..." His voice faded. He honestly thought they'd get into this house and find Josie huddled in a corner, freaked out but fine.

But now...the possibility that maybe, just maybe, whoever had taken her could've ended her life and thrown her body in the desert or buried her in a shallow grave, ate at him.

"You done?"

Millie's harsh question echoed through the small basement. She was standing at the top of the stairs, staring down at them.

"We need to regroup," Preacher said quietly.

"This is fucked up," Smiley said as his gaze scanned the room.

"Come on. The longer I'm in this house, the more I feel the need to shower," Preacher told them. He put a hand on Blink's arm.

He agreed with his friends. They *did* need to regroup, call Tex, maybe Kevlar and the others, figure out their next step. But something deep inside him didn't want to leave. He'd had such high hopes of finding Josie that the alternative was soul-crushing.

He turned and made his way back to the main floor, the hair on the back of his neck standing up as he traversed through the maze of trash and other crap Millie had collected.

"Told you," Gen crowed from her spot on the couch. She hadn't bothered to get up. Millie had gone to the front door and opened it. She was standing there, clearly indicating their time was up.

But still, the entire situation had Blink's internal radar screaming at him that the women were hiding something. Hiding *Josie*.

"Fuck—is that a diaper?" Smiley asked under his breath as he passed a plastic trash can balancing precariously on a pile of clothing and who knew what else.

"Disgusting," Preacher agreed.

Blink led his friends toward the door, stopping when he was next to Millie.

He looked into her eyes and said in a low, even voice, "We're going to find her."

Millie's lip curled. "The world is a better place without her in it. I hope wherever she is, the bitch is suffering. Regretting her role in killing my son. There's no torture too harsh to pay her back for what she's done to my family."

Something about her words made Blink freeze, but Smiley was at his back, pushing him forward.

"Josie didn't do a damn thing to your spoiled son, and you know it," Smiley said. "If she was guilty of anything, it was being too nice to someone who didn't deserve it."

"Get out!" Millie shouted, pointing to the door.

"Gladly," Preacher said.

Blink walked out into the dry desert air and felt an urge to turn right back around. He wanted to take every damn thing out of that hoarder house until he found Josie, or some sign of where she was.

Smiley pushed Blink again to keep him walking. Every step felt like his feet weighed four hundred pounds.

"Come on, we need to talk," Preacher said.

Blink walked as if in a trance back to the truck. He got into the back seat, and Preacher got in next to him. Smiley got behind the wheel. For a moment, they sat in silence.

Finally, Smiley said, "That was seriously fucked up."

Blink couldn't agree more.

"Now what?" Preacher asked.

"I'm not leaving. They know something," Blink said.

"I agree," Smiley said. "They were too quick to let us in."

"And the daughter seemed very tense. She tried to hide it, but she couldn't take her eyes off us," Preacher added.

He wasn't wrong. Blink had thought the same thing. "Josie's not dead," he said firmly. "I don't know how I know that, but I do. The mother was too willing to let us in, and I would've thought she'd dig in her heels and protest us stepping one foot inside her house."

"Right? She was pretty sure we'd come up empty-handed. Why? Because Josie isn't there? Because she knew we wouldn't find where they'd stashed her?" Preacher asked.

"Why is the daughter there anyway?" Smiley mused. "She has her own place, right? That's what Tex said, at least. So if she has her own apartment, why is she at her mom's house at," he looked at his watch, "eleven-thirty at night? And they're both completely dressed. Most people at this time of night, if they aren't getting ready to go party, are in their pajamas."

He wasn't wrong. Blink's mind spun.

"And did you see the look on Gen's face when she opened the door? She was definitely expecting someone, and she was shocked to see us instead," Preacher said.

"They're waiting for someone," Blink agreed.

"To bring Josie to them?" Smiley asked.

"Or to pick her up," Preacher said.

"The mom let us in, hoping we'd get in and out and leave. So that whoever they were expecting wouldn't arrive while we were there," Smiley said.

"So we stay. Stake the place out. See who's coming," Preacher decided.

Blink was on board with that plan. They were close to figuring out what the hell was going on. He felt it. These women weren't going to outsmart him. He had too much at stake—his entire future, his sanity, the love of his life.

Blink needed Josie. He wasn't sure he could survive losing her.

As hard as it would be to sit and watch, that's what he'd do if it meant figuring out what Millie and Gen Hitson were hiding. And they *were* hiding something, he had no doubt.

Smiley pulled away from the curb and headed down the street. They'd double back around and wait and watch...it was what they did best.

CHAPTER NINETEEN

Josie felt as if she couldn't breathe. She wasn't sure how long she'd been in the dark closet, but it felt like years. This was way worse than that damn cell somehow. She wasn't across the world in a foreign country. She was right here in the US. A place she should've been safe.

She second-guessed her actions from earlier. Should she have tried to escape? Run? Risked being shot to get away from Gen?

She hated that she once again needed to be rescued. She'd always thought she was extremely self-sufficient. She'd never relied on anyone else to give her what she needed. She'd clawed and fought her way to keep her head above water. Learned that from her mom. And yet, here she was. Locked away in another freaking hole as if she was nothing more than a piece of garbage. A throwaway person.

She might've fallen into a pit of misery already if it wasn't for Nate. He and his friends had accepted her, embraced her, made her feel as if she was worthy. Important to them. They wouldn't simply shrug after she disappeared and go on with their lives. No, Josie had no doubt they were moving heaven and earth to find her. She had to stay strong, the way Nate saw her.

The problem was, it wouldn't be as simple as confronting Millie and Gen—probably Nate's first thought. Because surely they weren't planning on leaving her in a closet in their home to die. They might think it was an appropriate punishment for what they considered her guilty of...killing Ayden. But they hated her enough to want her to suffer a far worse death.

Josie wasn't sure what was worse than dying from dehydration and lack of sustenance. Actually, that wasn't true; she could think of a *lot* of worse things. And Ayden's family had no doubt chosen something prolonged and painful.

It should've bothered Josie to realize she was hated so much. And if she hadn't met Nate and his friends, she would've been completely freaking out by now. But she'd been shown time and time again that she had value. Thinking about all that Remi and Wren had done for her since they'd met made Josie's heart swell. Not to mention Caroline, Fiona, and all the other women. And then there were the retired SEALs. Everyone had been so wonderful.

Millie and Gen were the bad people here—not her. *Screw them.* Whatever they had planned, Josie would do everything in her power to thwart them.

With that thought in mind, she reached out to run her hands over the walls around her. She needed to leave her DNA here. If she didn't make it out of whatever Ayden's family had in store for her, she wanted to be sure to leave signs for the police. Even if no one figured out where she'd gone for years, eventually *someone* would clear out this house, and they'd find this hellhole.

Josie ran her fingernails down the wall, then along the floor. She could feel the dirt building up under her nails.

Fumbling around, searching for something, *anything* she might be able to use to make some sort of mark on the wall, Josie gasped when her fingers closed around what she thought might be a coat hanger. A *metal* coat hanger, tucked into the corner behind her.

Even in the dark, it wasn't hard to twist it apart. It was more difficult to write what she wanted on the wall, since she couldn't see.

When she was done, she twisted the hanger into what she hoped was a sort of weapon. She didn't like violence, but if it came down to her or someone else dying, she'd do whatever it took to get back to Nate.

The thought of him made her breath hitch with a small sob. What was he doing right that moment? Was he pacing his apartment, wondering where she was? Was he driving around Riverton, hoping to catch a glimpse of her?

No, he wasn't doing either of those things. Her boyfriend had probably called in all the resources he had at his fingertips and was doing all he could to track her down. That thought gave Josie confidence.

She was going through different scenarios in her mind about what she could do if Millie or Gen opened the damn door, when it actually happened.

Caught unawares, she lost the element of surprise. And it

wouldn't have mattered anyway, because even the dim light in the basement was so bright after so long in the pitch darkness that Josie was basically blind.

"Get up," Millie growled.

Josie didn't want to. For all her wishing and hoping she could get out of that closet, suddenly it felt as if it was the safest place she could be. She had no idea what Millie had in store for her, but it wouldn't be good.

"What's that? Shit. Drop it!" Millie exclaimed. "I'll shoot you, I will! Drop the weapon!"

Her eyes had adjusted to the light coming in from the basement, and Josie's blood ran cold at the sight of Millie pointing the damn gun in her face once more. For a split second, she considered leaping out of the closet and doing her best to bury the sharp end of the coat hanger into one of the older woman's eyes. But instead, Josie put the hanger down.

She wanted to live. And all it would take was one twitch of Millie's finger and she'd have a bullet between her eyes. She couldn't live the rest of her life with Nate if she was dead.

Slowly, hoping not to spook Ayden's mom, Josie crawled out of the hole she'd been stashed in. The basement looked even more trashed now than it had when she was led to the closet. The path she'd taken had been obliterated. Millie and Gen must have scattered the junk all around them to hide the closet. To make it look as if walking through the years of accumulated crap was impossible.

Smart. And infuriating.

"Put those on," Millie ordered, pointing to a pair of handcuffs sitting on top of a plastic bag. They were rusty and looked ancient.

Josie hesitated.

"I'll shoot you and won't feel an iota of remorse," Millie warned. "But I won't kill you. A bullet in your brain would be too quick. Too painless. No, I'll shoot you in the knee and make you walk on it. Put on the fucking cuffs so we can get on with this."

Josie wanted to ask get on with *what*, but she wasn't sure she wanted to know. And her voice still wasn't cooperating anyway. Even if she wanted to plead for her life, once again try to convince Millie that it wasn't her fault Ayden had died, she couldn't.

Reaching for the handcuffs, Josie tried to think of a way that maybe she could pretend to put them on, but with Millie's impatience and her finger on that trigger, she couldn't think of any way to get out of having to shackle herself.

Slowly, feeling dread rise within her, she encircled one of her wrists and tightened the cuff. The clicking sound of the device locking was terrifying.

"Now the other one," Millie ordered, waving the gun at Josie's face.

The dread increased as she managed to get the cuff around her other wrist.

Millie laughed then. A sinister, horrible sound that would stick with Josie for however long she had left to live.

"Time to go, bitch. Just remember, you're getting everything you deserve. Karma will have her say. Upstairs. *Go*."

It was almost impossible to walk across the boxes, bags, and piles of trash around the basement, especially with her hands cuffed together. Josie's balance was thrown off time and time again, and she couldn't use her hands much to keep from falling. Every time she went to her knees or fell to the side, Millie laughed.

It felt as if it took hours to get to the bottom of the stairs, where there was finally a path leading up to the main floor. Josie had never been so grateful to step on a crooked, broken stair tread in all her life.

She cringed when she felt Millie poke the small of her back with the barrel of the pistol. "Hurry up. I want you gone before your boyfriend comes back."

Josie froze, and she whipped her head around to stare at Millie. Her mouth opened, but no words came out.

Millie cackled. "That's right, bitch, that ridiculous-looking redhead was here with two of his friends. We let them look around, but of course they didn't find you, just like we knew they wouldn't. Then they left. They aren't coming back, and they aren't going to save you from what I have planned for you. So if you're hoping for some sort of last-minute rescue, it's not happening. You're going to wish you were dead long before someone puts a knife through your stone-cold heart. He should thank me for saving him from the same fate as my Ayden."

Josie's heart was beating almost out of her chest. Nate had been here? She knew it. *Knew* he'd figure out who'd kidnapped her!

She rejected the rest of Millie's speech completely. Nate might've left, but he'd be back.

Millie's words were meant to demoralize her, but they had the opposite effect. They'd given Josie hope. Nate was here. In Las Vegas. She needed to be ready for anything.

The feel of the gun in her back had Josie hurrying up the rest of the stairs.

"Sit there," Millie ordered, gesturing to a pile of trash on the floor. It smelled horrible, but Josie did as she was told.

"The bitch give you any trouble?" Gen asked from her spot across the room on the couch.

"No. She's weak. Just like we thought," Millie answered breezily.

Josie sat completely still, not fazed at all by the older woman's insult. She wasn't weak. She'd proven that by surviving in Iran. All the times Nate had told her how strong she was, how impressed he was with her, echoed in her head.

"You tell her what's going to happen?" Gen asked her mom.

"No."

Gen grinned. "Can I? Please? I want her to know."

"Fine. But get up and watch out the door for him to arrive."

Josie didn't know who "him" was, but she assumed Millie didn't mean Nate.

Gen got up and made her way to the front door. She looked out the window beside it, then turned toward Josie.

"We sold you," she said bluntly, a glint in her eye. "To a guy who has connections in the sex trade. He knows a guy who knows a guy who likes fresh meat. Women who haven't been prostituted out already. He *used* to have a connection to someone in Peru, a man who took unsuspecting women from the casinos, but unfortunately, that guy's entire operation was taken down."

Gen laughed then. A deep sound that sent shivers down

Josie's spine. "You're going to be *fucked*—literally. Until you're bleeding out of every orifice. You'll be tied down, raped over and over. Given to anyone who wants to take a turn. And then you'll be shoved into a shipping container and sent to China. You'll be quite the novelty over there, and the whole process will start all over again. The rest of your life will be spent being fucked over, just like you did to *us*."

It sounded overly dramatic, like Gen had watched too many thriller movies, but Josie had no doubt that whoever she was about to be sold to didn't have plans to invite her over for tea and cookies.

"Did you hear me, bitch? You're about to live your worst fucking nightmare."

Josie simply stared at Genevieve. The last thing she'd do was give either of these women the satisfaction of knowing how terrified she really was. They *wanted* her to be scared. Wanted her to beg for her life. For that very reason, she refused to show any emotion whatsoever.

"A thousand bucks. That's all you're worth. It's more than we thought we'd get for you, though. Honestly, I would've given you to him for free, but Mom insisted we get some kind of compensation for our troubles. He had to make one other stop before he came here, but he's on his way now."

Josie felt cold inside, but she didn't let any of the turmoil coursing through her body show on her face.

Headlights flickered through the front window as someone pulled into the driveway outside.

"He's here!" Gen said excitedly.

Millie lifted the pistol again and pointed it at Josie. "It's time to pay for your crimes, bitch."

* * *

"Someone's pulling in," Smiley said unnecessarily from behind a car on the street, where he, Preacher, and Blink were crouching. They'd parked down the block and had been silently watching and waiting for something to happen. They didn't have to wait long.

A black four-door sedan pulled into the driveway and the headlights immediately turned off. A large man, about six feet tall and easily three hundred pounds, got out and walked up to the front door.

Blink got a glimpse of Gen at the door as she opened it, before the man disappeared inside.

His gut rolled. Everything within him was screaming for him to run up to the house, but his training forced him to stay right where he was.

"I'm going to go look in the car. I'll be right back," Smiley said.

"I'm going with you," Blink said quickly. He needed intel, and he needed it now. Whoever that man was who'd gone inside, he was up to no good. And if he was involved in Josie's disappearance, or if there was evidence of her being in the car, now or in the past, he needed to see for himself.

"I'll call Tex with the plate number," Preacher said. "Go."

Blink and Smiley crept across the dark road to the back of the car. They went around to the side of the car farthest away from the front door and leaned up to look in the window. Smiley took out a small pen light and turned it on, aiming it toward the back seat.

Blink inhaled sharply at the same time Smiley said, "What the fuck?"

Lying on the back seat was a woman. She had what looked like reddish-brown hair, and her eyes were huge in her face. She had a black eye, bruises all over her face, and a gag in her mouth. Her hands were bound with a zip tie, as were her ankles. If Blink had to guess, he would've said she was anywhere from her late twenties to mid-thirties, but it was hard to tell in her condition and in the darkness.

Smiley met Blink's gaze, then reached for the door handle. To both their surprise, it wasn't locked. And no overhead light turned on when the door swung open, another clear sign something seriously bad was going on.

Smiley reached into a pocket of his pants and pulled out the knife he always carried. It snicked open, and he reached for the gag around her mouth.

The woman flinched, but didn't jerk away from Smiley. He reached inside the car and cut off the offending material.

"Are you all right?" he asked.

It was kind of a stupid question, because of *course* this woman wasn't all right.

"No! Please help me!"

Without another word, Smiley leaned in farther and reached for her ankles.

Blink looked up at the house, then back at the woman. They didn't have much time. At any moment the man could return, and they needed to be ready.

"What's your name?" Smiley asked as he began to work on the zip-tie around her wrists.

"Bree. Bree Haynes," she said. "I...My ex sold me to this

asshole. He's here to pick up someone else. Then he said he's taking us to some underground brothel." She shivered. With fear or revulsion, Blink wasn't sure.

"I'm Jude Stark. My friends and I are Navy SEALs out of Riverton. You're okay now."

Blink had never heard his friend sound so...gentle. He wasn't known for his bedside manner, so to speak. But as Smiley cut off the woman's bindings, Blink was stuck on one of the last things the woman told them. The man was here to pick up someone else. And he knew in his gut who that was —Josie.

He'd been right. She *was* here. And no way was she being sold into sexual slavery. *Fuck no*.

"Come with me," Smiley said gruffly, holding out his hand to the woman.

She recoiled.

"I'm not going to hurt you. I just need to get you away from here. You *did* ask for help," he said brusquely, sounding more like the man Blink was used to.

The woman bit her already bleeding lip and winced. Then nodded. Without a word, Smiley took her hand in his and quickly led her down the street, toward where they'd parked, instead of heading back to Preacher.

The evidence of what Millie and Gen had planned for Josie sank in. Blink still didn't know who had actually kidnapped her, but at this point it didn't matter. They'd obviously sold his woman to this...monster, knowing what he had planned for her.

They were inhuman. He knew evil existed in the world, had given an oath to fight it on behalf of his country. But this...Blink was having a hard time wrapping his mind around it. Women knowingly selling another woman to a sex slaver was one of the worst things he could imagine. They wanted Josie to suffer in one of the worst ways imaginable.

He'd quietly closed the door of the sedan and was trying to figure out what his next move was going to be when Millie's front door opened. Silhouetted in the doorway was the large man who'd gotten out of the car, and a diminutive shadow at his side.

Blink would recognize Josie anywhere.

The man had her upper arm in his grasp, and Blink could see that her hands were cuffed in front of her. The sight made him hesitate for just the slightest moment.

That hesitation was something his training should've prevented. But this wasn't an op, it was personal—and the sheer relief of seeing Josie alive, combined with the rage over seeing her manhandled by the large man, was enough to make years of training fly out the window.

That hesitation caused him to fuck up...by not ducking back down behind the car fast enough, before the occupants of the house saw him standing by the back of the sedan.

Then all hell broke out.

CHAPTER TWENTY

The second the man walked into the house, Josie knew she was in deep shit. He was big. And he had a mean scowl on his face.

"This her?" he barked.

"Yes," Gen said.

"She's small," the man observed.

"I'm sure a lot of men will love that. You could probably lie about her age and charge people more."

"True," he said with a nod. "All right. Here's your money." He held out an envelope toward Gen, but Millie stepped forward and took it before her daughter could.

She flipped through the cash, then frowned. "It's only five hundred. You said a thousand."

The man shrugged. "That's what I've got. Take it or leave it."

Millie scowled but put the envelope into her back pocket.

"As long as I never have to see her again and she suffers, it's fine."

"She's not going to club med, that's for sure," the man said with a laugh that sent shivers down Josie's spine. He reached down and wrapped his huge hand around her upper arm and pulled her to her feet, almost wrenching her arm out of its socket in the process.

"She talk?" the man asked as he hauled Josie toward the door.

"Not much," Gen said with a shrug.

"Good. Got no use for bitches blabbering on and on. 'Please don't hurt me,'" he said in a high-pitched tone, mimicking what a woman might sound like. "'That hurts, stop.'" His eyes rolled. "It's hard for the customers to concentrate when they do that shit."

Josie felt sick. She trusted Nate and his friends, but they needed to hurry up and get here if they were going to prevent her from being taken away.

She tried to slow the man down as he neared the front door, but he was holding her so tightly, practically carrying her. Her efforts were useless. She wanted to yell at Millie and Gen. Tell them that they wouldn't get away with this. That they couldn't *sell* people! That it was Ayden who'd insisted on renting that boat, and he was showing off, getting close to the border just to scare her. But her vocal cords felt broken. Frozen.

The man pulled open the door and yanked her out onto the small front porch. He took two steps—then stopped suddenly.

Before Josie could figure out why, he'd pulled out a revolver and jammed the muzzle into the side of her head.

"Step away from the car," he said in an absolutely chilling tone. "Or I'll blow her brains out right here."

Looking up, Josie spotted the most beautiful thing she'd ever seen—Nate.

If she'd thought she was glad to see someone when she'd first lain eyes on him after he'd been dragged into that cell, she was wrong. *Nothing* made relief swim through her veins more than knowing he hadn't left her after searching Millie's house. That he was there. He'd save her. She had no doubt.

"I mean it," the man holding her growled, pushing the gun harder against her head.

With her hands cuffed in front of her, Josie couldn't do much more than try to lean away from the weapon. Not that it worked; the man was holding her too tightly.

"Oh shit," Gen muttered from behind her.

"Go get in my car. It's parked out back," Millie told her daughter.

Josie heard them, but all her attention was on Nate.

"Let her go," he said, coming out from behind the vehicle in the driveway. To Josie's dismay, she saw he wasn't holding any kind of weapon.

"Not a chance in hell," the bad guy said. "Fuck—where's the other one?"

"Her name is Bree. And she's already far away from here, you sick fuck," Smiley said, approaching Nate with a deadly look on his face.

"You're outnumbered, asshole," Preacher added, as he appeared at the side of the house, as if out of thin air.

Seeing the other members of Nate's SEAL team made Josie feel more confident, though this situation was anything but under control. She was more scared right this moment than she'd been at any point during their escape from Iran, which was messed up. Boat ride from hell, getting hoisted up into that helicopter, crashing, wandering through the desert mountains. Maybe because the man who held her had absolutely nothing to lose. If he allowed himself to be subdued, he was going to prison, probably for a very long time.

He was shuffling Josie off the porch, toward his car. But Nate and the others weren't giving up any ground. In fact, they were coming closer.

Suddenly, the man pointed his weapon at the sky and fired.

Josie's ears rang, but before she could even comprehend what he'd done, the barrel of the revolver was back against her temple.

She winced in pain. The heat from the weapon being fired felt as if it was branding her skin. Any attempt to pull back, to get away from the searing heat, was useless.

The fury on Nate's face was easy to see. Even from the ten or so feet that separated them, Josie could see the anger, the helplessness, the frustration.

"Back up!" the man ordered. "Or the next bullet will be in her brain."

In her peripheral vision, Josie could see neighbors starting to gather in the street, no doubt attracted to the scene by the gunfire—she would've thought the sound of a shot would've had them running *away*, but apparently she was wrong. She kept her gaze locked on Nate. If she was going to die, she wanted him to be the last thing she saw.

Even as she had the thought, anger welled inside her.

She was so mad. *Furious.*

That she'd been taken prisoner while she'd been in Kuwait visiting Ayden.

That she hadn't been given food or water.

That Nate had been tortured in those cells.

That she'd finally found a man who was kind and protective, and for some reason liked *her*, and this asshole was trying to take that away from her.

That Gen and Millie thought it was okay to sell her. *Sell her!*

That apparently there was another woman who'd been sold to this horrible man who was holding her with a grip that felt as if it would leave permanent marks on her body.

Josie was *done*.

She opened her mouth, and all her frustrations poured out.

She screamed as loud as she could. Letting the world hear her frustration, her anger, her sorrow. Life was unfair—and she didn't want to die!

Even as she continued screaming, Josie felt herself falling. The man had not only let go, he'd shoved her as hard as he could to the side. With her hands bound in front of her, she couldn't protect herself as she crashed to the ground. She hit the ground hard, her scream cutting off as abruptly as it started.

Pandemonium erupted all around her. Nate, Preacher, and Smiley charged the man the second he shoved her away. The sound of the damn gun going off again was loud but when Josie looked up, she couldn't tell if anyone was shot.

There was a tangle of arms and legs as the men fought for control. Josie tried to scoot out of the way, but her shoulder screamed in pain and all she could do was lie on the grass and watch with wide eyes.

The fight, such as it was, ended in seconds. Even though the man she'd been sold to outweighed the SEALs by a hundred pounds or more, Preacher and Smiley quickly had him on his belly with his arms wrenched behind his back and his legs bent in a kind of hogtie situation. They didn't have anything to tie him with, but he wasn't going anywhere as long as the two SEALs had a hold of him.

Then Nate was there, kneeling in front of her, blocking Josie's view.

"Are you all right? Were you hit?"

Hit? No, the man hadn't struck her. Why would Nate think that?

"Josie, look at me! Did you get shot?"

Oh! That's what he meant. She shook her head.

"*Fuck*!" Nate exclaimed.

And for some reason, hearing him say that, remembering back to the first time she'd heard him speak, when he'd said the exact same thing, made Josie feel safe.

Nate didn't say another word, just reached into his pants pocket and pulled out something small and shiny. To her surprise, the cuffs around her wrists fell off.

"You have a handcuff key in your pocket?" she asked. Now that Nate was here, she had no problem speaking.

Though, it seemed as if *Nate* had lost his words. He simply nodded, then put his hands on her cheeks and stared deeply into her eyes.

"I'm okay," she whispered, grabbing his wrists. They sat like that for several heartbeats, before the sound of a scuffle had them looking toward the side of the house.

Nate tensed, wrapping an arm around her.

"Hey! We saw what went down! They were trying to leave through the alley behind the house...figured that wouldn't be cool. So we pulled them out of the car and brought them back here." Four men held Gen and Millie between them. The women were struggling and trying to escape, swearing at everyone, but the men—who Josie could only assume lived in the area—had tight holds on both.

"A few of us have called nine-one-one," a woman called out from the street.

"I recorded it all on my phone!" a boy who looked to be in his late teens said. "Well, I missed the first gunshot, but I got everything else. That was so fucking lit!"

"You need help?" another man asked.

Before Josie knew it, the neighbors had come closer and were all talking at once. A couple knelt on the grass to assist Preacher and Smiley. The others stood around, talking excitedly as they waited for the police to arrive. Sirens were getting louder and louder as vehicles raced toward the scene.

Nate went to help Josie stand, and she moaned when the movement hurt her shoulder. He froze. "You're hurt?" he asked in a panicked tone.

Josie rarely heard him sound anything but calm and controlled. That, more than anything else that had happened, freaked her out. "I'm okay," she reassured him quickly. "It's just my shoulder. I think I landed on it wrong."

The next twenty minutes were a blur. The police arrived, guns drawn, and for a minute or two, Josie was afraid Preacher and Smiley were going to be shot. But the bystanders made sure the cops knew who was a good guy and who wasn't. Gen and Millie attempted to claim they had no idea what was going on, but the young man with the video was happy to share what he'd recorded with the officers— including Gen and Millie desperately trying to get away from the helpful bystanders, proving the two women were involved up to their eyeballs.

Nate had carried her over to the ambulance when it arrived, and an EMT looked at her shoulder and managed to massage it back into place, then put a brace on her arm. She was currently standing in the street, leaning against Nate, who had his arm around her. Josie soaked up his presence.

Eventually a detective arrived, and, after talking with the police officers who'd first reached the scene, he walked toward them.

"Mr. Davis and Ms. England, right?" he asked.

Josie didn't have time to do more than nod before Nate spoke. "I know you want to talk to Josie, but I need to get her to the hospital to be checked out more thoroughly. She's probably hungry and thirsty, and I really just want to get her out of here."

"I understand, but we need to figure out what happened here tonight," the detective said.

He really *did* look upset that he had to ask her questions. His compassion and understanding over the fact that she'd just been through something traumatic made Josie *want* to talk to him. The faster she got this done, the sooner she could go home. To Riverton. With Nate.

"It's okay," she told Nate, putting a hand on his arm.

"It's *not* okay," he said fiercely.

Ignoring the detective, Josie slipped around so she was facing Nate. She lifted her good hand and wrapped it around the back of his neck. "Look at me," she whispered.

It took him a second or two, but finally, he tilted his head down to meet her gaze.

"I knew you'd come for me," she told him. "That you'd find me. That you wouldn't let them get away with it."

"Spirit," Nate breathed.

Josie shook her head. "Even if that man had managed to take me away, I would've held on...for *you*. I love you, Nate. In a way I've never loved anyone else in my life. I wasn't going to let them win, not when I'd finally found everything I'd ever wanted. You, Nate. I found *you*. Or rather, you found me. I'm okay to talk to him. I want to. I want to make sure Gen and Millie don't get away with what they've done."

Nate closed his eyes, then nodded.

Josie turned to the detective. "I'm ready."

"If you wouldn't mind coming to sit in my car, it'll be more comfortable for you."

"I'm coming with her," Nate told the man firmly.

After they'd gotten as comfortable as possible in the back of the detective's vehicle, and he'd gotten her permission to turn on a recorder, Josie told her story. From the beginning. How Gen had shown up in disguise and kidnapped her, had been wearing an adult diaper so she didn't have to stop to use the restroom...about the gas, the phones, and how Millie was in Vegas sending texts on them to provide an alibi. How they'd kept her in that closet in the basement—and the scratches she'd left inside, as proof—the story about selling her to the man for a thousand dollars, and what Gen said would happen to her.

Finally, she explained the *why*—that they blamed her for Ayden's death, and hated her for it.

By the time she was finished speaking, Josie was a bit light-headed. It almost felt like she was in a dream, as if everything had happened to someone else.

"We've got all of them at the station now. The neighbors are being interviewed. Apparently they aren't well liked in the area, and no one is hesitating to speak up. We're also canvassing for security camera footage as well."

"We'll be staying the night here in Vegas, after I take her to the hospital. I'll leave you my contact info, as well as my friends' info. We're all Navy SEALs, stationed down in Riverton, California."

"Appreciate that. Thank you for your service."

Nate nodded, then reached for the door handle.

Josie scooted to the edge of the seat, and when Nate picked her up, said, "I can walk."

"I know. But I need this. Please."

Josie heard the anguish in her man's voice. She nodded, resting her head on his shoulder as he carried her toward his truck.

Preacher had been talking to a few officers, but when he saw them, he broke away and jogged over.

"She's gone," Smiley said when they reached the truck. He was standing next to the vehicle with a frown on his face.

"Who?" Josie asked.

"Bree."

"*Who?*"

"The woman who was in the car. The other woman who'd been sold to that asshole. She was tied up and beaten. I brought her to the truck and told her to stay here. But after everything happened, I came to get her...and she was gone."

"Oh no," Josie whispered. "Where'd she go? Do you think someone got her?"

"I don't know," Smiley said, sounding more worried than she'd ever heard him before.

"You want to stay here, maybe look around while we take Josie to the hospital?" Preacher asked. "We can come back after."

Smiley nodded. "If that's okay."

"It's fine," Nate told him.

"It's just...she was beaten all to hell. And terrified. Her ex fucking *sold* her. I don't know where she could've gone," Smiley said, running a hand through his hair.

Josie felt a kinship with the unknown woman. They'd both almost experienced something beyond horrifying. "I hope you find her," she told Smiley.

"Me too. I'm glad you're all right," he said gruffly.

"Thank you for coming with Nate to find me."

"Wouldn't have been anywhere else. Blink might be new to our team, but he's one of us."

Josie wanted to cry. She loved that Nate had friends like

these. That he had people who would have his back no matter what.

"Call if you need us," Preacher told Smiley.

The other man nodded. "I'm just going to hang out, maybe talk to some neighbors. She has to be around here somewhere."

He wandered back toward Millie's house and the groups of people who were still standing around. Even though it was the middle of the night, the adrenaline and excitement were keeping people at the scene.

Nate got Josie settled in the back of the truck, then climbed in after her. Preacher got behind the wheel and headed down the street.

Josie closed her eyes and leaned against Nate, fully relaxing for the first time since she'd opened the door to find Gen waiting for her.

"Fucking adult diaper," Preacher mumbled from the driver's seat. "Gross."

It was. But it also proved premeditation, which Josie hoped would mean she'd get a harsher sentence in court. Though she was well aware that by the time lawyers did their thing, the amount of time both Millie and Gen spent behind bars would probably be minimal. It sucked, but she had to hope that karma would take care of the heartless bitches.

CHAPTER TWENTY-ONE

Blink was having a hard time being away from Josie. He'd almost lost her. She'd been taken from right under his nose. He'd known that those fucking bitches were behind her disappearance. Even though Tex hadn't found any evidence, he'd *known*.

But even being right didn't make what happened any easier. Hearing Josie describe what Gen had said about her future had him wanting to puke. The thought of his Josie being forced into sexual slavery was horrifying.

And that scene at the house, when her captor had that gun against her head and was threatening to shoot her... Blink's life had flashed in front of his eyes. A life without Josie was cold and barren, and he wouldn't have been able to rebound if she'd been murdered in cold blood.

He and his teammates were about to make their move, to tackle the guy, when Josie had screamed. Blink would never forget the sound. It would haunt him to the end of his days. It sounded as if all her terror and anger and anguish came forth from her soul. The scream echoed around the quiet neighborhood as if a dark entity had come for vengeance on everyone's evil deeds.

But it had also been the distraction he and his teammates needed to be able to take the asshole out. As he shoved Josie away, they'd been able to tackle him before he could shoot them—or Josie.

Still, every time he looked at the woman he loved more than life itself, he was reminded of that damn revolver pressed against her head. The burn mark from the hot barrel on her temple would eventually fade, but Blink would never forget the despair and helplessness he'd felt during the short standoff.

To both their surprise, he was having a harder time with what had happened than Josie. She claimed it was because she knew he would find her, would come for her. But even though he had no doubt of who was behind her disappearance, he hadn't been as sure about the outcome. And knowing he'd searched that damn house and *missed* her, ate at him.

He'd been so close to her. If he'd only looked a little harder, hadn't given up so easily, she wouldn't have had to go through what she did. Wouldn't have been almost shot. It would be weeks, maybe months, before Gen, Millie, and the asshole they hired would face justice. But at least they'd be spending the time until then behind bars, as a judge had denied them bond.

The detectives wanted to find the people *above* the guy who'd come to collect Josie. Wanted to shut down the entire sex slavery ring, but that was much harder than it seemed.

The woman named Bree was in the wind, as well. Smiley hadn't been able to find her, even with Tex's help, and it bothered him more than he let on. Two weeks had passed since the incident, and he'd spent both weekends in Vegas, cruising the streets, visiting hospitals and calling women's clinics, attempting to find any sign of her. With no luck.

Today was the first day Blink was supposed to work a full shift on base. He and the rest of the team had a briefing to attend and an upcoming mission to plan. Josie wouldn't be alone, but even knowing she was spending the day with Jessyka and Benny wasn't enough to let Blink relax.

"She's okay," Kevlar said quietly during one of their breaks.

Blink sighed. "I can't stop thinking about going home and finding her missing, like last time."

"You texted her?"

"Only about a hundred times today already," he said with a small snort.

"Do it again."

"She already thinks I'm paranoid."

"Yeah. But she also probably needs to touch base with you, as much as you need to do the same with her. I know you said she's taking things really well, but you both went through something traumatic. It's not causing any harm to check in. For either of you."

Blink didn't need any more encouragement. He'd been trying to hold himself back from texting her...*again*...for the last twenty minutes.

He shot off a quick text and waited anxiously for her response.

. . .

Josie: I'm good. Jessyka is trying to teach me how to make some fancy mixed drinks...it's not going well.

Blink smiled at her note. She didn't sound upset that he'd texted her for the umpteenth time.

Blink: You partaking?

Josie: A chef can't make master status without tasting her creations. :)

Remembering the last time Josie had alcohol made Blink's cock twitch. They hadn't made love since she'd been kidnapped. Her shoulder had been sore for a long while, and all Blink wanted to do was hold her as close as he could against him all night. But for the first time, sexual desire rode hard and fast through his body.

"That smile must mean she's fine, huh?" Kevlar asked.

"Yeah."

"Good. I'm glad. None of us ever want to see you fall back into that depression you were in before joining the team. You need to text her, do it. Need to hear her voice? Call her. I guarantee she won't get mad. She needs it as much as you, even if she won't admit it because she's trying to prove how strong she is. How unaffected she is by what happened to her. She's definitely affected. How could she not be?"

Blink had been feeling guilty about needing to be around Josie so much, about needing to make sure she was safe. And while Josie insisted she was fine, she hadn't protested his hovering. Which made him think that Kevlar was onto something. "Thanks, Kevlar."

"Any time," his team leader said. "We have another hour or so of this briefing left, then I'm thinking you can head home early."

Blink wanted to take him up on the offer, but he felt bad because he definitely hadn't been holding his own on the team lately. He shook his head. "It's okay. I need to do my fair share of the work."

"You don't get it, Blink—this is what a team does. What *friends* do. They hold up the weak members until they can stand on their feet again. And I'm not saying you're weak, simply that you need a little more support right now. We've got this. We'll bring you up to speed tomorrow about the mission. It's not as if we can plan everything in a couple of hours. Take the time you need to come to terms with what happened. Go see Josie."

"Thanks. If it's really all right, I'll take you up on that and head out after we're done here."

"It's really all right. Remi's going over to your place tomorrow. She told me last night that Josie started taking some captioning jobs again, right?"

Blink nodded. They'd argued about it. He thought Josie should take more time off, and she'd insisted that working kept her mind occupied...that she actually enjoyed it, and her shoulder was feeling good enough to type. So they'd compromised, and she was working part time for now. Blink had a feeling that wouldn't last long. His Josie was stubborn; it was one of the many reasons why he loved her so much.

"Cool. Remi enjoys working at your place. Apparently, she likes not feeling alone while she works, but she's still able to get lots of drawing done because Josie doesn't talk her ear off while they're both working."

"Josie loves having Remi there. And Wren too."

"Right. So let's do this, then you can head home," Kevlar said.

Blink couldn't keep himself from sending one more text before he headed back to work.

Blink: I'm getting off work in about an hour or so. You want me to come by Aces and pick you up? Or will you get a ride home?

Three dots immediately appeared as Josie typed a response. He loved that she never made him wait for her to text back. Those dots made the tightness in his gut relax, knowing she was there, responding to him, was something he needed these days to keep from freaking out.

Josie: Benny said he'd take me home. And...yay! You'll be home early!

. . .

Blink couldn't keep the smile off his face. He loved that Josie didn't feel awkward about letting him know she was excited to see him. Kevlar's words sank in. She was probably feeling a little unsettled herself after everything that happened, and keeping an open and constant line of communication was as important to her as it was to him.

* * *

The worst part about coming home every day was the moment Blink approached his apartment door. He and Preacher had reinforced it, making it impossible to kick in, even with only the chain on, but the feeling of dread remained every time he walked up to the door.

He was relieved to see it shut and locked as normal as he stuck his key in the lock. "Josie?" he called out as soon as he entered, as he did every time he came home.

This time, there was no reply.

Immediately, Blink tensed. Memories flooded him of the last time that had happened and he'd found Josie missing

"Josie?" he called again, louder and a little more frantic.

"In here!" Blink heard her say from the back of the apartment, and he immediately breathed a sigh of relief. He had no idea how long it would take for his anxiety to ease in regard to Josie's whereabouts, but it was obvious today wasn't that day.

It was too early for her to have started dinner, but it was equally unusual for her to be back in their room in the middle of the day. If she wasn't working at the kitchen table, usually she was on the couch, watching TV or texting someone on her phone or simply reading a book.

He walked faster than normal as he headed for their bedroom. He pushed the door a little harder than necessary and it bounced against the wall when he stepped inside.

It took a moment for his brain to understand what he was seeing. He kind of thought Josie would be on the bed with a headache, or maybe her shoulder was hurting again.

Instead, she was propped up on some pillows, smiling at him, wearing a tiny piece of white lingerie.

"Hi," she said a little shyly. "I never did get to model what I ordered for you...before. I thought today was a good day to do that."

Blood rushed to his cock. The vision of the woman he loved on their bed, one knee bent with her foot flat on the mattress, the other angled outward, basically putting herself on display for him, made him dizzy with lust.

Blink began to rip at his clothes as he slowly walked toward her, memorizing the moment. He would bring this image of Josie out when he was knee deep in mud in some fucking jungle, or when he was sweating his balls off in a desert. She was his reason for living. For pushing through the hell that were so many of his missions. His reward.

Her small tits were bared as the white bodice framed her chest. It tapered down to a V toward her pussy, making his eyes go between her legs. The smallest scrap of white material covered her opening. All it would take was a flick of his fingers to move it aside so he could get inside her.

A trail of his clothes went from the door to the bed, but Blink didn't notice. He couldn't take his eyes off Josie. She was so beautiful...and he'd almost lost her.

He crawled onto the mattress and reveled in the way she reached for him.

"Are you sure?" he whispered as he neared.

"Positive."

That was all Blink needed to hear. He spread her legs farther apart as he crawled between them. He did exactly as he'd imagined, and flicked the strip of material to the side, baring her to his touch. She was soaked.

"What have you been doing while you were waiting for me?" he asked.

An adorable blush pinkened her cheeks. "Getting myself ready," she said firmly. "I want you. Now. Inside me. I need you, Nate."

The tip of his cock was notched between her legs before she'd finished speaking. Blink took a breath, trying to slow down. He didn't want to hurt her, and the way he was feeling right now, he was bound to.

Then Josie reached up and pinched her nipples as she stared at him.

That was all it took.

The iron control he'd been holding onto snapped.

Blink was balls deep inside her before he took his next breath. She was so damn tight, and just like that, he felt as if he were home.

He'd been desperate to come seconds earlier. Wanted to pound in and out of her, but now he was content to simply be deep inside her body, not moving...*living*.

"Nate?" she asked, as she attempted to shift under him.

"I love you," he said reverently, as he stared down at her.

"I love you too," she returned without hesitation.

Blink closed his eyes, memorizing this moment. Having Josie under him, around him, it was as close as he figured he'd ever get to experiencing what heaven on earth was like.

"Please," she whispered.

His eyes opened, and for a moment, all he could see was the damn mark on her temple, but then she pushed her hips up, trying to get him to move.

"I need more," she whispered.

At that, Blink moved. If Josie needed something, he'd give it to her. No matter what it was.

"Yes! Harder, Nate. Please!"

Their lovemaking was frantic and fast, and after Josie came, Blink was still hard. He turned her, taking her from behind. Then he put her on top. At some point, he came, but his dick didn't soften. He filled her with his come and kept on loving her.

By the time he orgasmed again, the very pretty but flimsy lingerie Josie had worn for him had been torn off and was hanging around her waist, and she'd come for the third or fourth time. The covers were hanging off the bed and they were both covered in sweat. Blink could feel their combined juices on his balls and thighs, and the sheets under him were soaked.

But he'd never been more content in his life. Their lust for each other slaked for now, Blink's cock still deep inside Josie's sheath. She was lying bonelessly on top of him, her breaths drifting over his chest as she did her best to regain her equilibrium.

"For the record...I liked the lingerie," Blink told her.

He felt more than heard her giggle, making him smile.

"Well, too bad that'll be the only time I wear it, since you ruined it," she said, propping her chin on his chest.

Blink shrugged. "So order more. A dozen. Two."

"I just might. You might like a little variety. More color. They have red, black, purple, even—"

Blink rolled them suddenly, cutting off her words. He reached for the drawer next to the bed, keeping Josie under him. When he returned to hover over her, he clasped a small object in his hand.

"I like you in white. No, that's not true, I like you in any color you want to wear, and in nothing at all. But white looks good on you. Maybe you'll wear it when we get married? White, that is, and not the sexy lingerie." He forced himself to shut up as he held up a ring.

Josie's eyes widened. She stared at the ring, then at him, then back at the ring.

Her hesitation made Blink sweat. He'd moved too fast. Rushed things between them. *Fuck.*

"Yes," she whispered. Then a huge smile crossed her face. "Yes!" she yelled, throwing her arms around his shoulders.

Blink was so startled, he dropped the ring. But he'd find it later. The only thing that mattered right then was that the woman he loved so much it was almost scary, had said yes.

Later, when Josie was once more draped across his chest, and the lost ring was poking into his ass, Blink stared up at the ceiling with a goofy smile on his face.

"Can we invite your brother? And maybe his pilot friends? I don't want a big ceremony, but I do want a huge party. I want all my new friends together in one place. Forgetting about the bad things in the world and just enjoying being together."

"We can do anything you want," Blink told her, pleased as hell that she'd thought about Tate. He'd been texting his twin more often. Almost losing Josie had made Blink more aware of how fleeting life was, and he needed to know those he loved were all right.

"You know, when I was in that cell, I couldn't think about the future. Literally, all I could think about was living through the next minute, then hour, then day. My body was trying to shut down, but for some reason I refused to give up. To just lay down and die. Now I know why. It's because I was waiting for you. You've changed my life, Nate, and I can't imagine you not being in it. I love you."

This woman. She'd changed *his* life. "I was the same way," he admitted. "I spent day after day sitting at Aces, lost within myself. All I could think of was what I should've done differently, and how my team didn't have to be killed or hurt. When I was sent back to the place where it happened, I believed I was meant to be there. At the time, I thought it was so I could do what I should've done before, sacrifice myself for others. But now, I realize I was meant to be there to meet you."

"Nate," Josie said with a sniff.

"No. No crying," he ordered gently.

He was rewarded with her small chuckle. Then she said, "That cup? The one I wanted on the shelf on the wall, so we could see it every day?"

Blink frowned. He hadn't been so sure about putting a reminder of a horrible event on display, but he'd done it, because she'd seemed so adamant. "Yeah?" he asked when she didn't continue.

"It represents hope to me. Resiliency. Not giving up. That's why I want to see it every day. To remind me that even when things seem hopeless, they aren't."

His Josie. Stronger than anyone he'd ever met.

He lifted his head to kiss her...but just then, her stomach growled. Long and loud.

She giggled. "Ignore it," she ordered as she kissed his lips.

But he couldn't. His woman was hungry, and Blink would be damned if he ignored her needs for his own. Lifting her off his cock, he bit back the moan of complaint that threatened to leave his throat. If he had his way, he'd live deep inside her hot, wet heat, but he needed to feed her.

"Don't bother showering," he informed her bossily. "Because I'm just going to haul you right back here after we eat. Besides, I love seeing *that*." He'd put her on her feet next to the bed, and he couldn't take his gaze away from the bead of come that was making its way down her inner thigh.

Josie rolled her eyes. "You're weird," she complained, as she licked her lips and stared at his erection covered in their combined juices.

Blink walked over to the dresser, ignoring his clothes strewn all over the floor and pulling out a pair of boxers and one of his T-shirts. He stepped into the underwear, then walked back to where Josie was struggling to remove the ruined lingerie from around her waist. When she managed it, he eased his shirt over her head, helping her find the arm holes.

She should've looked ridiculous in his shirt, which was

four sizes too big for her tiny frame. But he loved seeing her in his clothes. Resisting the urge to kiss her, knowing it would lead to him throwing her back on the bed, Blink reached around her for the ring that was reflecting the sun coming through the window.

He picked up her hand and slid the ring down her finger. The small princess-cut diamond looked amazing. And would look perfect once it was paired with the matching wedding band he'd picked out to go with it.

"Nate, it's beautiful," Josie breathed.

It dawned on Blink that this was the first time she was seeing the ring properly, since he'd dropped it before he could get it on her finger.

"*You're* beautiful," he countered, leaning down and kissing the ring on her finger. "Hamburgers okay for dinner?"

"Perfect," she said. "Give me a minute in the bathroom and I'll come help."

Blink could handle making the meal without help, but he'd never turn down spending time with this woman. Ever. "Sounds good."

"Nate?" she asked, putting her hands on his chest and leaning into him.

"Yeah?"

"Put on a shirt so you don't burn yourself," she said with a smile, then turned and headed for the bathroom. Her giggle echoed in the room around him.

Life would never be boring with his woman. She'd keep him on his toes. And Blink had no problem with that. None.

EPILOGUE

Maggie took a deep breath the moment she stepped outside.

Freedom.

It was something she'd never take for granted again.

The one year and ten months she'd spent behind bars was hell. And nothing she'd been prepared for. It didn't matter how many times she claimed she hadn't done what she'd been accused of—no one had believed her. And why would they? With the evidence against her, she'd known she was fucked from the very start.

Resentment welled inside her once more. She wanted nothing more than to get revenge against the man who'd set her up, had her thrown in jail. But she knew better than most that he wasn't a man to fuck with. If she'd thought the last twenty-two months were bad, they'd be *nothing* if she snitched.

No, the only thing she could do was try to get on with her life.

A car pulled into the small parking lot outside the building where Maggie had spent almost two years of her life locked up. The woman behind the wheel smiled and waved.

Grateful for her friend Adina, Maggie hurried down the steps of the prison.

Adina had gotten out of the car, and now she greeted Maggie with a huge hug. Nothing had ever felt better. Maggie had been starved of basic human contact while incarcerated.

"I'm so happy you're out!" Adina said.

"You and me both," Maggie told her with a small smile.

"Come on. I've ordered takeout for your first night, and I have my guest room all set up for you. I have a bunch of stuff to tell you before I head out next week."

"Head out?" Maggie asked as she got into the passenger side of the older-model Honda Accord.

"Yeah," Adina said with a small frown. "I didn't want to stress you out before you were released, but I'm leaving for a six-month deployment next week."

Shit. Maggie did her best not to panic.

"As I told you before, you're more than welcome to stay at my apartment for as long as you want to get back on your feet," Adina said quickly. "It'll be nice to have someone there looking after the place while I'm gone."

Maggie swallowed hard. She and Adina had met just a few months before...the incident, as she was calling it. And it was a huge surprise when the woman had actually kept in touch while she'd been behind bars. Maggie had lived for her letters. All her other friends had disappeared. The fact that Adina had offered her a place to stay when she got out...it meant the world to Maggie.

But free rent or not, California was expensive. She needed to find a job. And now that she was a felon, Maggie had no doubt that would be easier said than done.

That was a worry for tomorrow. Today, she would revel in the fact that she was free. Away from the hell she'd been living for almost two years.

"Thanks for coming to get me," Maggie told her friend.

"Of course! You didn't deserve to be there in the first place."

She didn't. And it felt amazing to have at least one person believe that she hadn't done what she'd been accused of. She didn't even think her own lawyer believed her when she'd told him she'd been set up.

"I wish we had more time together before I have to leave. I was going to set you up."

Maggie recoiled as if she'd been struck. "No! No set ups. I'm going to be single for the rest of my life. The very last thing I want is any kind of boyfriend."

"Ever?"

"Ever," Maggie said firmly. She'd learned her lesson the hard way. Men were dogs.

"So, I guess going to Aces Bar and Grill is out for tomorrow night?" Adina asked.

"It's out," Maggie confirmed.

"Well, darn. Fine. But if you change your mind, all you have to do is say so. I know some single, good-looking Navy SEALs."

"Nope. No guys. *Especially* not ones who are in the Navy."

Adina spent the rest of the drive to her apartment happily

talking about all the things she had planned for them for next week, before her deployment. All Maggie wanted to do was hole up and get her wits about her again. To reacclimate to being outside the prison walls. But she wouldn't say a word against her friend's plans. The fact that Adina was willing to let her live with her, rent-free, for as long as it took for Maggie to get back on her feet, was a small miracle. She'd do anything the woman wanted.

By the time Adina got back from her six-month deployment, Maggie was determined to have a job and be self-sufficient again.

Then she was leaving California. Going somewhere that didn't have a naval base. Somewhere she'd be guaranteed *never* to see the asshole who put her in jail, ever again.

In the back of her mind, Maggie had a feeling if the man knew she was out, he'd do whatever he could to make sure she was sent right back behind bars. He was an asshole of the first degree, one with power. She hadn't seen him for who he was before, but she did now.

When Adina turned off the engine in her parking lot, Maggie got out and took another deep breath. The fresh air smelled so good.

She wasn't going to mess up this new start her friend was giving her. She'd make the most out of it. Or die trying.

* * *

As you all know, nothing in my books ever goes smoothly, Maggie's new start is no exception...starting with the no Navy guys thing. Preacher and Maggie are about to cross paths and take them both on a journey filled with ups and downs. Read all about how it plays out in *Protecting Maggie* the next book in the SEAL of Protection: Alliance series!

Scan the QR code below for signed books, swag, T-shirts and more!

Eagle Point Search & Rescue

Searching for Lilly

Searching for Elsie

Searching for Bristol

Searching for Caryn

Searching for Finley

Searching for Heather

Searching for Khloe

Game of Chance Series

The Protector

The Royal

The Hero

The Lumberjack

SEAL of Protection: Legacy Series

Securing Caite

Securing Brenae (novella)

Securing Sidney

Securing Piper

Securing Zoey

Securing Avery

Securing Kalee

Securing Jane

Delta Force Heroes Series

Rescuing Rayne

Rescuing Aimee (novella)

Rescuing Emily

Rescuing Harley

Marrying Emily (novella)

Rescuing Kassie

Rescuing Bryn

Rescuing Casey

Rescuing Sadie (novella)

Rescuing Wendy

Rescuing Mary

Rescuing Macie (novella)

Rescuing Annie

SEAL of Protection Series

Protecting Caroline

Protecting Alabama

Protecting Fiona

Marrying Caroline (novella)

Protecting Summer

Protecting Cheyenne

Protecting Jessyka

Protecting Julie (novella)

Protecting Melody

Protecting the Future

Protecting Kiera (novella)

Protecting Alabama's Kids (novella)

Protecting Dakota

Delta Team Two Series

Shielding Gillian

Shielding Kinley

Shielding Aspen
Shielding Jayme (novella)
Shielding Riley
Shielding Devyn
Shielding Ember
Shielding Sierra

Badge of Honor: Texas Heroes Series

Justice for Mackenzie
Justice for Mickie
Justice for Corrie
Justice for Laine (novella)
Shelter for Elizabeth
Justice for Boone
Shelter for Adeline
Shelter for Sophie
Justice for Erin
Justice for Milena
Shelter for Blythe
Justice for Hope
Shelter for Quinn
Shelter for Koren
Shelter for Penelope

Ace Security Series

Claiming Grace
Claiming Alexis
Claiming Bailey
Claiming Felicity
Claiming Sarah

Mountain Mercenaries Series

Defending Allye

Defending Chloe

Defending Morgan

Defending Harlow

Defending Everly

Defending Zara

Defending Raven

Silverstone Series

Trusting Skylar

Trusting Taylor

Trusting Molly

Trusting Cassidy

Stand Alone

Falling for the Delta

The Guardian Mist

Nature's Rift

A Princess for Cale

A Moment in Time- A Collection of Short Stories

Another Moment in Time- A Collection of Short Stories

A Third Moment in Time- A Collection of Short Stories

Lambert's Lady

Special Operations Fan Fiction

http://www.AcesPress.com

Beyond Reality Series

Outback Hearts

ABOUT THE AUTHOR

New York Times, *USA Today*, #1 Amazon Bestseller, and #1 *Wall Street Journal* Bestselling Author, Susan Stoker has spent the last twenty-three years living in Missouri, California, Colorado, Indiana, Texas, and Tennessee and is currently living in the wilds of Maine. She's married to a retired Army man (and current firefighter/EMT) who now gets to follow *her* around the country.

She debuted her first series in 2014 and quickly followed that up with the SEAL of Protection Series, which solidified her love of writing and creating stories readers can get lost in.

If you enjoyed this book, or any book, please consider leaving a review. It's appreciated by authors more than you'll know.

www.stokeraces.com
www.AcesPress.com
susan@stokeraces.com